NOBODY GETS
THE GIRL

NOBODY GETS THE GIRL

A Comic Book Novel

JAMES MAXEY

PHOBOS BOOKS
NEW YORK

phobos

Published by Phobos Books
A Division of Phobos Entertainment Holdings, Inc.
200 Park Avenue South, Suite 1109
New York, New York 10003
www.phobosweb.com

Distributed in the United States by National Book Network, Lanham, Maryland.

The characters and events in this book are fictitious. Any similarity to actual persons, living or dead, is coincidental and not intended by the author.

Library of Congress Cataloging-in-Publication Data

Maxey, James.
   Nobody gets the girl : a comic book novel / James Maxey.
     p. cm.
   ISBN 0-9720026-2-6 (pbk. : alk. paper)
   1. Heroes—Fiction. 2. Quantum theory—Fiction. I. Title.
PS3613.A89 N63 2003
   813'.6—dc21

                                 2003007748

♾️™ The paper used in this publication meets the minimum requirements of American National Standard for Information Sciences—Permanence of Paper for Printed Library Materials, ANSI/NISO Z39.48-1992.
Manufactured in the United States of America.

For Tony St. Clair.
Even though he's wrong about Thor
being stronger than the Hulk.

ACKNOWLEDGMENTS

To properly acknowledge everyone who's helped me over the years would require this book to have twice as many pages. To save space, I'll have to thank some of the people in groups. I couldn't have done this without help from the *Writers Group of the Triad*, *Orson Scott Card's Writer's Boot Camp*, the *Odyssey Fantasy Writer's Workshop* and the spin-off *Odfellows Critique Group*, the short story forum at the *Zoetrope* website, and, of course, the wonderful crew at Phobos. In addition, special thanks go out to Ken Ward, Greg Hungerford, and Lisa Marler for their heroic efforts at reading my first (thankfully unpublished) novel way back when. Greg also put in reading duties on the first draft of *Nobody*, as well as Paul Schilling, Thomas Seay, and Rob Cooper. Later drafts were read by Christine Koyama, Luc Reid, Marcus Belk, Chris Young, Sherri Rapp, and Anne Abrams. Special thanks go to Jeana Martin for facilitating my attendance of various workshops,

ACKNOWLEDGMENTS

and to Anjela Indica for making *Odyssey* possible. Jeremy Cavin and Chris Woodcook deserve special mention for their hard work and dedication over the years. Elizabeth Lustig and Phil Levin have spent the better part of a decade now reading almost every word of fiction I've written and putting in superhuman effort toward improving it. Jeanne Cavelos, Harlan Ellison, and Orson Scott Card all spent at least a week trapped in a classroom with me and deserve medals. You wouldn't be holding this book in your hands without the work of Christian O'Toole, Keith Olexa, and Sandra Schulberg. Thanks also to Dona Nova, Ian McDowell, and Eric Buchanan for helping show that dreams can become reality. *Parts Unknown, the Comic Book Store* gets a special mention for keeping a steady stream of funny books coming my way. Thanks to the Mountain Goats for providing a soundtrack during the rewrites. Thanks to my family for all their support over the years. And, finally, my thanks and love to Laura Herrmann, the girl who got this nobody.

PUBLISHER'S NOTE

With the publication of our first novel—James Maxey's *Nobody Gets the Girl*—Phobos Books comes of age . . . comes of age in a time as turbulent as the one described in this book. Comes of age during a time when Somebody— somebody with eerie similarities to Dr. Know—may destroy the world under the guise of saving it. Who is that Somebody? The President? The American nation? Or is each one of us that Somebody?

The multivoiced citizenry, struggling to be heard as individuals, is relentlessly herded by pollsters and politicos into a giant chorale so as to sing a single song of Patria. How many of us can remember when we all, as a nation, sang the song of War as though the words and rhythm sprang spontaneously from our own just hearts? How many of us can remember when millions from around the world joined voices to chant the song of Peace?

Shall we choose to be citizens of the New World, America; or shall we choose to be citizens of the New World, Earth?

Science fiction has plotted the evolution of governing principles and government bodies from national to planetary, from planetary to extraplanetary. Holy scripture may seem predictive of the future to some; but at Phobos we prefer our science fiction hard. Our scriptures are literary, and our scriptures tell us: The Future is Here.

It is time for each of us to navigate, as we do daily on the Internet, towards and with our planetary brethren until we find a way through these treacherous narrows, where voices from the banks fill the air with cries for our custom: "$2 dollar, $2 dollar, we get you secure nation with manned borders, good GNP, and long-range missiles."

James Maxey has a gift for creating high amusement as he contemplates serious subjects. He proved that with his story "Empire of Dreams and Miracles," which we published in 2002. This book is written in quite a different style, but with the same dark humor. It uses certain conventions from the world of classic comics, so we are calling it a "comic book novel," and it may be seen as the literary first cousin to the graphic novel. If you underestimated comics in the past (as I did for many years), this delightful satire may help you break through.

As publisher, I want to credit Keith Olexa, Editor of Phobos Books, and Creative Director Christian O'Toole, whose enthusiasm for this book gave everyone the confidence to proceed. Other members of the Phobos crew—Doni Farkovits, Sabrina Levavi and Bill Kabel—echoed their convictions. When those on the cutting edge develop the eloquence and ammunition to transform the old paradigms, risks are worth taking.

Together, we want to acknowledge Jim Shooter. He may call himself an old man, but that's only because he became a man as a youth, at age 13, when, despite what the Torah proclaims, most boys in our society are still playing at being boys. We've said it before: Jim thinks like a Superhero, and, *cogito ergo sum*, that makes him one.

This book would not exist without a triumvirate of men—Stanley Plotnick, Steve Klein and Jed Lyons—whose companies are funding the Phobos mission. Like flight directors on Earth, they've allowed us to take the controls and pilot our craft beyond their orbit into unknown space. It takes inordinate faith and trust to let us go, and they do.

The fact that *Nobody Gets the Girl* is in bookstores all over the country and can be ordered via the Internet from anywhere in the world is a testament to the prodigious support we get from the team at National Book Network. We are particularly grateful to Michael Sullivan, Miriam Bass, Spencer Gale, Mark Cozy, Vicki Metzger, Tressa Shelko, Jen Linck, Candy Busey, Ginger Miller, Cassie Copper, and Lynn Humphries.

The book you hold in your hands was manufactured courtesy of Rowman & Littlefield Publishing Group; and we are indebted to Julie Kirsch for her ever-sensitive attention to our imprint's output. We also value the artistic guidance of Gisèle Henry. Underlying their work is that of our stalwart proofreader, Debbie Wolf. To create the marvelous cover, Jim Shooter gathered two of his trusty MARVEL artists, Bob Wiacek and JayJay Jackson. Thanks for making it zing!

The investment from our original group of partners—Mark Buntzman, John Roche, Sybil Robson Orr, Jack Hyland, and especially Rajesh Raichoudhury—continues to ferment. The Phobos culture they seeded is sprouting in all the areas we had hoped—books, movies, games, the Internet.

Being a fledgling publisher and head of Phobos mission control is a glorious, difficult challenge. I didn't fly solo. There is a corps summoned during the dark hours, who bring forth a light, sometimes harsh, sometimes soft, that is always illuminating. My thanks to Amichai, Anne, Betsy, Chris, Diane, Dieter, Fiona, Jane, Jennifer, Joe, Lia, Lindsay, Lynn, Mike, Nancy, Naomi, Roly, Whitney, and my cherished band of brothers, K.C., Peter, & Jon.

Whenever we are tempted to contemplate the prospect of War—of ritualized, institutionalized killing—it is time to contemplate Peace. We may still opt for War, but the debate must be won in each of our hearts, not by some "Somebody" out there. Let *Nobody Gets the Girl* entertain you in the process.

This is for you, James. May you do us proud.

SANDRA SCHULBERG
Publisher
New York City
March 2003

INTRODUCTION

James C. Shooter

Certain Tibetan wise men and lamas can create living beings out of pure thought. These beings are called *tulpas*. Alvin Schwartz, a brilliant, charmingly cranky gentleman and a wise man in his own right, taught me that in the pages of his marvelous book, *An Unlikely Prophet*. This isn't some bogus "mysterious East" mythology of the ilk seen in the *Kung Fu* TV series. This happens right here in the world we think is real. Ask any Tibetan.

Alvin Schwartz has had a varied, distinguished and successful career. For 17 years, during what aficionados call the Golden Age, he wrote comic books, most notably *Superman*.

My pal Bob Burden created *The Mystery Men*. I say "my pal Bob Burden" because he is, and because his business card reads "Your Pal, Bob Burden." Bob created a number of other things as well. His first hit, I believe, was a zany, madcap hero called the Flaming Carrot. The Carrot became a superhero by reading 5,000 comic books in one sitting to win a bet. Too many comic books. Something inside his brain snapped.

This happens right here in the world we think is real. Ask any comics pro who's been to a comic book convention.

Which brings us to James Maxey. No, he's not a tulpa. He may have read too many comic books, I don't know, but in our one brief meeting, I didn't notice any of the seven deadly warning signs. James Maxey wrote *Nobody Gets the Girl*. As you'll soon learn, the title is a cutesy word-play, but that's okay. I checked the shelves at my local bookstore. Books that deal in the fantastic often have word-play titles. Maxey was only following form, a perfectly respectable and professional thing to do. Mark Twain, in his wickedly funny essay entitled "Fenimore Cooper's Literary Offenses" lists ". . . nineteen rules governing literary art in the domain of romantic fiction . . . ." If Mark Twain endorsed following form, then it's all right by me.

Said another way, as I learned while in the Bronx, when on Jerome Avenue, do as the Jeromans do.

But don't do it the way anybody expects. In *Nobody Gets the Girl*, James Maxey has done it in proper form in a way that nobody, not even Nobody, expects.

Without giving too much away, this tale is predicated upon a major change in the world we think is real. It's the same but different in startling ways. God, that sounds lame-o-same-o when I say it just like that, but only because in trying to be coy and not blow any surprises, I'm forced to hint at what happens in bland generalities. *Wait till you see what happens!*

The idea behind Maxey's tale is one of those crystalline concepts that seems like it ought to be one of the SF staples. It isn't, as far as I know. My knowledge of SF literature is far from encyclopedic like, say, that of Keith Olexa, the excellent editor of this book, but only one other writer

I'm aware of has attempted a tale based on a concept similar to that of *Nobody Gets the Girl*. That would be me.

If you've read enough comic books, or too many, you may be familiar with "Alpha and Omega," "Second Death," and all other VALIANT comic books up to and including *UNITY*, which combined to form one vast tale. The concept behind that tale is cousin to the concept behind *Nobody Gets the Girl*. Aside from a roughly similar concept and the few inevitable coincidences, however, the stories are very different. To say that one is like the other would be like saying that *Easter Parade* is just like *Romeo and Juliet* because they both involve romances. Nonetheless, I can assure you from my somewhat related experience that it's a high degree of difficulty dive, which may account for why it's pretty much unexplored territory.

Maxey's exploration of it is startling. He will surprise you. If you're one of those perversely analytical people who try to outguess the storyteller, you will lose. Every time you start to cry foul and claim that Maxey yanked a bunny out of his bonnet, you will no doubt suddenly realize that he's gotcha. You *should* have expected it, but you didn't.

Maxey's protagonist—hard to call him a hero—is a self-made man, you might say. That is, he's a *tulpa* that he himself created and maintains in existence by his own thoughts. Nobody, for real.

Don't give yourself a headache trying to figure that out now. You'll see.

The world Nobody thinks is real is strange and yet everything that happens there is as logically founded and reasonable as everything that happens in the world we think is real. It is a world that, like the Flaming Carrot, seems to have gone mad from reading too many comic books. And yet, in ways it is chillingly too familiar. The world Nobody thinks is real exposes the strangeness and madness of the world we think is real.

Nobody Gets the Girl soars from the heart to the skies. From deeply personal to super-sized epic. Nobody is just an ordinary Joe except for the not-existing thing. You can feel his pain and occasionally his lust. You can rise with him to his finest moments and wallow with him in some really shameful behavior. When push comes to shove, the scale of the action is awesome. Yet, there too, is all the darkness and nobility of humankind.

James Maxey won the hotly contested Phobos Award for a short story he wrote entitled "Empire of Dreams and Miracles," which then was further honored by its selection as the title feature of *Empire of Dreams and Miracles: The Phobos Science Fiction Anthology*. Find it, buy it. Maxey built a world in that story. In *Nobody Gets the Girl* he tops himself.

And, he gives new meaning to the lyrical phrase, "You're Nobody till somebody loves you."

NOBODY GETS THE GIRL

A DAMN FINE
ACT OF TERROR

Seattle burned. The night sky smoldered a hellish red, as flames reflected off dust and steam. The horrible smoke rendered most senses useless. People stumbled over debris on the sidewalk, unable to see through teary eyes. The fumes burned their lungs, filled their mouths and noses with a sickening chemical stench of burning carpet. There were too many noises. People were screaming, sirens and alarms blared over the waterfall roar of the inferno. Glass shattered and crashed upon the city streets.

And above it all, explosions. Just when the roar of the last blast fell silent, another would follow, throwing people to the sidewalk. The Earth shook as if a giant were stamping its feet.

Which, in fact, was exactly what was happening. Those people who through luck, good or bad, had a vantage point above the smoke and destruction were greeted with a disturbing sight this night. Waddling through the

1

downtown streets of Seattle, with a swaying, tottering rhythm, was a one-hundred-foot-tall baby doll. Where the doll's head should have been was a pistol, a gleaming Saturday night special the size of school bus. The doll would toddle forward a few blocks, knocking down walls and shattering glass as it swayed, then, bracing itself, would turn its gun-gaze on a nearby skyscraper and let fly with an enormous bullet.

The doll had been wandering the streets for half an hour. It seemed to have no plan or purpose other than destruction. It was impossible to say whether it was by chance or design that it arrived at the most famous structure of the Seattle skyline, the Space Needle. For a moment, it waddled past the Needle, seemingly oblivious to its presence. Then it turned its horrible muzzle toward the structure.

Half a world away, a man with his feet kicked up on the coffee table chuckled with pleasure as the Needle tumbled to the ground. His name was Rex Monday.

"That, my friend, is a damn fine act of terror if I do say so myself," said Monday, waving toward the TV.

His "friend" was an old man, very thin, dressed in clothes so worn and dirty any civilized person would have burned them. The old man watched the carnage playing out on the screen as he crunched on the unpopped kernels he had dug from the bottom of the bag of popcorn in his hand. "I reckon. Sure. But what's in it for you? I'm grateful for the work, Mr. Monday. Not much work for a carny geek these days. But, as long as you're going to be tearing up buildings, shouldn't you be stealing stuff? Send me in. I bet I can find a bank to chew into or something."

"You think small, friend," said Monday. "What's in it for me is that *he* hates it. He hates that he can't outthink me, that he can't predict me, that he can't protect the world from me."

"Who?"

"*Dr. Know.* Haven't you been paying attention?"

"Oh yeah," said the old man, who held the bag up to make sure he'd finished the contents. Seeing that he had, he wadded up the bag, and ate it in one mouthful. As he chewed, he said, "Your, uh, enemy. Still think it couldn't hurt to scoop up some jewelry or something."

"Petty baubles," said Monday. "Worthless. Meaningless. There's a grander prize at stake in this game."

"What's that?" asked the old man.

"The *world.*"

NONE OF THIS had anything to do with Richard Rogers. Richard would read about the rampage in Seattle in the paper tomorrow, just like the rest of the world. The news these days sometimes seemed like an unending chain of tragedy and despair. But by lunch he would be firing off e-mail jokes about it to his friends, feeling only a little guilty. He was the first to admit there was nothing funny about it, nothing at all. Richard knew that in the wake of these attacks there were people left homeless, spouses widowed, children orphaned. Only an insensitive clod would be writing jokes before the dust settled. Still, gee whiz, how could you not laugh at the idea of a freakin' *giant doll* tearing down the Space Needle? It helped that these things always seemed to happen far away, in cities a lot bigger than his. They didn't touch his life directly.

At least, not yet.

CHAPTER ONE

NOBODY HOME

"Yeah, all my life I've been lucky," Richard said, transitioning from driving jokes into current events jokes. "Lucky I don't live in D.C., for one thing. You been following this? The Dome?"

There were maybe twelve people in the audience now. A few were still laughing from the last punch line. A handful nodded their heads at the mention of the Dome.

"I mean, talk about a waste of money," said Richard. "Seventeen billion dollars this thing's costing. Gonna put a big old dome over the entire city. Climate control year round. There's, what? Two million people living under this thing? Three million? You could buy umbrellas for everybody for a lot less than seventeen billion. Or maybe not, if the Pentagon was in charge of it. Then we'd be buying the XJ-11 combat ready umbrella. Not only rainproof but bulletproof. They'd weigh forty-five pounds each."

He wielded the mike-stand like a very heavy umbrella and staggered a few feet across the stage, grunting under its weight. The audience laughed hard. One of the first lessons Richard had learned about stand-up comedy was that he could make anything seem funny if he attached it to a silly walk.

He straightened up and put the mike back into the stand. "Thanks! You've been a great audience! I'm Richard Rogers! I'll be back here next month!"

He bounded from the stage and shook a few hands. He felt wired, buzzing, full of the same manic energy that always hit him after a set. The charge was the same with twelve people in the audience as with a hundred. This is why he'd drive four hours on a weeknight to perform at the Stokesville Ramada's comedy bar open mike.

Making his way through the small crowd, he arrived at the bar.

"Good set," said Billy the bartender, who was already filling a glass with Richard's usual beer.

"Thanks," said Richard as he took the glass. "Small crowd though."

"Eh," said Billy. "It's raining. Never a big crowd when it's this nasty out."

"Maybe I'll start driving to D.C.," said Richard. "Not many nasty nights there anymore."

"Thought you didn't like the Dome," said Billy.

"Ah, who cares. It's too weird to get really worked up about. Every day I watch the news and think, 'They're just making this stuff up.' They've got a bunch of ex–comic book writers sitting in the back room cranking out these stories. Probably cheaper than hiring reporters. I mean, right now the government is telling us that the most wanted terrorist in the world is somebody named Rex Monday. Pardon me, but didn't he fight Dick Tracey?"

Richard grew aware of a presence behind him stepping a little too much into his personal space. He looked over his shoulder. It was a woman. She had caught his eye a few times when he was onstage. She was tall, good looking, maybe a few years older than him, but very attractive.

"You were good up there," she said, taking the stool next to him. "My name's Rose."

"Thanks," he said. "I'm Richard."

"So what are you doing here on an open mike night?" she asked. "You're better than most of the pros I've seen in here. You should be paid for this."

"Thanks again," said Richard. "I don't suppose you'd happen to be an agent, would you?"

"No. I'm the district sales rep for Oxford Financial. I travel a lot. When I'm in town I usually come here. Really, I've seen a lot of comedians, and you're very talented."

Richard shrugged. "I've thought about turning pro, but it's not likely to happen."

"Why not?"

"Oh, you know. I didn't really discover I enjoyed doing this until I was already neck deep in something else. I'm a network manager at FirstSouth. I can't afford to quit that and hit the circuits in hope of some big break. For the time being, the Stokesville Ramada's as far as I travel."

"I wish this was as far as I traveled," said Rose. "My counterpart in the Carolinas quit so I'm covering four states now. But it's not all bad. Some parts of life on the road I really like."

"Such as?"

"Meeting new people," said Rose, moving even closer to Richard. "I feel more like who I want to be when I'm talking to someone for the first time."

"Hmm," said Richard.

"You must understand," said Rose, lightly touching his arm. "You're a different person when you're onstage? On the road, you can be anyone you want to be."

Richard nodded. "Yeah. I do feel like a different person up there. Only it's not really different. It's like who I really am. It's everywhere else in my life I feel a bit out of place."

She touched his arm again. "So you do understand. Funny people are often the most insightful."

Richard looked at her hand which was lingering on his arm. He suddenly felt rather warm.

"So," she said. "Do you have a room here?"

"Um," said Richard. "No. Actually I have to work in the morning. I'm driving home tonight."

"In this weather?" she asked. "Wouldn't you rather spend the night in a warm bed than out in that mess?"

Richard placed his left hand on the bar, making sure his wedding ring was visible. "My wife would be worried," he said.

"Call her and tell you you're staying over because of the weather," said Rose.

"I'd never hear the end of it. You don't know my wife," said Richard.

"And you don't know my husband," said Rose with a sly grin, leaning closer. "Isn't it marvelous we have so much in common?"

She was looking directly into his eyes. Richard had a strong sense of déjà vu. This was a fantasy he'd played in his head many times over, being approached by a beautiful woman after he'd finished a set, a woman who found him sexy based purely on his ten minute routine. Now here his fantasy was, in the very attractive flesh.

He looked down at his wedding ring.

OUT ON THE interstate, Richard kept thinking he should turn the car around. Maybe Rose would still be at the bar. Maybe she would find it charming that he had changed his mind and come back.

He kept driving. He did have to work tomorrow. And Veronica, well, Veronica already hated his late nights. Affair or no, she would hold it over his head for a month if he didn't come home. A month if he was lucky.

When it's pouring rain and you're the only car on the interstate, it's difficult not to feel a little introspective. Was his life so terrible? He had a good job, a nice house, a devoted wife. Why did he feel this craving to throw all that away and live on the road, traveling state to state, bar to bar, just to have people laugh at him?

As he got off the exit near his house he kept thinking he should turn back. Rose would be gone by now, but what did that matter? He didn't think he could take another day of watching the clock at work. He knew he would snap if Veronica complained about his being out an hour later than he had promised.

He had made his decision by the time he pulled into his driveway. He would go inside and write Veronica a letter. He'd been composing it in his head for some time now. "I'm sorry," it would start. "I'm not happy anymore. I'm living the life I wanted five years ago, but five years ago I was an idiot." He would pack his toothbrush and hit the road.

"Never look back," he whispered as he closed the door behind him and stepped into his darkened living room.

But he knew that 3 A.M. is a terrible time to contemplate such things. He tossed his coat on the couch. Not hanging it up was a minor act of rebellion. He looked around at the carefully groomed living room, with the throw pillows thrown to millimeter accuracy and the single large art magazine sitting on the coffee table at a carefully calculated angle to convey casual intellectualism. He sighed, picked up his coat, and placed it in the closet. He pulled off his shoes and crept into the bedroom. He undressed by the dim LED light of his alarm clock. He could still get four hours sleep. Four and half if he went to work unshaved and slightly rumpled. Or, he could put his clothes back on and—

But before he could even finish the thought he was in bed and Veronica's warmth and smell was the only thing he was aware of in the darkness. Would Rose have felt as warm? What would she have smelled like? He closed his eyes and breathed through his nose very, very slowly. He had to put this out of his head. He would be the same person tomorrow that he was tonight. These fantasies of walking out of his life, a life that had grown so comfortable and familiar that it bored him, and into a new, exciting unknown one, would never do him any good.

Then again, these fantasies also did no harm. Richard knew in his heart he would never act on them. Whether that represented courage or cowardice on his part he could not say. He was too drowsy to think about it anymore. He scooted closer to Veronica, till his back touched hers, and fell into sleep.

THE ALARM WENT off. Richard rolled from his bed groggily, reaching out to click off the alarm. But the alarm clock wasn't there. It was ringing behind him, on the other side of the bed. He looked over his shoulder. A man's hairy arm slipped from the covers on the far side of the bed and slapped the snooze button.

Richard leapt up and spun around. *Who the hell . . . ?* he thought. There were two strangers in his bed. Only it wasn't his bed. Veronica and he shared a queen-size bed, and he was now standing at the foot of a king-size one. He froze, afraid even to breath, as he studied the room in the pale morning light.

The room had a spooky familiarity to it. The closet, the windows, the hall door . . . in fact, every single architectural element of this room was an exact match of his own bedroom. Except the furniture, the paint, the curtains—those were all different. He was in someone else's house.

In the bed was an old man of considerable girth and a skinny old woman, their snores resuming in the aftermath of the alarm.

OK, he thought. *This is plain weird.*

Was this his house, or wasn't it? Should he be outraged at the intruders, or was he the intruder?

His head hurt. Rubbing his temples, he realized what was happening. He was dreaming. He had done this before, dreaming that he was awake, growing increasingly confused and panicky before truly waking. There was even a name for this: hypnagogic sleep. His comedian's mind held onto little bits of trivia like that. But this level of awareness of his dream state gave him a chill. It was almost magical.

He laughed. Loudly. The sleeping couple didn't stir.

"Ain't this a hoot," he said. The couple continued to snore. He was very aware of the sound of his own voice. It seemed so real.

"Am I dreaming?" he said. "I must be dreaming."

He turned and looked in the dresser mirror. His hair was messed up from sleep, his eyes baggy and dark. He needed a shave.

"You can wake up now," he said.

He closed his eyes.

When he opened them, he was still in the strange room.

So maybe he couldn't wake up. His heart raced as he swallowed hard. No, no, no, he thought. He was already awake. Which meant he was in some stranger's house. How?

The alarm went off again. The man smacked it into silence, and slowly rolled his great bulk into a sitting position. He rose, and lumbered off toward the bathroom, never even looking in Richard's direction.

Richard silently let out a long, slow breath and tiptoed toward the hall door. He opened it gently, and stepped out of the bedroom. The hall was exactly like the one in his house. Richard scratched his head.

He could rule out the dream thing. His senses were fully engaged. His legs were cold, standing in the hallway in only his underwear and socks. With every breath, he could tell that the residents of this house smoked, and weren't particularly fastidious in cleaning their cat's litter box. In the bathroom, the old man was making sounds on the toilet that Richard hoped were real, and not emanating from some dark and disgusting part of his subconscious.

He left the hall and entered the living room, now prepared for the sense of déjà vu. The house, structurally, was a perfect match.

Weird, but not impossible, he thought. Suburban architecture wasn't exactly known for individuality. But what were the odds that he had gone sleepwalking and wound up in a different house built on exactly the same plan?

Then it hit him. This must be Bert's revenge. About a month ago, he had played a semi-harmless prank on the guy at work. He had loaded a gag font onto Bert's system, one where all the letters were reversed. Then he'd set that to be the default system font on Bert's machine. Bert had spent hours trying to discover what kind of killer virus had wrecked his computer before figuring it out. Bert had been to his house before. What if Bert had a friend with a house built to the same plan? Bert could get his friends in on it, could get Veronica to play along, could . . .

Richard stared at the fireplace. When he and Veronica had moved into the house, they had discovered a small heart carved into the mantelpiece by some previous occupant. Richard took a step closer. The heart was there. This was his house.

He had seen enough. He stormed back down the hallway and slammed opened the door.

"Does someone want to tell me what the hell is going on?" he yelled.

The old woman sat up with a start, staring at the door. She looked as confused as Richard felt.

"Henry!" she called out.

"What," Henry grunted from the bathroom.

"Did you just hear something?" she asked.

Richard stared at the woman's face. She was looking right through him. Was she blind? Being the victim of a bad joke didn't make him feel good about terrorizing old blind women. His anger fizzled.

"Look," he said softly. "I'm sorry I startled you. I'm not a burglar, or—"

Henry came out of the bathroom, naked. Richard once again hoped that this situation wasn't a dream. If he was going to be dreaming of a naked person this night, it should be Rose or Veronica, shouldn't it?

"What?" said Henry.

"I said did you hear something? It sounded like the bedroom door slammed."

Henry stared at the door, with no acknowledgment of Richard's presence.

"I didn't open it," said Henry.

"Neither did I," said the woman.

"Huh," said Henry.

Richard sighed. "If this is a joke, it's a great one, except for one tiny detail: it's not funny!"

Henry walked over to him, not in a menacing way, but with a speed and trajectory that showed very little respect for Richard's personal space. Richard held his ground. Henry stepped up to him. And then stepped right through him.

Richard felt dizzy. He stumbled forward, and leaned against the dresser.

Henry stood in the hallway, looking around.

"Maybe it was Pooky," Henry said.

"Pooky," the woman called out. "Where's my Pooky?"

With a plaintive meow, a large gray cat ran into the room from the hall and leapt up onto the bed. Then the cat looked at Richard. Its eyes widened, its fur bristled, and it hissed loudly.

13

"Pooky!" the woman exclaimed, reaching for her cat.

Pooky eluded her grasp and fled the room.

"What's gotten into that cat?" she asked.

"Who knows, Martha?" said Henry, stepping back into the room. "Pointless to try to figure it out."

"OK," Richard said. "This has gone far enough. You've taken this gag a long way, but the cat just blew the act. Who are you and who put you up to this?"

Henry didn't answer. He went to the dresser and opened his underwear drawer.

"Answer me, damn it!" Richard yelled, reaching out to grasp the old man's shoulders. But his hand passed right through Henry as if he were a ghost.

Or as if Richard was.

Richard began to laugh. He fell to his knees, tears in his eyes. He had figured it out. This was his house.

And he was haunting it.

"I WONDER HOW I died," he said to Martha.

Martha kept ironing clothes.

"I mean, it seems like my death should have been memorable, huh? It's, you know, one of life's big events."

When Martha finished her ironing, she went into the living room to watch *The Price is Right*. She lit up a cigarette.

"You shouldn't smoke," Richard said. "It'll kill you."

He sat down next to her on the couch and looked at the television. "So will this crap. I mean, c'mon Martha. Don't make me spend my afterlife with Bob Barker. You hear me?"

She didn't hear him.

He sighed. "I figure I went in my sleep. That's why I don't remember it. But, I was so young! Pretty healthy, too. At least I thought so. Christ, I never even got colds."

He crossed his legs on the coffee table and sank back into the couch, making himself comfortable. Bob Barker revealed the correct price of the stainless-steel refrigerator.

"Twenty-two hundred dollars?" said Richard. "You know why refrigerators cost $2200? Women. Me, I was happy with my $50 dorm fridge. 'Why do we need a big refrigerator?' I asked. 'It just means we'll have more stuff going bad in it.' But Veronica had to have the top of the line. Our refrigerator had to make four different kinds of ice and have water on tap. I mean, ice is ice, and the water coming out of the refrigerator was exactly the same stuff coming out of the sink. But did any of that matter to her?"

Richard looked over at Martha. She didn't answer.

"Huh," said Richard. "Wonder what she spent on my funeral?"

The funeral. He imagined looking down on himself in the casket. It was almost like a memory. Was it a memory? He wondered where his body was now, moldering away in some grave. Or would Veronica have had him cremated? Was he sitting in perfect *feng shui* harmony on a mantle-piece in a new living room? The bank had pretty good life insurance. It was probably a very large living room. Maybe with a big screen TV. Just his luck to be stuck here.

A commercial started playing and Martha got up and went into the kitchen. Richard grabbed the remote control and changed channels the second she was out of the room, clicking through crap until he found CNN. From the kitchen, he heard the beeps of a microwave.

"The Washington, D.C., Dome was the target of another bomb scare today," the announcer said. "The bomb was discovered and diffused by a UN peacekeeping squad with the assistance of the mysterious adventurer known as Rail Blade." The screen shifted to stock footage of a woman lifting a tank over her head. This was the kind of stuff that made Richard assume that the line between journalism and fiction had been forever erased. "There were no injuries," the announcer continued. "The terrorist group Monday's Revelation claimed credit for the failed attack, and vowed further acts of violence during next week's opening ceremonies."

This news gave Richard pause. He could recall the last day of his life, and he was pretty sure the D.C. Dome celebration was about a week away then. Just how quickly did Veronica sell the house once he'd died?

The smell of popcorn filled the room as Martha came back from the kitchen. As she neared the couch, Richard's fingers turned to smoke around the remote, and it fell to the couch, right through his lap.

Martha looked at the television, confused.

"Pooky?" she asked, looking around.

Richard felt more than a little confused himself. His on-again-off-again tangibility was frustrating. And, if he was dead, why was his stomach rumbling now that he smelled the popcorn? He got up and went into the kitchen. He opened the refrigerator (definitely not a $2,200 model). To his relief, he found a pack of bologna and some cheese. To his greater relief, there was also a six-pack of beer. A loaf of bread sat on top of the fridge.

He finished his second beer by the time he had assembled a sandwich. He sat down at the kitchen table. The chair made a rasping sound as he scooted it closer to the table.

A moment later, Martha cautiously peeked around the doorway. Richard waved at her, then returned to his sandwich. He was a little surprised that the sandwich didn't fall from his fingers. He wondered what Martha saw. Did it look as if the sandwich was just floating in mid air?

Martha took a step forward. Richard reached for his beer, to wash down his food. His fingers passed right through the can.

"Well, damn," he said, spitting crumbs.

Martha crept toward the table. She reached out and touched the can of beer, then pulled her fingers away.

The phone rang, and both of them jumped.

Martha smoothed down her hair, before answering the phone.

"Henry! Oh, thank God! No, Henry, listen to me! I think there's someone in the house!"

She paced back and forth as she spoke, casting her eyes warily around the room.

"Well, I was watching channel 6, then went into the kitchen, and when I went back, the remote had moved, and the TV was on channel 32. And then, when I came back into the kitchen, there was a can of beer on the table. And . . . and someone's moved the bread from the top of the refrigerator to the counter."

Martha twisted the phone cord around her fingers until Richard thought she might pull it from the wall. He felt bad about scaring her, but it wasn't like he meant it. He was just trying to get on with his afterlife.

"No!" said Martha. "I mean, sure, Pooky could have stepped on the remote. But how did she get a beer out of the refrigerator? No, it isn't one you left out last night. It's still cold!"

Richard finished his sandwich. Since he was unable to touch the beer, he thought he'd try to get some water from the sink. But, for some reason, he couldn't scoot his chair back. It seemed nailed to the floor. He tried again, pushing harder, and suddenly tumbled to the floor, as the chair became intangible. He sat up quickly, rubbing his right elbow. The floor was still solid enough. And it was filthy. Martha and Henry weren't the best house-keepers. He got up, brushing away dirt.

Martha was telling Henry she planned to call the police then go over to Mrs. Green's house. This bugged Roger. Mrs. Green was his neighbor. She was a sweet little old lady who deserved better neighbors than slobs like Martha and Henry.

If Martha were going to call the cops, he'd give her something to call about. He went to the dishes in the sink. Martha was looking away, craning her neck to see if anyone was in the living room.

Richard picked up a plate, and hurled it against the wall by her head. It shattered with a satisfying crash.

He flinched as Martha shrieked at an octave he didn't know the human voice could reach before she fled the house through the kitchen door.

"Martha!" Henry shouted from the phone.

Richard picked up the phone.

"Hi," he said.

"Martha! What's happening?" said Henry.

"Can you hear me?" asked Richard.

"Martha! Say something!"

"Sorry," said Richard, hanging up the phone. "Nobody's home."

Chapter Two

HEY! I'M ON TV!

In retrospect, Richard felt kind of bad about how close the plate had come to Martha's head. In life he hadn't been short-tempered. He'd always been able to take consolation in the fact that today's frustrations could be turned into next week's stand-up comedy.

But his current situation didn't strike him as particularly funny.

He took a shower to wash away the grime of the kitchen floor, although the grime of the shower tiles prevented him from feeling clean. It made him wonder again just how long he'd been dead. Veronica had been such a neat freak. The shower tiles used to sparkle. How long would it take to build up so many layers of soap scum and mildew?

He got out of the shower and toweled himself dry. He thought he heard something like footsteps in the hall. Had Martha come back? They sounded too heavy for Martha.

A voice called out, "Anybody here?"

"Yes!" said Richard, bounding out of the bathroom with the towel wrapped around him.

Two police officers stood in the door of the bedroom. The first one, a middle-aged black man, crept into the room cautiously, seemingly oblivious to Richard. He was followed by a young Hispanic woman who seemed much more relaxed.

"Search the closet," the man said, pulling out his flashlight and lowering himself to his knees. He clicked the light on and looked under the bed.

The woman shrugged and went to the open closet door. She half-heartedly pushed the clothes around with her flashlight.

"Look at the size of these pants," she said. "Whoever lives here must be a real lard-bucket."

"I don't suppose you can see me," Richard said, waving his hand in front of the woman's face. She turned from the closet and walked through him.

"Just testing," he said.

"Why are we wasting our time with this?" the woman asked.

"It's our job," said the man, sounding annoyed.

From outside, there was the sound of squealing tires, followed quickly by a slamming car door.

"Martha," Henry screamed, bursting through the front door.

The older cop stepped into the hallway, his gun drawn.

"Freeze!" he shouted.

"Don't shoot!" Henry cried out from the hallway. "I live here! What's happened to my wife?"

"She's OK," said the woman, cautiously slipping past her partner. "Just stay calm. I believe that you live here, but we're going to need to see some ID."

Richard followed to watch events unfold, toweling his hair dry. No one seemed to see a towel floating in mid-air. He wished he understood the rules of this ghost business a little better. This bit about being able to touch stuff unless someone was looking at it . . .

Was that it? Was it as simple as that?

He stepped back into the bedroom and turned on the light. Then, just for the hell of it, he picked up the lamp on the nightstand and threw it against the wall.

The cops were in the room in seconds, guns drawn.

"Come on out!" the male cop shouted.

"With your hands up!" the woman added. "We know you're in here! Give up!"

"I'm trying, OK?" said Richard.

They swiveled around, placing their backs together, studying the entire room.

Richard went to the lamp. He couldn't budge it. He could feel it, but it seemed made of lead. With a grunt, he tried harder. Once more either he or the lamp seemed no longer solid. His hand passed right through.

"Curious," he said.

Then, just for the heck of it, he threw his towel into the air.

It fell to the bed. The woman cop jumped, and looked in his direction.

"You see that?" she said.

"What?" the guy asked.

"That towel on the bed. It wasn't there a second ago."

She reached out and picked it up.

"It's damp," she said.

"You sure?" the guy asked.

"Yes, it's damp," she said.

"No. I mean, maybe it was there. I think I saw it there earlier."

"I don't know," she said. "It . . . I don't know what I saw. It was like it moved."

Suddenly, the male cop relaxed. "OK. OK. Whoever you are, I know you can hear me. So far, you haven't hurt anybody. I don't think you want to hurt anybody. I think this is all a joke to you. Come out right now, before I change my mind about how serious this is."

"It's breaking and entering," said Henry, from the hall.

"Sir, it's probably safer if you go next door with your wife," said the woman.

Richard stepped through all three of them on his way into the hallway. Martha and Henry could go next door. Could he?

He opened the back door and stepped into the sunlight, leaving the door open.

He stretched his arms over his head, luxuriating in the warmth on his naked skin. He walked a little further into the backyard. The lawn had really gone to hell. But it really didn't matter. Why had he wasted even one Saturday morning mowing it? What did an unmown lawn matter in the grand scheme of things? Then he noticed that his feet itched, and he worried that he might have stepped on something bad in the tall grass. So, OK, maybe his life hadn't been a complete waste.

Before he had time to further ruminate on the cosmic significance of his life, the cops followed him out the door.

"Told you I heard the door open," the woman said, with a smug tone that indicated she had won some small argument.

"Gloat later," the guy said, sprinting around the edge of the house. The woman raced in the opposite direction. Henry came out onto the back deck, and Martha called out to him from the neighbor's yard.

Richard decided to go back inside. He wasn't used to being barefoot. Maybe Henry had some sandals that would fit.

A few minutes later, he joined the crowd that had gathered in the front yard. He was dressed in Martha's pink silk robe with Henry's neon green flip-flops. No one paid him any attention.

The lady cop was on the radio, reporting back to the dispatcher. "Whoever it was got away. Ray thinks it might have been a runaway kid hiding out. We're pretty sure he slipped out the back door and is long gone."

"So, you're not going to do anything?" Henry asked the male cop.

"We did do something," the cop answered. "We searched the house. Nobody's in there. All we can do now is keep an eye on the place."

Martha looked wild-eyed, half-afraid, half-angry. "I can't go back in there," she said. "What if he's still inside? Maybe he just opened the door, then went back into hiding."

"Ma'am," said the male cop, "if anyone's hiding in that house, they're either the size of a rat or invisible. We searched everywhere."

"Well, he must be invisible then," Martha said. "Because, I swear, there's someone in that house!"

"Sorry lady," said the cop with a shrug. "Invisible people aren't really a police matter. Maybe you should call a priest."

RICHARD WOKE UP feeling wonderful. He'd had the most awful dream. Then he looked around the room and realized he was still in Henry and Martha's bed. He owed his good night's sleep only to exhaustion and the fact that Martha had insisted on sleeping in a hotel.

"So, you're not going to wake up from this," he said. "This is real, Richard, deal with it."

First, he wanted to deal with some coffee. He wandered into the kitchen and found a coffeemaker. Unfortunately, he didn't find any coffee.

So he grabbed a beer.

He went into the living room and stretched out on the couch, then clicked on the TV with the remote.

Somehow, he had imagined the afterlife would provide a sharper contrast with life. Was he really going to spend the rest of eternity wandering around the house in a bathrobe, drinking beer, and watching TV? Was death like a Saturday morning that would never end? If so, was that Heaven, or Hell?

"I'm getting real tired of this," he said, casting his eyes toward the ceiling. "I mean, shouldn't I be here for a reason? To avenge some injustice or something?"

It occurred to him that this would probably make for a pretty good Jerry Springer show. "My boyfriend don't do nothing with his afterlife but keep his ass glued to the couch," he said in his best redneck woman voice.

But instead of finding Jerry Springer as he flipped through the channels, he found a local news show, with a picture of his house on the screen.

"Police say the strange occurrences could have been caused by a runaway child. But the owners of the house have another theory."

Martha's wrinkled visage suddenly flashed on screen. "Poltergeist," she said. "I've read all about them in *Fate*. Our house has been possessed by an unquiet spirit."

The camera cut to home video of the crowd gathered in front of the house the day before. And there, plain as day, was Richard in his pink robe.

"Hey!" he said, sitting up. "I'm on TV!"

The report ended with the news that Martha and Henry planned to contact a priest.

"OK," Richard said. "OK, OK, OK. I was on TV. The camera saw me, even if no one else did. OK. OK. So what does that mean? I mean . . . I mean . . . what does this mean? What on Earth?"

He got up and paced around the room, running his fingers through his hair.

"I can touch things, I can't touch things. I can't be seen, but I can be filmed. I can't be heard on the phone, but . . ."

He noticed something out the living room window. There was a paper on Mrs. Green's sidewalk. At least now he could know once and for all how long he'd been dead.

Standing on the sidewalk, he unfurled the front page of the paper. July 9. He'd played the comedy club open mike on July 7.

He wasn't dead.

At least, being dead didn't add up. There wasn't enough time for him to be buried, for Veronica to sell the house. There wasn't enough time for the grime on the kitchen floor. So he wasn't dead, and he wasn't dreaming.

Insanity began to climb pretty high up the list.

Only, he wasn't insane, either. He was certain of it. As crazy as his situation was, it was the situation that was screwed up, not him.

He went back into the house. Maybe Martha had a video camera or at least a tape recorder. Maybe there was some way he could send a message. Especially if a priest really was coming, maybe a priest would have some clue as to Richard's condition.

He tore apart the front hall closet.

He scattered the contents of the kitchen hither and yon.

He pulled out all the bedroom drawers and emptied their contents on the floor.

Nothing. Not even a camera.

Then he noticed the tube of lipstick on the dresser. He looked at the mirror.

He uncapped the tube, and wrote as calmly and legibly as he could on the mirror. "My name is Richard Rogers. I'm trapped in this house, like a ghost, but I'm not dead. Help me."

RICHARD LIKED THE priest.

Father Leibowitz was a young man, but one accustomed to the authority and respect due his position. He took command of the situation from the moment he stepped in the door. Henry and Martha didn't have time to introduce themselves before Father Leibowitz gave his first order.

"The mirror," he said. "Show me."

"I apologize that the place is such a mess," Martha said, leading him down the hall. "What with all—"

"Unimportant," Leibowitz said with a dismissive wave. He drew up in front of the mirror, and read its message. He pulled out a cell phone and punched a button.

"April," he said. "I've got some names for you to do a search on. Our ghost says his name is Richard Rogers, and his wife's name is Veronica Rogers. If you find her, get her on the phone to me. Also, he says his parents are named Bill and Florence Rogers, and they live in Salem, Virginia. He has even been obliging enough to give us a phone number, but do a search to see what you come up with. I don't want to call this number until we get a little more information."

Richard received this news with a bit of frustration. He had already dialed the number, and had the heartbreaking experience of hearing his mother's voice but being unable to speak to her. Still, Father Leibowitz seemed confident and professional. Richard took a seat on the bed and decided to be patient.

"Richard?" asked Father Leibowitz. "Can you hear me?"

"Sure," said Richard.

"Richard, if you can hear me, give me some sign."

Richard got up and went to the mirror. He reached for the lipstick. It slipped through his ghostly fingers.

"Figures," he said. But, he wasn't beaten yet. He walked past the priest and went to the kitchen, picked up two pots and banged them together, twice.

"How 'bout twice for yes, once for no?" Richard called out.

But then Father Leibowitz stepped into the kitchen and the pots slipped through Richard's fingers, clattering on the floor. Richard thought this was strange. Normally things he was holding, like the towel, stayed solid to him and invisible to everyone else until he let go of them.

"April," Father Leibowitz said into the phone. "I think we can definitely rule out a hoax. I just saw two pots levitating, no doubt in response to my request."

Richard realized this was a perfect opportunity to move back into the bedroom and add to his message on the mirror, to let them know that he would cooperate however he could.

But as he stepped into the hall, he stopped when he heard Father Leibowitz's words.

"Right," said Leibowitz, in response to April. "No record of a Richard and Veronica Rogers in this city. I'm not surprised."

Richard decided that April wasn't very good at her job. He went back to the mirror, smeared away a clean surface with one of Henry's undershirts, and wrote down his Social Security Number, his work phone number, and his birth date. Then, he had a clever idea. He ran the lipstick along his fingertips, and left a perfect set of fingerprints on the mirror.

"That should make it easier," he said. "Assuming Father Leibowitz has a fingerprint lab in the trunk of his car. But what the hell." Then he banged his fist against the wall several times, until Leibowitz came running, and his fist went through the wall without leaving a mark.

"April," said Leibowitz. "Let's try again. I've got some more—what? You do have a listing in Salem for Bill Rogers? Yes. Yes, that's a match. No, don't call yet. Check out this Social Security Number first."

Richard smacked his forehead. "Look, just call my folks, OK?"

Then he thought about it. Call and say what? Your son is invisible and intangible and we were hoping you might help? What good would a phone call to them do?

"Maybe April could look up Stephen Hawking's phone number," Richard suggested.

Instead, April was giving Father Leibowitz the results of the Social Security search.

"Yes. Yes that is a strange coincidence," said Leibowitz.

"What," said Henry.

"The Social Security Number belongs to an Alan Leibowitz in New Jersey," Leibowitz said with a shrug. "Could be a cousin."

Richard took another look at the mirror. That was his number. He was sure of it.

The priest addressed Henry and Martha. "This is only a minor setback. This sort of confusion isn't uncommon among the dead."

"Father," said Martha.

"Yes?"

"Can I ask a personal question?"

"Go."

"Isn't Leibowitz a, um, Jewish name?"

"I'm asked that all the time," said Leibowitz. "I think it's time to call the parents. It's the only information our ghost has given that April's been able to get a confirmation on."

"Finally," said Richard. He started to bite his nails, until he realized he had lipstick under them. Just what would Leibowitz say to his parents?

"Is this Bill Rogers?" Leibowitz asked, as April set up a three-way call.

"Mr. Rogers, my name is Father Leibowitz, and I'm call—yes. No problem. I'm asked that all the time. But, let me get directly to the point of my call. Do you have a son named Richard? I see. Second question: Does the date March 9, 1969, have any meaning to you? I see. No, not a joke. No. No, you've been very helpful. Sorry to have disturbed you. Have a nice day."

"Well," said Henry.

"They don't have a son," Father Leibowitz said.

"What?" said Richard.

"We're left with only one possibility," said Father Leibowitz.

Richard's knees grew weak. He braced his back against the wall and slowly slid down into a crouch. "This can't be real," he whispered.

"The spirit that haunts this house is quite likely a fallen angel," Father Leibowitz explained. "From time to time, the damned delude themselves into thinking they are something they are not. In this case, the demon has made up elaborate details about a former human life, in an effort to strengthen his delusion. But, as we've just determined, all of these details are lies."

"Lies," Richard said. "Oh God, this can't be. This can't be. My name is Richard Rogers. I'm real. I have a life. I have a wife. Her name is Veronica. I . . . can't believe this!"

"No doubt, the demon is listening even now," said Father Leibowitz. "It's important, no matter what happens, that the two of you keep faith. God watches over us. No demon can touch you."

"I am not a demon!" Richard screamed. He wanted to grab the priest by the throat. He stalked from the bedroom, back to the kitchen, flung open the cabinets and started throwing pots and pans around the room. He wasn't sure why this seemed like a good idea, but his present state left him so few options for venting his frustration.

"Stop this now!" Father Leibowitz shouted as he entered the kitchen.

"Screw you," said Richard.

Martha peeked her head into the kitchen, and shrieked.

"What?" asked Father Leibowitz.

"I see it!" she cried.

Richard raised his eyebrows. Throwing pots and pans might work out for him after all.

"It's right there," said Martha, pointing to where Richard stood. "It's like . . . like a pink haze."

Richard looked down at his housecoat.

"You do see me!" he said. "Oh, thank God!"

Henry stuck his head slowly around the corner, and caught his breath.

"I see it, too," he whispered.

"Can you hear me? Can you hear me?"

Apparently, they couldn't hear him.

"Martha, Henry, listen to me," said Father Leibowitz. "You must not turn away from what you see. You must have faith in God."

Father Leibowitz took a step toward Richard. "Demon! Your presence is revealed to us. Show yourself!"

"I'm freaking trying, OK?"

"Show yourself!" Father Leibowitz commanded once more.

Richard's stomach twisted into a tight knot. His skin suddenly felt hot.

"Show yourself!" Leibowitz demanded.

Richard fell to his knees, staring at his hands. His flesh writhed and crawled, twisting his hands into blood-red claws with long black nails.

"Gah," he cried, choking, as he felt his face stretching, till it seemed like it would split open.

He knelt submissively before the priest, too weak to hide his shameful, distorted body, too frightened to even try to speak.

"Pitiful wretch," Father Leibowitz said, his voice seething with disdain as orange slime dripped from Richard's body and slithered about the filthy linoleum.

"Look at yourself," Father Leibowitz said. "You are not the ghost of a man. You never were. You are a fallen angel. You do not belong here."

Richard squealed as he forced his misshapen jaw into action. His forked tongue flicked across his lips. "My . . . name . . . is . . . Richard Rogers."

"No," said Father Leibowitz. "We both know that isn't the truth. Tell us your true name."

Richard didn't know. Richard didn't know if anything was true anymore. Acid tears rolled down his cheeks, burning small holes in the floor where they fell.

"Be. . . Beelzebub," he said, unable to think of anything else.

Before Father Leibowitz could respond, the door from the kitchen to the back porch swung open. A tall, gray-haired man in a white lab coat stepped into the room.

"You monsters," he said, contemptuously. "Leave this man alone."

"What kind of demonic trick is this?" Father Leibowitz asked angrily.

The gray-haired man pulled out what looked like a high-capacity water gun from his coat and pointed it in the face of Father Leibowitz.

"This won't be painful," he said, and pulled the trigger. A cloud of green gas engulfed Father Leibowitz who slumped to the floor like a puppet with its strings cut.

The gray-haired man looked at Henry and Martha.

"Leave," he said.

With hurried footsteps, they left.

Richard screamed. He was changing once more, his skin and muscles and bones sliding to new configurations. In a dozen heartbeats the transformation was complete. He was himself again.

The gray-haired man placed a hand upon Richard's shoulder.

"Hello, Richard. I'm sorry I didn't make it here sooner."

"You . . . you see me," said Richard, still trembling from his ordeal. "You know my name."

"Yes. I am Doctor Nicholas Knowbokov. I'm here to help you."

"A doctor," said Richard, placing a hand on a chair to steady himself. "Oh God. Oh God, I'm crazy aren't I? And you're going to help me get better. Please help me get better."

"Your sanity is quite intact," said Dr. Knowbokov. "And better is a subjective term. But I'll do what I can to help you come to terms with your new reality."

"Not crazy. My skin was freaking melting into puddles a minute ago, but I'm not crazy? You sure you're a psychologist?"

"Actually, I'm a theoretical physicist," said Dr. Knowbokov. "And I'm responsible for your condition."

CHAPTER THREE

ONE MINUS ONE

They left through the back door, cutting across the neighbor's yard to the street beyond. A long black limousine waited. A very tall black woman got out as they approached. She was bald, with an elaborate tattoo of a dragon on her scalp. She wore a black uniform, with her eyes hidden behind sunglasses.

She opened the door as Dr. Knowbokov approached.

"Thank you, Mindo," the doctor said. He paused, and motioned for Richard to enter. "We have a guest, Mindo. An invisible man."

Mindo nodded, but said nothing.

Dr. Knowbokov followed Richard into the limousine. Richard slid across the soft leather seats, whistling as he looked around at the trappings of wealth.

"Theoretical physics must pay better than I thought," said Richard.

"I've lived a fortunate life," said Dr. Knowbokov.

"This thing have a bar?" asked Richard. "I could really use a drink."

"Of course," said the doctor. "Bar, open."

With a whir, a minibar unfolded out of the wall separating the passenger compartment from the driver's cab. Richard quickly accessed the contents. Every kind of juice he could think of (and some blends he'd never imagined, like kiwi-tomato-carrot), four different kinds of bottled water, and not a drop of booze.

"You wouldn't be Southern Baptist by any chance?" asked Richard.

"No. Why do you ask?"

"Not important," he said, deciding to sample the banana-celery-cranberry. "You say you're responsible for my condition. How? What's happened to me?"

"It won't be easy to explain," said Dr. Knowbokov.

"Try me."

"Two days ago, I made the maiden voyage with my time machine, and—"

"Stop," said Richard.

The doctor stopped, smiling gently.

"Try again. You can't expect me to believe any story that starts with a time machine."

"Very well," said Dr. Knowbokov. "And what, pray tell, would you accept as a reasonable explanation for your condition?"

Richard sipped on the juice. It was hideous. He took another sip, imagining it mixed with vodka. He could get used to it.

"OK," he said. "I'll play along. Time machine."

"I built my time machine purely for research. I never intended to interfere with the past. I experimented carefully. My intention was to travel back to a point just after the creation of the universe to search for my enemy before he had time to conceal himself."

"Your enemy," said Richard. "At the creation of the universe. Is God really pissed off at you or something?"

"I was looking for the terrorist known as Rex Monday. But this detail is unimportant," said Dr. Knowbokov. "A detail that matters, however, is that my time machine causes a rapid displacement of air when it's used. It makes, if I may be crude, a sound rather like a loud fart."

Richard stared at the doctor, expecting him to crack a smile. The doctor continued.

"I traveled to July 4, 1968. I chose a remote, rural location to minimize the chance of interacting with people of that time. Unfortunately, a man named William Rogers was out hunting that day, less than two hundred yards from the location I materialized in."

"My father," said Richard.

"Not at that time. I sensed him instantly. I knew he had heard the noise that accompanied my arrival, and was curious about it. He began to walk in my direction. Due to the roughness of the terrain, I still had several minutes. I conducted the search for the man I sought. I failed to find him. I left, with time to spare before William would have seen me."

"Hmm," said Richard. The insanity theory was rising high on his list of explanations again. "Didn't even see you, huh?"

"Still, his search for the source of the sound he had heard delayed him. He returned to his car twelve minutes later than he would have had I not made my trip."

"And this is responsible for my present condition how?"

Dr. Knowbokov shifted in his seat, looking slightly uncomfortable. With a deep breath, he continued. "Your father visited a pharmacy that evening. He purchased a package of prophylactics. A different package than the one he would have purchased had he arrived twelve minutes earlier. And, in this package, all the prophylactics functioned properly."

"What are you saying?"

"You were conceived as a result of a ruptured condom. With my visit to the past, I erased the time line in which you existed. You were never born."

"Uh-huh. Right." Richard took another sip of his juice. "And just what am I then? I'm real. I'm alive. I'm not some figment of your imagination."

"True," said Knowbokov. "It may be more accurate to say that you are a figment of your own imagination. Reality has a certain elasticity in response to consciousness. You were, and still are, aware of your own existence. You are apparently a man of great willpower, to continue believing in your own reality in the face of so much evidence against it. Most people would have succumbed to doubt and faded away."

"This is pretty tough to swallow," said Richard, glancing at the juice box.

Dr. Knowbokov didn't catch the double entendre. "You will no doubt discover in the coming days that your own perceptions of reality fail when they conflict with the shared reality of others. This is why you are able to touch and manipulate objects only when no one is observing them."

"But . . . but the priest saw the pots I was holding."

"He expected to," said Dr. Knowbokov. "And when he convinced Martha and Henry they would see a demon, you responded physically to this."

"OK. OK," said Richard. "Fine. Let's say I believe you. You've erased my life with a time machine. When are you going back to fix things?"

"I'm not," said Dr. Knowbokov.

"What? Why?"

By now they had reached an airfield on the edge of town. The limousine pulled to a stop near a mid-size jet.

"Come," said Dr. Knowbokov. "Let's continue our conversation aboard my plane."

"Let's finish it now. Why won't you go back and fix things?"

"I have materials to show you on the plane," said Dr. Knowbokov. "Photographs that will help me explain our dilemma."

"Visual aids, huh?" said Richard. "Fine. I'll play along."

The jet was nothing like the commercial aircraft on which Richard had traveled. Instead of the normal rows of seats, the mid-part of the cabin was laid out like a living room, with two huge leather couches facing an elegant coffee table. Veronica would have loved it. On the table were several manila envelopes.

"Have a seat," said Dr. Knowbokov.

"I feel like standing," said Richard.

"That won't be safe during take off."

"Take off? Where exactly are we going?"

"The Caribbean. My estate is located on a private island."

"Ah," said Richard. "Of course it is. You kin to Bruce Wayne?"

Dr. Knowbokov looked slightly confused. "The Bruce Wayne that lives at 47 Stanton Street in Tulsa, Oklahoma?"

"Um. Sure."

"No. Why do you ask?"

Richard sighed, then took a seat on the couch opposite the doctor. The plane's engines began to roar, and the cabin lurched.

"The Caribbean, huh? I guess I'm along for the ride. Has to be better than where I was."

"Indeed. I think you will like my home," said Dr. Knowbokov. "I hope you will be a frequent guest. I would like to propose a partnership between us."

"Partnership?"

"I would find a man of your talents quite useful. You would be the perfect spy."

"And who, may I ask, would I be spying on?"

"My enemies, of course. Perhaps even, should the need arise, my allies."

"That sounds a little paranoid, Doc," said Richard. "But, maybe not all that paranoid. I guess being rich enough to own your own island does involve a little crooked dealing."

"Nothing of the sort," said Dr. Knowbokov. "My wealth has been obtained through careful investments and numerous patents on my discoveries and inventions."

"Oh yeah," said Richard. "And there's that time machine. Must make lottery picks a breeze."

"I hadn't contemplated that," said the doctor. "If the acquisition of wealth were my focus, I suppose I could use the time machines for selfish purposes. But I have lived my life in service to mankind. The wealth that has resulted is quite incidental, and used mostly for philanthropy."

"And Caribbean estates."

"I provide what comforts I can for my family," the doctor said, sounding apologetic.

"I had a family once," said Richard. "And you screwed that up. Care to take a stab at explaining why you aren't going to fix it?"

Dr. Knowbokov handed him a manila envelope.

"This file contains information about Lisa and Linda Rogers. They are, in a way, your sisters."

"Sisters? I was an only child. Dad always joked that I was so much trouble they didn't want another kid."

"Lisa and Linda were born in 1970 and 1972. Your parents were more emotionally and financially secure than they were when you were born."

Richard emptied the envelope, and looked through the photos of two bright-looking, happy women. They seemed very familiar, like relatives he should recognize, but couldn't quite recall.

"Sisters, huh?"

"There's more," said Dr. Knowbokov, handing him another envelope. "Your former wife, Veronica, married before she finished college. She has two children now, a boy, age seven, and a girl, age eight."

"I don't believe you," said Richard. "Veronica hated children. She viewed them as little dirt magnets. She would never have found a diaper bag that meshed with her wardrobe."

"The girl was unplanned, but is loved," said Dr. Knowbokov. "Look at the photographs."

Richard fumbled with the clasp. His hands were trembling. He left the envelope closed, and said, "I don't care."

"What don't you care about?"

"Any of this. Any of these people."

"They are real people," said Dr. Knowbokov, his voice very calm and gentle. "As real as you once were. More real than you are now. If I were to tinker with time again, even if I had the talent and wisdom to make things exactly as they once were, I would be condemning these people to non-existence."

"I don't care!" Richard rose, flinging the envelope across the room. It came open, sending a flurry of photos and papers drifting through the air. "You're going to put me back!"

"No," Dr. Knowbokov said calmly.

With a feral growl, Richard lunged forward, his hands aimed at the doctor's throat.

Still seated, Dr. Knowbokov raised his leg high above his head and delivered a kick to Richard's chin. Richard crashed to the coffee table, stars before his eyes. He rolled to the floor, tasting blood in his mouth.

"Any attempt at physical assault is most unwise," said Dr. Knowbokov. "I have black belts in seven styles of martial arts."

"Of course," Richard said, his hands clutching his throbbing jaw. "Goddamn."

"I understand your emotional distress," said Dr. Knowbokov.

"Sure," said Richard, swallowing blood. "Why wouldn't you understand? This is your fault. You destroy my life. You tell me that my parents really did decide against kids because I was so horrible, and my wife would have welcomed the opportunity to breed, just not with me."

He sighed, rubbing his jaw. "Sorry, DNA. Guess I let you down."

Dr. Knowbokov laughed. "You possess a sharp wit, Richard. This is evidence of your intelligence. I have faith in your ability to adapt to your condition."

Richard ignored him. "And to top it all off, I'll have to eat through straws for the rest of my life. Man, it feels like my teeth are about to come out."

"Unlikely," said Dr. Knowbokov. "I didn't kick you that hard."

Richard shook his head. He didn't know what to say. This was just too much to think about, especially with his head throbbing. So he said, "I have a headache."

"Perhaps it would be best if you rested. I have sleeping quarters in the rear of the plane. There is medication in the bathroom. Some anti-inflammatories will help ease your pain."

Richard chuckled joylessly. "Any pills in there that will make me real again?"

"Richard, you are real. It's vitally important you remember that, and believe it. I have told you these things because I believe that the truth will help you come to terms with your new circumstances, and actually reinforce your identity."

"Yeah," said Richard. "Self-esteem, believe in yourself, blah, blah, blah. You sure you're not a shrink?"

"Come," said Dr. Knowbokov, offering his hand. "Let's get you to bed. After you rest, we can further discuss my offer of employment."

"Spy, huh?" said Richard. "Won't be as cool as in the movies. I'm unlikely to get the girls, being intangible and all."

"There are rewards in life far greater than 'getting the girl.'"

"Gee, thanks for the pep talk, Dr. Know-it-all."

Richard took the doctor's hand, and was pulled to his feet. The doctor led him to the next room. The sleeping quarters weren't the cramped bunk he expected but a plush canopy bed, covered with hand-sewn quilts. The bathroom beyond was spacious, with a full-sized toilet, a bidet, and a claw-footed tub.

"Swank," said Richard. "Doc, you may be a time-traveling, life-wrecking scumbag, but you got taste."

"Here," said the doctor, handing him some pills. "These will prevent swelling in your jaw, and help you sleep."

Richard popped the pills and swallowed them without waiting for water. He collapsed onto the bed. It was soft and warm, and smelled freshly laundered. He shut his eyes, and felt like he was at his grandmother's house.

When he opened his eyes, Dr. Knowbokov was gone.

He closed his eyes again. His head felt full of static. Images flashed across his eyelids, words echoed through his head.

Echo. That's all he was now. An echo of someone who used to be. How long before he faded away to nothingness?

It was absurd. Everything, the time machine, the photos of sisters he'd never known, the private jet, the island, the seven-foot-tall bald chick driving the limo, all of it was just a joke. Any minute, someone would yell, "Surprise!" He could grin and say, "You got me!" Or maybe he would open his eyes and realize that the soft bed he lay upon was the floor of a padded cell.

But he had gone too far into this now to question his sanity. Lying in the bed, his jaw still throbbing, he had a very good sense of what was real, and what wasn't. This wasn't a joke. He wasn't real. And, yet, of course, he was.

41

He could feel himself drifting. He wondered if something in the pills was putting him to sleep. He felt too full of questions to sleep. And yet, little by little, he drew deeper inside himself, floating in memories.

He remembered sitting on his grandmother's bed. Her bed had always smelled so wonderful. He was very, very small. She held his hand in hers.

"And when you add another one you get . . . ?" She folded out a second finger from his fist.

"Two!" he said.

"And when you fold it back you have?"

"One!" he said.

She folded the remaining finger back into his palm.

"And now you have?"

He looked at his hand. He wasn't sure what he had.

"One minus one is zero," his grandmother said.

He stared at his fist, unconvinced. After all, his fingers were still there.

"Zero," he said, knowing it would make her happy.

"Good boy," she said.

Drifting to sleep in his memories as well as here and now, Richard felt his grandmother's kiss upon his brow.

Chapter Four
STRONG GENETIC COMPONENT

When Richard opened his eyes again his jaw no longer hurt. He touched it carefully, then more firmly. It was like he'd never been kicked. Rich people apparently got better pills than the rest of us.

He sat up on the most comfortable bed he'd ever slept on, and stepped onto the nicest carpet his feet had ever touched. Piano music drifted into the room, serene and introspective. An eerie red light seeped through the drapes. He went to a window, pushed aside the drapes, and opened the shade.

They were over an ocean, gleaming with the last sunlight of the day. For as far as he could see, there was only water and sky merging as one on the horizon. The plane seemed to hang in perfect stillness.

On the window, he could see the faint trace of his reflection.

"Never born," he said. "Huh."

In the distance he could see a flash of light, a boat perhaps, or a low plane. Whatever he saw, it was moving rapidly, leaving a wake of gleaming silver.

He focused his attention on the approaching object. Could a boat move that fast? The wake wasn't dispersing like a boat's. It remained a perfect, shining, razor-sharp line. It was definitely moving above the water, not across it. A plane? It seemed too small. Whatever the object was, it was keeping low and gaining on them.

Low, fast, and small. A missile? Suddenly, Richard wondered just how tough Dr. Knowbokov's enemies were.

He left the bedroom and found Dr. Knowbokov playing a grand piano in the room where they had held their earlier discussion. The couches and coffee table were gone. Had they changed planes? Richard's brow furrowed. Somehow this bothered him much more than the thought of an approaching missile.

"Ah, Richard," said the doctor. "My playing didn't disturb you, I hope?"

"Weren't there couches in here just a little while ago? Or have you been tinkering with the time machine again?"

"Nothing so exotic," said the doctor. "The furniture can be raised and lowered from the holds via hydraulic lifts."

"Does Martha Stewart know about this?"

Dr. Knowbokov's eyes closed, and he seemed briefly lost in thought. He opened his eyes.

"No," he said.

"How about the missile coming our way? She know about that?"

"Missile?"

"Maybe. Take a look out the window and tell me my eyes are playing tricks on me."

Dr. Knowbokov went to the nearest window and raised the shade. A woman stood outside the plane, only a few yards away. The wind whipped at her hair and clothing as she skated along beside the plane astride a pair of polished steel rails. Her clothes reminded Richard of a drum majorette's, with a tight red jacket fastened by twin rows of gold buttons, a short skirt, and a tall, flat-topped hat, which fastened with a strap beneath her chin. She smiled and waved.

Dr. Knowbokov waved back.

"I don't see a missile, Richard," he said.

Richard pinched himself on his arm. The woman veered off, descending. The steel rails she rode seemed to materialize from the air before her.

"Oh. My. God," said Richard, fully grasping what he'd seen. "That was . . . that's . . . that's the woman who's always on the news. I mean, she's always fighting giant robots and . . . I don't believe this. I thought she was just a joke! What's her name? Blade Something? I . . . I mean, she's real?"

"Rail Blade," said Dr. Knowbokov. "She's not only real, she's my daughter."

Richard slapped his forehead with his palm.

"Of course," he said. "Of course she's your daughter. You have a time machine. You've got a private jet, furniture on hydraulic lifts, and a gun that shoots knockout gas. You have a seven-foot-tall bald woman for a chauffeur! Why wouldn't you have a comic-book hero for a daughter?"

Dr. Knowbokov smiled. "Two daughters, actually. The media has christened my other daughter 'the Thrill.'"

Richard went to the window and stared. Rail Blade was nowhere to be seen now, though the gleaming rail she had ridden remained visible as a shining line across the ocean.

"OK," he said. "You're the physicist. Where does that rail come from? How does it stay up like that? I'm no engineer, but shouldn't those rails she rides buckle under their own weight? There's nothing holding them up."

45

"It is curious. By all the known laws of physics, not to mention the laws of biology, the ferrokinesis my daughter exhibits is categorically impossible."

"Must have made for interesting family arguments," said Richard. "Young lady, since you insist on breaking the known laws of physics, there's no dessert for you tonight."

Dr. Knowbokov shrugged. "She had an answer for that."

"Oh?"

"She said it wasn't her fault I didn't know all the laws of physics."

THEY ARRIVED AT the island moments later. Richard emerged from the plane into a tropical wonderland, with bright flowers and even brighter birds almost everywhere he looked. Reaching the tarmac, he felt as if he were stepping into a scene from a postcard.

"Having the weirdest time," he said. "Wish I were here."

"Come now," said Dr. Knowbokov. "Things will look up soon. You'll find that even in your condition there are still many pleasures to enjoy in this world."

"'In my condition' makes me sound pregnant."

"You'll feel better once we go to the mansion and have a nice meal. Afterwards, we can discuss your situation further."

Suddenly, in utter, eerie silence, a pair of railroad tracks sliced through the air heading straight toward Richard. Richard jumped as the ends of the tracks plunged and bit into the ground mere feet from where he stood. Then, with a whistling roar, Rail Blade shot toward him, leaning back as she approached, sending sparks shooting from her steel boots.

Richard cupped his hands over his ears and winced at the horrible squeal the rails made as she slid to a halt beside him.

"Father!" said Rail Blade, in cheerful greeting.

"Amelia," said Dr. Knowbokov, somewhat coolly, thought Richard. "How was the mission?"

"Things went as planned," she said. "The subject is safe and secure in the bank."

Dr. Knowbokov nodded knowingly.

"Aren't you going to introduce me to your friend?" Rail Blade asked.

Dr. Knowbokov's mouth dropped open. He cleared his throat, and said, "You can—"

"—see me," finished Richard. "You can see me!"

Rail Blade looked more than a little confused.

"Yes?" she ventured.

"And hear me?" asked Richard.

"I think I may be missing the point of your questions," she said.

"This is a wonderful development," said Dr. Knowbokov.

"I'm cured!" said Richard.

"No," said Dr. Knowbokov. "But I suspect that other descendents from my bloodline may share my ability to see you. After all, consciousness does derive from brain function, which of course has a strong genetic component."

"You make this stuff up as you go along, don't you?" said Richard.

"Father never makes anything up," said Rail Blade, with an oddly humorless tone.

"Amelia, may I introduce you to my new associate Richard Rogers? Richard, this is my eldest daughter, Amelia."

Richard held out his hand. Amelia nearly crushed it with her grip. She stared at him as they shook hands, and he became acutely aware that he was dressed in a pink robe with neon green flip-flops.

When they ended their handshake, he ran his hand across his uncombed hair, then scratched the three days' worth of stubble on his cheeks.

"I'm sorry if I acted a little spaced out," he said. "It's just that, thanks to your father, I've kind of never been born."

"I'm sure Father has his reasons," said Amelia.

"Richard's condition is an unfortunate side effect of one of my experiments," said Dr. Knowbokov. "While he may not seem extraordinary to you, to almost everyone else in the world, he doesn't exist."

"I see," said Amelia. "This could have advantages, I suppose."

"Advantages?" said Richard. "Have you been reading your father's script? He was telling me what a wonderful life I have in store for me. But all I want is to be normal again."

Amelia shrugged. "Normal is only a state of mind. You can be normal anytime you want."

Richard didn't have a comeback to that.

"We were just going up to the mansion," said Dr. Knowbokov. "Richard is in need of a good meal. Go and find your mother and sister, and tell them we'll be having a guest for dinner. I've phoned ahead to Paco. He'll be ready to serve us in an hour."

"I doubt Sarah will come," said Amelia. "You know her."

"Tell her Richard tried to strangle me earlier today," said Dr. Knowbokov. "She'll come."

Amelia cut her eyes toward Richard, with a brief, dismissive glare. She turned. The rails she had rode in on crumbled to blood-red dust, swirling in the wind. New rails shot into the air before her. She leapt up onto the rails, and was gone.

RICHARD ENTERED THE dining room feeling more alive than he had felt in a long time. He had showered and shaved, and he was wearing new clothes. But the thing that really brightened his mood was that he had brushed his teeth with a toothbrush he could call his own for the first time in days.

But it wasn't just his recent ordeal that he felt was improving. He was genuinely intrigued by the events swirling around him. He felt as if he had finally mastered the horrible wave that had been drowning him, and was now surfing atop it.

Of course, he couldn't help but remember—eventually all waves crash.

Dr. Knowbokov rose from his chair as Richard entered the room. The doctor wore a white linen suit and smiled brightly. There was a woman seated next to him.

"Richard," he said. "Welcome. This is my wife, Katrina. Katrina, this is the young man I was telling you about, Richard Rogers."

Dr. Knowbokov motioned to the woman. She was regal looking, with a strong jaw and dark eyes. Diamonds flashed upon her fingers and ears. She looked in Richard's direction, then back to her husband.

"I assure you this is not amusing," she said.

"Um, pleased to meet you," said Richard.

Richard reached out to take a chair. His hand passed right through it.

"Mumble grumble gripe," said Richard.

"Katrina," said Dr. Knowbokov. "Would you be so kind as to close your eyes?"

Katrina sighed, and closed them.

Richard pulled out the chair and took his seat.

"Thanks," he said.

"May I open them now?" she asked.

"Please," said Dr. Knowbokov. "Our guest is seated."

"Hate to be a bother," said Richard.

"Nonsense," said Dr. Knowbokov.

Katrina scowled at him. "I suppose I'm expected to believe our invisible guest pulled out the chair."

"He did. He's sitting before you right now."

"I would have expected something more elaborate from you, Niko."

About this time, Amelia entered the dining room. She had changed clothes and now wore a sundress and sandals. Her hair was pulled back in a ponytail. She carried herself with an unnaturally perfect posture.

"Mr. Rogers," she said. "I trust you feel refreshed?"

"Yes, kind of. I think all the stress of the last few days has just sort of numbed me."

"Amelia," said Katrina. "I would expect this from your father. But I would have thought you would be above this sort of petty torment."

"Pardon?" said Amelia.

"She can't see me," said Richard.

"Not yet," said Dr. Knowbokov.

"Not yet?" asked Richard.

"The couple whose house I found you in eventually came to believe in you, and were able to see you, after a fashion."

"Don't remind me."

"My hope is that Katrina will also come to accept you as real."

"I think this has gone on far enough," said Katrina, pushing back from the table.

"What's gone on far enough?" a woman asked from the next room.

Richard turned to the sound of the approaching voice. He saw an angel. The Thrill had decided to join them for dinner.

On television, the Thrill possessed the same trumped up beauty possessed by models and actresses. She looked too good to be real. And yet, here she was, tall and slender, with a short tee shirt exposing her midriff and torn jeans that revealed more skin than they concealed. She was barefoot, with toenails painted red. Her feet hovered inches above the ground. She literally floated into the room. Richard tried to remember what the news had said about her. He knew she could fly, and that she was some kind of siren; few could resist her slightest requests.

"Don't tell me I've missed something," she said.

"Have they brought you in on it, too?" asked Katrina.

"In on what?" she said. "I heard that there was some guy here who wanted to kill Dad."

She looked at Richard. "You him?"

"Yep," said Richard.

"Sarah sees him, dear," said Dr. Knowbokov to Katrina. "Do you really believe she would play along with any joke of mine?"

"What joke?" asked Sarah.

"Mother thinks we're playing a joke on her," said Amelia. "She can't see Mr. Rogers."

"You're Mr. Rogers?" asked Sarah. "Funny, you look a lot older on TV."

Richard rose from his chair, and held out his hand.

"Richard Rogers," he said. "And you look . . . Wow! I mean, I've seen you on TV, and . . ."

Richard couldn't think of a clever way to end the sentence. Sarah didn't reach for his hand.

"So what did Dad do to you?" she asked.

"Thanks to his time machine, I was never born," said Richard. He furrowed his brow. "That doesn't sound at all crazy, does it?"

"Around here?" said Sarah. "Wait until Dad tells you the bit about destroying and recreating the universe."

Katrina stood up and threw her napkin to the table.

"Enough," she said. "I will not talk around your 'invisible guest' any longer. I'm going to the library."

"Don't leave," said Sarah, turning her gaze toward her mother.

Katrina stopped dead in her tracks, smiled cheerfully, if a bit glassy eyed, and immediately sat down.

"Sarah!" shouted Dr. Knowbokov.

"How dare you!" shouted Amelia.

"You are not to use your powers on your mother, young lady," Dr. Knowbokov said firmly.

"Chill out," said Sarah. "I just didn't want her to leave because she thinks we're joking. Mother, there really is a man sitting across the table from you."

"If you insist," Katrina said wearily.

Sarah turned to her father. "I could use my powers to make her believe us, she might see him then."

"No," said Dr. Knowbokov. "You gave your word it would never happen again. I will not condone it for even the most benign reason."

"I really feel bad about this," said Richard. "I would have offered to eat alone if I'd known my presence would cause an argument."

"Feeling like you've caused an argument around here is a little like an Eskimo shaman feeling he's caused snow," said Sarah.

Sarah looked at her mother. "Sorry," she said. "I did kind of nudge you to stay—but just lightly. It should wear off any second."

Katrina rose from her seat once more, looking pale.

"We'll speak further of this tomorrow," she said to her husband, before stalking from the room.

"I said I was sorry," said Sarah.

"Never do it again," said Amelia. "Or I may do something we'll both regret."

"Oooh," said Sarah. "Gonna cut me? Gonna go railblading on my ass? Try it."

"Sarah," Dr. Knowbokov said. "Language. Both of you calm down. Neither of you will be using your powers in the house. Period."

"She's flying," said Amelia, plaintively.

"Oh, grow up," said Sarah, stepping down from the air to the floor as if she were stepping from a stair.

"So," said Richard. "Flying. Is it like in *Hitchhiker's Guide to the Galaxy*? Throwing yourself at the ground and missing?"

"Not really. It's tough to describe," Sarah said with a shrug. "Dad didn't know all the laws of physics."

CHAPTER FIVE

RIGHT BETWEEN THE EYES

A week later, Richard Rogers became Nobody.

They were standing on the White House lawn, getting ready to fight Baby Gun, and the Thrill said: "Hey, we need to give you a code name. Get you into the spirit of things. How about 'Ghost Man?'"

"How about 'Nobody?'" said Rail Blade.

"I like it," said the Thrill.

"Whatever," said Nobody. The relaxed mood of the two sisters seemed jarring to him. There were a million people on the Mall for the Dome celebration. And Monday's Revelation had made good on their threats. Over the screaming crowd a giant figure loomed, a hundred feet tall, with a body like a toddler. But where the head should be, the giant sported a gleaming black pistol. To Nobody this seemed more pressing than deciding on a code name. He asked Rail Blade, "You going to stop God's personal handgun, or what?"

"You do your job, we'll do ours," said Rail Blade. "Ready for armor?"

"Hit me," said the Thrill. From thin air, strips of metal slinked and slithered, thickening into plates that covered the Thrill like a second skin. The outfit was completed with a large round shield with a mirrored finish for her right hand, and a long, slender, white-hot sword for her left.

Ready for battle, the Thrill zoomed above the crowds, shouting, "Keep down! Stay calm!"

The churning crowd's screaming changed into a relaxed, upbeat murmur.

Rail Blade raced off along her tracks, a dozen razor-sharp metal half-moons spinning in rapid orbit around her.

"It's not just a job, it's an adventure," muttered Nobody. He settled the radio headset that he had been given more firmly onto his head. "How did I get into this mess?"

"FOR THE LAST three decades, I have worked to make our world a better place," Dr. Knowbokov had told him on his second evening at the mansion. They stood on the balcony, overlooking the sea. "Environmental destruction, war, hunger, disease . . . I view their existence in the world as a personal failure on my part, and dedicated myself to their elimination."

"Noble of you," said Richard. "But wouldn't giving to the United Way be more practical than building a time machine?"

"Richard, I'm going to ask you to take a leap of faith. I have unimaginable resources at my disposal. You must trust me. I can eliminate these evils from the world. I have the knowledge. I have the plan. Work for me, and you will work to usher in a Golden Age."

"Sounds like you've got it all figured out. Why do you need me?"

"Because there are forces in this world working in opposition to my plan. Have you ever heard of a man known as Rex Monday?"

Richard nodded. "Terrorist. He's behind that whole 'Monday's Revelation' thing."

"He's behind far more than that. Over the years he has become an increasingly violent and formidable obstacle to my work. While I fund the research that eliminates disease, he funds labs in rogue nations developing new viral weapons. Where I arrange for diplomatic missions to bring long warring enemies together, he is busily trafficking horrible weapons to those least interested in peace."

"He doesn't seem to like the Domes any either," said Richard. "There's been, what, seven bombings at the D.C. Dome?"

"The Domes are crucial to my plan to protect Earth's ecosystem without abandoning the technological advances that make human life comfortable. With domes over our cities, we can filter out harmful gasses before they can warm the atmosphere or harm the ozone. With domes over croplands, we can provide year round food production in even the harshest climates, and protect the surrounding environment from agricultural chemicals or genetic pollution from engineered crops. Without the domes, Earth could face ecological collapse in less than a century. Rex Monday's opposition to them is proof of the darkness in his heart."

"Actually, I'm not a big fan of the domes either. I mean they're big, expensive, and ugly. There must be a better way to save the Earth."

"Richard, did you know you are under a Dome now?"

Richard looked up. The sky was bright with stars.

"No way," he said.

"They are big," said Dr. Knowbokov. "But not ugly. They are barely even visible under most conditions. As for expense, what price can you put on the health of the Earth?"

Richard strained his eyes, searching for some evidence to the truth of the doctor's words. "Maybe the domes aren't the worst idea I've ever heard. OK, I'll play along. You want an invisible spy, you've got an invisible spy. It's not like I have a life to get back to. What do you want me to do?"

"Obviously, I want you to find Rex Monday," said Dr. Knowbokov. "And then, I want you to kill him."

AFTER A WEEK witnessing wonders, Richard thought he had seen it all. He was hanging out with a woman who could fly and another who could lift tanks with her thoughts. He was the personal guest of the closest thing to a mad scientist he had ever met. He kept thinking he should be used to weird stuff by now. But he couldn't help staring at Baby Gun. He had seen Baby Gun on TV once, and had assumed he was just some kind of special effect. But, there he was, toddling around, bigger than any of the buildings that surrounded him, shooting car-sized bullets from his head. Baby Gun had already shot three gaping holes in the D.C. Dome, and knocked a siz-able chunk out of the Washington Monument before Rail Blade reached him. In seconds, the giant's flesh was marked with a cross-hatching of red slashes as Rail Blade's weapons tore into him. He turned his bizarre gun-barrel face in her direction and fired. Rail Blade raced away, but the huge bullet shattered her rails, send-ing her into a spin.

The Thrill sped in to help her. But before she could reach her sister, there was a blinding flash of light, as a bolt of white-hot energy struck the Thrill in the center of her back. Following the flash back to its source, Nobody could see a woman, with flaming hair and glowing skin, soaring aloft on enormous wings of flame.

"Who's that?" Nobody asked into his radio headset.

"Sundancer," said Dr. Knowbokov. "Rex Monday is using his most powerful agents for this attack. But make no mistake—any damage these two do will be inconsequential compared to Rex Monday's real plan. I've found more of his agents on the other side of the mall, near the Air and Space Museum. Get over there quickly. The easiest one to find will be the Panic. Anyone who sees him is instantly overcome with blind fear, but I think you will find his power cannot affect you. He's accompanied by someone we haven't encountered before. He looks like a street person, very dirty, ragged clothes. I can't read him, so he must be under Monday's influence. Find them and follow them. I will make sure my daughters keep their distance. With any luck, they can lead you to Monday."

"On it," said Nobody. He started to make his way across the mall, moving slowly at first, carefully avoiding the thousands of people who were keeping low and staying calm. But after failing to bump into a few people who took unexpected turns into his path, he realized caution wasn't needed. He began to run, straight through the crowd, often straight through individuals. He wondered if he would ever get used to it.

Overhead, Rail Blade and the Thrill were making progress. Baby Gun had been brought to his knees near the Washington Monument. Enormous iron chains now bound his limbs and bent his howitzer shaped face low to the ground. He was blasting craters in the Mall, but doing no harm to anyone but the earthworms.

Sundancer was proving more difficult. The Thrill was effectively deflecting her heat bursts with her mirrored shield, but couldn't get close enough to her agile opponent to land a blow. Her shouted commands to hold still proved ineffective.

But Nobody could no longer pay attention to the fight. He had left the area of calm the Thrill had created, and entered into a panicked mob. Around him, people lay trampled and broken on the ground. Others fled headlong into trees, into benches, and into each other. Nobody pressed on, into the eye of the storm.

The Panic was just a kid, no older than thirteen or fourteen. He wore blue jeans, a black tee shirt, and new white sneakers. Nobody recognized him because he was serenely calm amidst the sea of fear, strolling along, smiling as he chatted with his companion, a gray-haired, snaggle-toothed bum with filthy trousers riding halfway down his skinny, boil-ridden butt.

"Lovely," said Nobody, gasping for breath as he pushed to catch up to them and listen in on their conversation. He wasn't in luck. As he reached them, they ran out of things to say.

He followed them closely as they left the Mall and wandered down the side streets. People continued to flee before them. A police car appeared, heading in their direction. The streets were closed to traffic for the inaugural celebration of the D.C. Dome's completion, so the car was creeping forward through the fleeing crowds, with lights flashing and sirens blaring. Suddenly, the last of the crowd dispersed, and the car sped forward for about a dozen yards. Then, with a squeal of brakes, it slid to a stop near the Panic and his companion. The tires whined, leaving rubber streaks as the car shifted into reverse and raced backwards in a swaying, drunken line. The car veered sharply, smashing tail first into the side of a building. It then lurched forward, straight into a fire hydrant. The air bags deployed.

A pair of cops tumbled, clown-like, from the car. One fled instantly, streaking off after the fleeing crowd. The other had his feet snared in the spent airbag. The more he struggled, the more he tangled himself up in it. As the Panic grew closer, the cop pulled his gun. Tears streaming down his face, he closed his eyes and fired. Two bullets ricocheted from the pavement. The third bullet struck the old bum squarely between the eyes.

"Ow, goddamn it," the bum cursed, sticking his dirt-blackened finger into the hole in his head.

The cop kept pulling his trigger long after his gun was

empty. The Panic and the bum walked up to him. The cop began to squeal like a frightened pig as he gazed upon the Panic's white sneakers.

The old bum squatted down next to the cop, his pants ripping as he did so. "Right between the eyes is just the goddamn meanest place to shoot a fella," he said. "I'm gonna go all cross-eyed staring at it. Why would you wanna do somethin' like that? What'd I ever do to you?"

The cop vomited and began to claw at the sidewalk in an effort to get away. In seconds, wet red trails were left where his fingers scraped the pavement.

The Panic picked up the cop's fallen gun. "Cops are all the same," he said. "Guns are like penises they wear on the outside of their pants, lording their manliness over everyone else. Why don't you show him your trick?"

"Hold his eyes open," the bum said, taking the gun.

Nobody uselessly reached out to grab the Panic as he knelt over the frightened man. The Panic dug his nails in just below the cop's eyebrows and pulled his eyes open.

"Folks call me Pit Geek," the bum said. "You know what a Pit Geek is, Cop? We're carny folk, the meanest of the lot. And you know why folks pay to see us? 'Cause we can eat anything."

To prove it, he stuck the barrel of the gun into his mouth and bit down. He gnawed the barrel like it was a particularly tough piece of beef jerky, tearing it off. He chewed twice, then swallowed.

Nobody felt ashamed. "Yeah," he said. "I guess I *would* pay money to see that."

Pit Geek finished off the gun. Then he took the cop's bloody right hand into his own hand, and shoved it, up to the wrist, into his mouth.

"Jesus God!" shouted Nobody, vainly grabbing at Pit Geek's hands.

The cop fainted as the bloody stump of his wrist fell limp upon the pavement.

Pit Geek tapped him on the forehead. "Wakey, wakey."

The Panic dropped the cop's head. "Forget it," he said. "We need to hurry. The boss says they're getting the evacuation ready now. Children first."

The two of them moved on. Nobody lingered behind. Now that no one was looking, he ripped long strips from the airbag and made a tourniquet around what was left of the cop's wrist. Satisfied that the blood loss was abating, he jogged off after his two targets, who were entering a parking garage filled with school buses.

"Bomb," said the Panic.

Pit Geek began to retch. His mouth and throat bulged as he vomited forth a large rectangular package. Richard wondered how someone as thin as Pit Geek could have held such a thing in his body. "Good thing the bullet didn't hit this," Pit Geek said, wiping his mouth. "I got blowed up once back in '83 and it took damn near a year to work all the shrapnel out." He held the still dripping bomb out to the Panic.

"I'm not touching that," the Panic said. He pointed to the nearest bus. "Get under there."

Pit Geek dropped to his knees and crawled under the bus.

"Always gotta do the dirty work," he grumbled.

Nobody spoke into his radio once more. "Found out part of their plan," he said. "They're going to blow up school buses. Any idea on how to stop them?"

"Stopping them isn't your priority," said Dr. Knowbokov. "Just don't let them out of your sight."

"You're going to call the cops or something, right?"

"Of course," said Dr. Knowbokov.

By now, Pit Geek had vomited up another bomb, and was crawling toward the next bus.

"It's those damn corners that get to me," Pit Geek complained. "Couldn't the boss have rounded them off or something?"

"Keep working," the Panic said, placing a hand to his

left ear. "Boss says they've gathered the children at the Air and Space Museum auditorium. We've got ten minutes, tops, before they start loading the buses."

Nobody crawled under the first bus and looked at the bomb, which Pit Geek had jammed between the transmission and the body. The package was about a foot long, eight inches wide, and maybe four inches deep. It was wrapped in what looked like tin foil. The corners did look unnecessarily sharp. There were no dials, wires, or counters.

He radioed Dr. Knowbokov once more and described the bomb.

"These are fairly common works for Rex Monday," said Dr. Knowbokov. "They will be motion sensitive, so they won't need a timer. They just need a good jolt, like a pothole, or a speed bump."

The garage had speed bumps everywhere Nobody looked.

"But the cops can disarm these things, right?"

"Of course," said Dr. Knowbokov.

By now, Pit Geek was flat on his back beneath the tenth bus in the row, groaning. "Goddamn," he said. "I need a better line of work."

"Let's get going," said the Panic.

Pit Geek rolled from under the bus and rose shakily.

"Hold on," said the Panic.

"What now," said Pit Geek, belching.

"It's OK. Kids are on the way. The first group's just a block from here."

"Why are the kids on their way?" asked Nobody into the radio. "You've contacted the police, right?"

"I've taken care of everything," said Dr. Knowbokov. "The police are very busy right now, but they've dispatched people to help. Concentrate on following your subjects. Keep them within arm's length if possible."

"Boss," said the Panic. "I swear, nobody's in the garage

with us. It's like a ghost town in here."

Nobody moved close enough that he could now see the tiny earpiece and microphone the Panic was using.

"Sure. It's stupid, but sure," said the Panic.

The Panic looked around, bending to look beneath the buses.

"Hey," he called out. "If you're following us, boss says I should tell you Dr. Knowbokov never called the cops. He was worried we would monitor police bands and get tipped off someone was following us."

"This true?" asked Nobody into the microphone.

"Don't be absurd, Richard," said Dr. Knowbokov.

"They know I'm here. Call the cops."

"They've already been called. Right now we're trying to reach the teacher accompanying the children on her cell phone. Follow your targets," said Dr. Knowbokov.

The Panic shrugged. "Boss says we're done. Let's see if we can help Sundancer."

The old man and the kid began to wander back toward the garage entrance. Nobody followed. Then he heard voices around the corner, still a good distance away. Children.

"Goddamn you," he said, running to the nearest bus. He slipped underneath, and dislodged the bomb with a grunt. He crawled back out and shouted after Pit Geek and the Panic, "Hey! You dropped something!"

They didn't turn around.

Nobody banged his fist against the cowling of the bus engine, creating a satisfying thump.

He spiked the bomb like a football in the end zone as Pit Geek and the Panic turned their eyes toward him.

And then there was fire. It engulfed him, it filled him, and it flowed from him and through him. But it did not touch him. He leapt from the nearest ledge of the parking deck, suddenly feeling the heat as he fell to the ground. Pit Geek seemed tough, but even he couldn't survive this, Nobody surmised. Debris bounced all around him.

A red stop sign from one of the buses buried itself into the ground inches from his head.

He rose and stumbled out to the street. Half a block away, children were shouting and pointing at the smoke.

"You've lost them," said Dr. Knowbokov.

"Actually," said Nobody, "I have a pretty good idea where to find them. Parts of them, at least."

"I assure you, their bodies will never be found. They have exited, just as Sundancer and Baby Gun have."

"Exited? Like, exited stage left? Escaped?"

"You had an opportunity to follow them and you squandered it."

"I just saved, I dunno, like four hundred kids or something. Also, I kept a cop from bleeding to death. I think I did pretty good for my first time out."

"We will finish this discussion later," said Dr. Knowbokov. "Rendezvous with Rail Blade and the Thrill at the Washington Monument."

Nobody sighed, contemplating the long walk back to the monument. He looked around. There was an ambulance at the scene of the crashed police car. He could see the officer sitting up, staring at his absent hand, but alive.

"Humph," he said. "Pretty damn great."

CHAPTER SIX

I LOVE THIS PLACE

The following day, Richard sat on the beach, rubbing the blisters on his feet. He hadn't noticed how badly his feet hurt during all the excitement. He missed his old sneakers, the high top ones with the busted seams that he'd owned for years. Veronica had always nagged him to throw them away. His continued possession of them was the only fight he'd ever won with her. Now they were lost forever, vanished like everything else he had valued in life. He looked out over the pale blue waves, and the white sand leading to them. This looked like paradise. But his feet hurt, he was lonely, and he had every reason to believe that this was going to be a really bad day.

He glanced sideways as a shadow moved across the sand. The Thrill floated toward him, walking on air. The slight breeze caused her long blond hair to flow behind her. She wore a very revealing bathing suit with a pack of cigarettes stuck into the waistband. Richard noticed she was barefoot, and her toenails were painted emerald green.

"Hi," he said. "I'm guessing you don't get a lot of blisters, huh?"

"That's the strangest conversation starter I've ever heard," she said.

"I mean, on your feet. Seems like you always fly everywhere."

"Wouldn't you, if you could?"

"Sure," said Richard. "I can't even imagine it, though. It must be a real thrill. No pun intended."

"Call me Sarah when I'm not on one of Dad's missions," she said. "Give me your hand."

Richard reached up. She closed her hand around his. Suddenly, he was weightless, drifting upward to her side.

"Holy cow!" he said. He twisted in her grasp, trying to orient himself properly. He wound up with his feet over his head as he flailed his free hand around uselessly.

"You're trying to use your muscles," said Sarah. "Go limp. Let your mind move your body."

Richard tried to relax, but couldn't. He felt nauseous, and the sensation of looking at his feet and seeing sky beneath them made him instinctively tense up, preparing for a crash landing. He kicked his feet around, bringing them earthward, but they kept going, twisting him skyward again. His momentum pried him from Sarah's grasp. He fell with a grunt to the warm sand.

"I guess I'll stick to walking," he said, sitting up and rubbing his neck. "Ow."

"In that case, you need better shoes," said Sarah, glancing at his blistered feet.

"You're telling me," said Richard. "For all the money your dad has, I swear he bought my shoes from Bulgarian Army Surplus."

"I'll call Mindo and tell her to get the helicopter ready," said Sarah.

"For what?"

"Let's pop over to Miami," Sarah said. "Time to go shopping!"

RICHARD WAS SURPRISED when the helicopter took them to the Sunshine State Mall off of I-95. He had figured that Sarah would be heading someplace a little more upscale.

"I love this place," Sarah said as they stepped onto the rooftop. "Four hundred and twenty-three stores of pure middle-class kitsch. Thirty-eight of them are shoe stores, so we'll definitely find something that works for you."

"Promise we won't go to all thirty-eight," said Richard.

"Sure," said Sarah. "Once you've been to twenty or so, they all just run together anyway."

She held out her hand to him once more. "Wanna try again? This time, just relax. Let me do the driving."

"Relax," he said, letting out a deep breath. "I'll try."

He mimed relaxation, arms flopping at his sides, his knees bent. He swayed gently.

"You call that relaxed?" she asked. "You need some yoga lessons."

"Nah," said Richard. "I've always had a solution for when I really needed to relax. Medical scientists call this solution tequila."

She took his hand. He closed his eyes. Again, he felt weightless, but he didn't fight it. He peeked. They were floating over the edge of the mall, down to the parking lot. People were pointing at them. He began to feel disoriented, but he tried to shove the feeling from his mind. They landed safely seconds later, before he'd had time to really freak out.

"Was that so bad?" she asked.

"Landing was the best part," he said.

By now, a dozen people had run up to them.

"Oh my God!" a teenage girl yelled. "You're the Thrill!"

An older man said, "Miss, my brother was in Washington yesterday. You saved his life! Can I have your autograph?"

"Step back," the Thrill said.

Everyone near her smiled and took one step back.

Sarah paused for a second to take out a cigarette and light it. The crowd stared silently, anticipating her next words. She blew out a stream of smoke, then said, "For the rest of the day you'll leave me alone. You won't tell anyone you saw me."

The small crowd murmured in cheerful assent.

"Flying and mind control," said Richard. "What kind of radioactive insect has to bite you to get that combination of powers?"

"It's not mind control," Sarah said, her eyes narrowing. "People just like to do what I ask them to do."

Richard thought it wise not to respond to that. They went into the mall. It was about 11 A.M. on a Sunday, and the stores were just opening.

"I love getting here first thing in the morning," said Sarah. "With all the chain gates clattering up, and all the different music coming on, it sounds like the warm-up of a symphony."

"That's an interesting way of looking at it," said Richard.

"My sister never does stuff like this," Sarah said. "She has a team of personal shoppers and wardrobe experts who buy her clothes for her. I like to get down into the nitty-gritty. It helps keep me grounded."

Richard looked down. Sarah was almost touching the ground, but not quite.

"Your sister does seem a little . . . restrained," said Richard.

"My sister is fucking crazy, as is my father, and my mother. I might be, too. The life I've lived, it warps any sense of perspective, y'know?"

"I'm not the best person to ask," said Richard. "I went crazy about ten days ago and still haven't come to grips with it."

"I don't know," said Sarah. "You seem OK to me. Kind of admirable, actually, given the crap Dad's put you through. Oh, hey, let's get cinnamon buns."

"Sure," said Richard. The cinnamon buns on display at the nearby shop did smell wonderful.

"Two of the big buns," said Sarah to the cashier. "And two large lemonades."

"That will be $5.70," said the cashier, a skinny teenage guy who seemed very nervous.

"No," said Sarah. "You'll just give them to me."

"With pleasure!" the kid said, smiling broadly.

"So," said Richard. "You use your amazing gifts to take food from children."

"With pleasure," said Sarah. "Besides, it's not like I'm stealing from this geek. I'm stealing from a corporation somewhere. Probably one my father owns, with any luck."

The kid gave her a tray with the buns and drinks.

"Anything else?" he asked.

"Study hard and do well in school," Sarah offered. She handed a bun to Richard. Tentatively, Richard tried to grasp it. To his relief, he could.

"I have a theory about how your powers work," said Sarah. "I think you'll do really well here in the mall, because here most people are invisible anyway. Even if people were looking right at me holding out a cinnamon bun to an invisible man, no one would notice because no one really looks at anyone else in the mall."

"Maybe," said Richard. "But you seem to be turning a few heads. I doubt a woman as beautiful as you ever really blends into the crowd."

"I don't know," said Sarah. "I try to fit in. I sometimes feel like I'm fitting in. But I guess I'll never know how the rest of the world sees me. That's Dad's superpower by the way."

"Your dad knows how the rest of the world sees you? That's a superpower?"

"He was bitten by a radioactive pollster," said Sarah. "No, really, Dad's like this super-telepath, right? He sees what's going on in everyone's head."

"Everyone? In the whole world? All at once?"

"Well, not everyone, I guess. His power doesn't work on Amelia or me. I don't think it works on you."

"Why wouldn't it work on me?"

"Well, you didn't step back earlier. My powers don't have any effect on you, so you're probably immune to Dad. Neither of our powers works on Amelia, either."

"Are you immune to Amelia's power?"

"Not the sharp steel blades part. But she can't pick me up by my blood."

"She what?"

"She does this thing where she picks people up by grabbing the iron in their blood."

"This is just too strange," said Richard. "You're pulling my leg."

"Nope. Hey, did I tell you Amelia and I have a code name for Dad? Dr. Know. Catchy, huh?"

"Copyrighted, probably." Richard realized that this new information about his employer explained a lot of apparent non sequiturs in their conversations. And it meant something else. "So, your dad knows about your stealing cinnamon buns?"

"I assume so. He hasn't mentioned it before. But, also, I think his power gets more focused the fewer people he concentrates on. He can get vague impressions from millions of people at once, or concentrate on a hundred and know their every last secret. But that's not the worst thing Dad can do with his power."

"Do tell."

"He can take over people's brains entirely. Use them like memory chips in a computer, to take over some of his thinking for him."

"Must come in handy when he's designing time machines and domed cities."

Sarah sat down on a bench and motioned for Richard to follow.

"You can't imagine what it's like," said Sarah. "Having a father who can watch your every move through the eyes of whomever it is you're with. When I was seventeen, right? There was this guy named Vance I met at a Nine Inch Nails show. He was like, twenty or something, really cool, with long hair and dark eyes. Just the most awesome guy I'd laid eyes on, really. And Vance starts hitting on me, and I'm digging it, and we go back to his van and smoke some pot, and he, you know, starts doing stuff to me. And I like it. It was my first time even kissing a guy, and already he had my bra undone, and I'm just totally in the flow, no doubts whatsoever. But then the van lurches, like a car's hit it or something, and the top of the van just peels off like it was tin foil, and there's Amelia, wearing her nightgown, looking all pissed.

"Dad sent her. He knew what I was up to because he was inside Vance. My father was inside the head of a guy who had his hands in my panties."

"Shit," said Richard. "I mean, wow, shit. That's horrible."

"You can't imagine," said Sarah. "Dad grounded me, of course. But it didn't matter. I mean, what was I going to do after that? I could never let another guy touch me again."

"That's awful," said Richard. "What a lousy hand to be dealt."

"Have you been with a lot of women, Richard?" asked Sarah.

"What?"

"You were married, right?"

"Yeah. In a different lifetime. Her name was Veronica."

"Was she your first?"

"Um," said Richard. "No. No, I'd dated a few women in college. Look, I don't want to seem evasive, but I'm trying not to think about my old life. I need to put all those memories as far behind me as I can if I'm going to get through this. Whenever I start remembering things, then realize that those things never happened as far as this world is concerned, it makes me feel like my head might split in two."

"The hand you've been dealt is as fucked up as mine," said Sarah. "Do you mind if we do a test? Just to make sure you're immune to my powers?"

"Sure."

"Take off your clothes," said Sarah.

"No," said Richard.

"Hmm. How about . . . you take off my clothes?"

"Here? In public?"

"Oh, I guess not," said Sarah. "You do seem immune to my charms."

"Well, immune to your powers at least," said Richard. "I still find you charming."

"One last try: kiss me."

She closed her eyes and puckered.

Richard couldn't believe this was happening. He decided to fail her test. He moved his lips to hers. They were warm and slightly sticky, with a hint of cinnamon. He could feel her trembling.

"I've dreamed about someone like you," she whispered as they parted. "Someone my father can't get inside of. You can't know what it's like to look into your eyes and not worry that my father might be looking back."

"I'm flattered," said Richard. "I really am. But, things have been so crazy for me. My life is in such a strange spin. What do you really know about me? What do I know about you? I don't know if I'm ready for a relationship right now."

"Who said anything about a relationship?" asked Sarah. "Let's just go someplace and make out."

Richard stared at her. He didn't know which was easier to believe, that he'd never been born or that a woman as sexy and powerful as Sarah was coming on to him. He grinned like a man taking a second glance at his winning lottery ticket. He leaned forward and kissed her once more. He drew the kiss out this time, placing his hands in her silky hair.

He pulled away and they sat in magical silence, savoring the moment.

Sarah grabbed his hand.

"Come on," she said.

She dragged him into the nearest shoe store, which sold athletic shoes. The clerk stared slack-jawed as she approached.

"You," she said. "Go home early."

"Hell yes!" said the clerk, jumping over the counter.

"What size do you wear?" Sarah asked Richard.

"Nine."

She quickly found the section with that size shoe and grabbed the first one that caught her eye.

"Try these on."

He took the shoes and sat down on the bench. She sat down next to him. They were out of view of any passersby in the mall. She kissed him again.

The shoe fell from his hand.

She broke off the kiss.

"So do they fit?" she asked.

"What?"

"The shoes."

"I haven't—"

"Say 'yes.'"

"Yes," he said.

"Good. Let's take them. We're done shopping. There's a store on the upper floor that sells big, black, overstuffed leather couches. I've always wanted to make out on a big, black, overstuffed leather couch."

Richard picked the shoes up and stuck them under his arm.

"Done shopping in thirty seconds and now you want to make out," said Richard. "My God, Sarah, you're like my dream woman."

"Enough chitchat," she said, taking him by the hand once more. Once again, they were flying, his feet several inches from the ground. It felt perfectly natural to him, completely sensible. This was turning out to be a really good day.

CHAPTER SEVEN

MORE ELABORATE
WAYS TO BREAK
MY SANITY

The following week turned into one of the best of Richard's life, old or new. He and Sarah had spent the rest of the day hanging around the mall, stealing stuff and making out in full view of an oblivious public. Any qualms he had had about using Sarah's powers to swindle shopkeepers quickly vanished. It wasn't like they would accept his credit cards anyway.

"The world is good," Sarah had said, "and made for our pleasure."

Richard subscribed to her philosophy very quickly. Why shouldn't he take every pleasure the world offered? Especially when life with Sarah offered so many pleasures. The island offered endless miles of pristine beaches for them to walk upon and talk of life. In the landscaped gardens of her father's estate, the grass was like soft bedding as they lay together. In the middle of the night they would slip from her bedroom and raid the enormous kitchen and eat delicacies prepared by Paco,

Dr. Knowbokov's personal chef. Even if all the luxury of wealth had been stripped away, Sarah alone would have made his life heaven. She was wonderful to talk to, so open and honest. Her cynical wit matched and often exceeded his. He hung on her every word.

On those rare moments when he and Sarah weren't together, Richard would roam the vast mansion. One of the odder things Richard noticed was how few people lived there. As near as he could gather, outside of the Knowbokov family, only two other people inhabited the island—Mindo and the chef, Paco.

The person he most often ran into was Mindo, Dr. Knowbokov's seven-foot-tall personal assistant. In fact, Mindo was nearly ubiquitous. Richard would go to the garden, and there would be Mindo practicing martial arts with Amelia. He'd walk to the spa, and find Mindo giving Sarah a massage. Moments later, in the library he would spot Mindo serving Katrina tea.

He once asked Dr. Knowbokov if he'd cloned Mindo and the Doctor had laughed and complimented him on his imagination. When he asked Sarah if Mindo had a twin sister, she looked at him oddly, dismissing his question. And he never actually saw two Mindos at the same time, so eventually he just stopped worrying about it. He was invisible to Mindo, so it wasn't like he was ever going to sit down and chat with her.

As near as Richard could determine, all maintenance work on the island was done by machines. Solar powered, robotic mowers crawled silently over the lawn. Foot-long, crablike robots scuttled through the rooms of the mansion, gathering up discarded laundry and empty plates. He even wandered into a room where a larger robot was repairing the smaller robots. Richard took the presence of the robots in stride. They just seemed a natural fit in Dr. Knowbokov's little mad scientist universe.

One thing the robots couldn't do well, apparently, was cook. Which explained Paco. Paco was Mindo's exact opposite. Mindo was tall, muscular, and never spoke unless spoken to. Paco was a doughy, squat man who jabbered ceaselessly even when no one was around. While Mindo turned up everywhere in the mansion, Paco was never seen outside the kitchen.

Richard liked to sit in the kitchen and nibble on snacks as Paco waddled around his domain, giving a running commentary on his every move. It was like a cooking show on the Food Network.

"Look at this tomato," Paco would say as he prepared a salad. "Nature's artwork has never been finer. Look at the red glow, the gentle curves. Smell it."

Then Paco would sniff the tomato and sigh before attacking it with his knife, at which point he would deliver an editorial on the virtues of a good knife.

Richard understood why all of the Knowbokovs were so trim. It was easy to eat right with someone like Paco working round the clock to feed you. That, and there weren't any fast food joints on the island.

The other thing that Richard liked about Paco was that while Paco was certainly a little odd, he was well within the acceptable realms of oddness that Richard understood. He didn't fly or fight crime or build time machines. He just talked to himself while cooking.

One morning he went into the kitchen and found Katrina there with Paco. Katrina was someone who rarely entered Richard's thoughts. He had to admit he enjoyed the guilty pleasure of having a girlfriend whose mother didn't know he existed. Katrina kept to herself, and when he did see her she was usually reading.

Even this morning, as she sat at the small table in the corner of the kitchen drinking tea, she had a book in front of her. But she was talking to Paco, and Richard deeply wished he hadn't entered in the middle of the conversation, as the first words he heard from Paco were, "As you say, he would know if you asked me to put poison in his food."

"He knows we're talking about this now," said Katrina, who looked like she hadn't slept well. "But he won't mention it. He's never mentioned it in the past. I'm no longer of any consequence to him."

"Your husband is a good man," said Paco. "If you would talk with him, I'm sure he would listen."

"Why should he listen when he knows every word I'm going to say?"

"I know this is difficult for you," said Paco. "But the man saved my life. I love him. I love you, too, and your daughters. And it's because of this love that I must ask we not discuss these drastic fantasies of yours."

"Paco, you're the only normal person I have left in my life. Can't you understand me at all?"

"You've been stressed by all of this joking by your daughter about her invisible boyfriend," said Paco. "Let me make you something that will take your mind off your troubles. Something comforting; dumplings, perhaps."

Katrina sighed. "Food isn't going to make me feel better."

"What you are saying," said Paco, "contradicts my life-time's experience."

Katrina left the room as Paco silently set to work mixing dough, looking worried. Richard followed Katrina, unsure of what to do. Should he tell Dr. Knowbokov about Katrina's feelings? On the other hand, if Dr. Knowbokov really was telepathic, didn't he already know?

Katrina went to the library, to the furthest wall with its rows of thick, leather bound reference books. After a moment's study she reached out and tilted one of the books forward. Richard was struck by how much her action reminded him of triggering a secret door in an old movie. Then, the shelf began to slide apart, revealing a passage beyond.

Richard laughed. Dr. Knowbokov's humor was singular.

Richard followed Katrina into the enormous room beyond. The first thing he noticed, high overhead, was a rocket ship that looked like it had been lifted from the pages of a 1930s comic strip. It was painted cherry red, and had chrome fins on the tail.

The room was filled with countless odds and ends, like the attic of a museum. Everything had a label, or a little metal plate describing it. For a moment he forgot about Katrina as he looked around the room and whistled. In one corner of the room was a fifty-foot-long construction crane arm tied into a bow. He leaned over to gaze into a microscope on a nearby table. In the petri dish below it, flea-sized dinosaurs grazed among a forest of hair-width trees. Next to this stood a suit of medieval armor, crafted for a warrior ten feet tall with four arms. Richard leaned over the plate, and saw that the armor had once belonged to a "Dr. Alterman" from the "Mirror Dimension."

He remembered Katrina, and hurried through the maze of exhibits mentally cataloging things he wanted to examine further when he had the time. Just what did one do with a radioactive skateboard? An anti-sound piano? A warp-monkey?

Katrina was standing in front of a skeleton of a football-field-sized snake with wings. When Richard reached her, he saw she was crying. He felt awkward, even though he knew she couldn't see him. He wondered if he should leave.

Then, Katrina took a deep breath, threw her shoulders back, and wiped her tears. She walked past the snake to an exhibit of a crib in an aquarium. Richard didn't have time to read the plaque in front of it before Katrina rushed it, and pushed it over with a shattering crash that echoed throughout the huge chamber. Water poured across the floor and Richard took a step back, worried this might be mirror dimension water that could turn him into a warp-monkey.

Katrina moved on to the next exhibit: a petrified baseball bat in a case. She flipped the lid open, grabbed the bat, raised it over her head, and took aim at a globe containing glowing gold fish.

But before she could swing, Dr. Knowbokov slipped up silently behind her and snatched the bat away.

"Katrina," he said. "We should talk."

Katrina spun around and slapped him. Richard winced. The doctor stood stoically, unfazed by the blow.

"How dare you?" Katrina said. "How dare you tell me we should talk when you know every word I will say?"

"I knew you would strike me," said Dr. Knowbokov. "And chose to receive the blow, in hopes you would feel better for having struck me. Whether I anticipate your words or not won't negate the therapeutic effects of saying them."

"Sometimes I think you've spent the last thirty years dreaming up ever more elaborate ways to break my sanity," said Katrina. "How can you stand there so calmly and tell me we should talk?"

"What other path would you have me follow?" asked Dr. Knowbokov.

Katrina brushed the hair back from her face and set her jaw as her lower lip trembled.

"No matter how you feel," said Dr. Knowbokov, "it's unwise to start wrecking exhibits. Breathing the fumes of the *aqua regia* fish could damage your lungs. And there are things you could unleash here that would be even more dangerous to you."

"Nothing could be more dangerous to me than you," said Katrina, slipping past Dr. Know, walking quickly, though gracefully, back toward the library.

Dr. Know knelt down, sighing. He tilted the overturned crib back onto its rockers. He said, "I'm sorry you had to see that, Richard."

"I feel like I should be apologizing," said Richard. "I didn't mean to spy on your wife. She just seemed so upset. And in the kitchen, she was . . . I mean she—"

"She was talking about killing me," said Dr. Know-bokov. "I know. I fear we have entered a terrible downward spiral, she and I. The more I know and understand what she is feeling, the more I attempt to react to it, to offer my help. But this only serves to further remind her that I am aware of her thoughts. Sarah didn't help matters when she used her powers on Katrina the night you first joined us. That hadn't happened in years. It stirred up unpleasant memories, I fear."

"Unpleasant memories?"

"I can only say that life has not been easy for Katrina. Sarah and Amelia both demonstrated their powers from childhood. Sarah was especially challenging for Katrina. Imagine having your will subverted to the needs and desires of an infant. I attempted to isolate Katrina from Sarah, but this seemed to trigger even greater pain for her."

"I can see how this would lead to marital strife," said Richard. "But, if I may ask a blunt question, why doesn't she just leave you? Better still, why don't you send her away? Set her up in a nice little house someplace far away from your crazy little world and let her get back to a normal life?"

"She would never be safe from my enemies if she left this island," said Dr. Knowbokov. "Her situation is difficult, but I continue to have faith that one day she'll be able to accept my 'crazy little world.'"

LATER THAT NIGHT, he went back to the museum with Sarah.

"I don't even know where to begin asking questions," said Richard. "What is all this stuff? Heck, let's start with the winged snake."

"Quetzalcoatl," said Sarah. "It was some kind of god to the ancient Aztecs or Incas or whatever. Rex Monday triggered a spell that brought it back to life. Amelia killed it. When it died, all of its feathers and flesh just turned to dust and blew off, leaving the skeleton. And this isn't even close to the strangest thing I've seen in my life."

"As long as we're on the big exhibits, what's up with the rocket ship?"

"Is that a joke? Up? Rocket?"

"Uh, no," said Richard.

"It's not a real rocket," said Sarah. "It doesn't have any engines. Amelia just picked it up and moved it around with her mind the only time she had to use it."

"OK. How about the dinosaurs in petri dishes?"

"Some weird side effect of Dad's earlier attempt at a time machine. I can only say that you've never really itched until you've had microscopic velociraptors in your pubic hair."

"Ew," said Richard.

Sarah took out a cigarette. Within five seconds of her lighting it, a silver bumblebee-sized robot swooped down from the ceiling and extinguished it in a puff of lemon-scented mist. It buzzed away before Sarah could swat it.

"Damn it," she said. "Dad couldn't be satisfied with a simple no smoking sign?"

"Would you obey it?" asked Richard.

"Don't give me grief," said Sarah. "I smoke. It's a bad habit. It pisses Dad off maybe even more than me using my powers on Mom. But I'll stop on my timetable, not his."

"They say that every cigarette you smoke takes a day off your life," said Richard.

"If that were true you wouldn't be the only person in the room who'd never been born. I'd be, like, negative forty-three by now."

Richard laughed, but then was hit by a serious thought. "About your mother," he said. "Look, I don't know if I should tell you this, but she seems to really hate your dad."

"Duh," said Sarah. "She hates me, too. She's been scared of me since before I can remember."

"Do you hate her?"

"No. Of course not. Jeez. She's my mother. I feel sorry for her more than anything, I guess. When she married Dad he was just a normal guy. A very smart physicist normal guy, but he wasn't telepathic. When they were planning to have babies, she definitely wasn't planning on the freak show she got. On the other hand, Amelia and I didn't exactly get to pick whether or not to have weird powers. I wish Mom had learned to deal with it. I mean, some mothers give birth to babies who are blind, or who have no hands, or who are retarded, but they still love their kids. Is it mean of me to want my mother to display even a tiny fraction of this acceptance?"

"No," said Richard. "It's not mean."

"How about this," she said. "I sometimes wish my parents were dead."

"Now you're veering into mean," said Richard.

CHAPTER EIGHT

RED AND WET

Mean or no, Richard enjoyed Sarah's honesty. Sometimes when he was with her, he could completely forget he had ever had another life. Waking up next to her was like waking up in his proper place in the universe. Then, one morning, he woke up in the dark and found only a note by his side.

"Father called with a mission," the note said. "Will be gone for a week. Would have woken you but you looked so peaceful. Plus, I think that if you looked at me right I would have told my father to do his own dirty work and spent the day here with you. I don't know that I'm ready for that confrontation yet. I'll think of you constantly. Love, Sarah."

He couldn't go back to sleep. It was 4 A.M. Nothing was on television. He decided to spend a little time in the gymnasium he'd spotted on his ramblings around the mansion. Sarah's energy had really been pushing him to his physical limits, and he felt like perhaps he should start doing a little weight lifting. Comic book heroes always seemed to be packed with muscles no matter what their profession, even before they gained their powers. Rocket scientists, geeky students, and physicians were revealed to have already sent off for the Charles Atlas course the second they ripped away their shirts to reveal their colorful underwear. Richard felt a little cheated. He was the same skinny guy he'd always been. Sarah and Amelia both could probably take him in arm wresting.

As he opened the door to the gym, he was greeted with the solid thumping sound of someone murdering a punching bag.

Amelia stood in the far corner of the gym, in old sweats with her hair pinned atop her head. Her hands were bound with tape, and she was dripping sweat and grunting as she lay into the heavy bag.

"Kick its ass," said Richard. "America's safe if Rex Monday ever attacks with an army of radioactive, intelligent punching bags."

Amelia stopped and wiped her brow.

"What?" she asked. "You going to talk them to death?"

"Was that a joke? I don't think I've heard you tell a joke before."

"There's not much in this world I find funny," she said.

Looking at her sweaty, stern face, with her hard, steel-gray eyes, Richard believed her.

"You're not much like your sister," he said.

She leaned over and grabbed her water bottle. "My sister's going to get herself hurt or killed one day. She doesn't train like she should. She doesn't push herself."

"She seems healthy enough."

"Healthy doesn't count for much in this game. Her powers are useful for certain missions, but when there's real fighting to be done, the burden falls to me. I have to watch both our backs. Now, I'll have to watch out for you as well."

"I guess," said Richard. "I didn't ask for this life, you know."

"You signed on voluntarily," said Amelia. "And you blew your first mission. All you had to do was follow your target."

"Am I the only one who thinks that saving those kid's lives was important?"

"My sister approves, apparently," said Amelia. "She seems to have become fond of you."

"Fond isn't quite the word," Richard said with a grin.

"You don't seem to take much seriously," said Amelia.

"Why try? I'm some sort of time-ghost, my girlfriend flies, and I'm talking with a woman who can pick up trains with her mind but still feels like she might have to rely on her fists in a fight. It's easier to just roll with it."

Amelia took a drink from her bottle. "Have you ever been in a fight, Richard?"

"Not really," he said. "Don't guess I'm likely to, since no one can touch me."

"I can touch you," said Amelia.

"You wanna fight?" said Richard. "I don't. You'd whip me from here to next week."

"Worth one shot," said Amelia.

Before Richard could even blink, she had crossed the twenty or so feet that separated them and planted a punch squarely on his jaw. Stars flashed before his eyes. When his vision cleared, he was flat on his back. Amelia knelt over him.

"You're sleeping with my sister," she said. "I don't approve."

"Ow," said Richard, shaking his head to clear it. "I don't care what you approve."

He sat up, looking at Amelia warily. "That's the second time I've been taken out with a shot to the jaw lately. I don't like it."

"I suspect you'll grow used to it."

"What? You really think threatening me is going to make me stop sleeping with Sarah?"

"No," said Amelia. "I'm not threatening you. I'm making you an offer. Right now you're weak and have zero combat skills. You're more dangerous to yourself and my family than you are to any of our enemies. You need martial training. I can provide it. Who knows? I might train you well enough that I won't be able to knock you out with one punch."

"You must learn your negotiating style from your father. He destroys my world then sells me on what a great opportunity it is to make this world a better place. You knock me out with one punch then want to train me until you can hit me three or four times before I go down."

She held out her hand to help him to his feet. "You went along with father's plan. You want to sign onto mine?"

"Let me think about it," he said taking her hand. "I'm not all that eager to be your full-time punching bag. Why don't you approve of Sarah and me? She's a grown woman. Let her live her own life."

"As I said, you're weak. I don't want Sarah getting killed because she's looking out for you in battle."

"Does your father know about Sarah and me?"

Amelia shrugged. "I don't know. For a man who's close to omniscient he can sometimes be blind to the obvious."

"So he didn't send her off on some solo mission just so you'd have a chance to punch me in the jaw?"

"Father has sent Sarah to Jerusalem. He's decided to bring her unique talents into play in his efforts to broker peace."

Richard scoffed. "Christ. Your father wasn't joking about wanting to save the world. But, c'mon, how long do you think a peace she negotiates using her powers is going to last over there? A week, tops."

Amelia walked away from him, back toward the punching bag. She placed her hand on it to steady herself as her muscles slackened. She took another swallow of water.

"You're right," she said. "Father hasn't given up hope, but I'm starting to. I've been fighting for my father's dream of a perfect world all my life. But I've been to Jerusalem. I helped bring a riot under control in the Old City. You can see it in people's eyes. The old grudges there can only be satisfied with blood. But Father thinks Rex Monday is supplying arms to the factions there. He'll do whatever it takes to stop Monday's schemes. If my sister fails, it's only a matter of time before my father sends me there."

"What can you do that Sarah can't? She is the, um, persuasive one."

"I can kill people," said Amelia. "Eventually, it will all boil down to killing people."

The door to the gym opened. It was Mindo.

"Your father sent me for you," Mindo said. "A situation has developed."

"WOW," SAID RICHARD. "You must make the stock holders of Circuit City very happy, Dr. Know."

Monitors and instruments filled the room. Along the far wall, a bank of televisions displayed broadcasts from all over the world. In the center of it all was a large padded chair in which Dr. Know sat.

"This is the first time you've been to my command hub, Richard," said Dr. Know. "This is also the first time you've called me by that irritating nickname Sarah finds so amusing."

"Ah, hell. I knew it was only a matter time before I slipped up and said it to your face. I'll watch out for it." Richard silently resolved to use the nickname anytime the doctor was in earshot.

"What's happening, Father?" asked Amelia.

"One of our transports has been intercepted. The prisoner is now missing."

"When?" asked Amelia.

"One hour ago in Austin, Texas."

"An inside job, obviously," said Amelia. "How many people will you need to check before you find a lead?"

"Only three people knew the truth," said Dr. Know. "I've checked them all, and they're shocked and worried by what has happened. I've done a broader search of the area without results. I can't find anyone who knows about this. Which means—"

"Monday's involved," said Amelia. "I'll suit up."

"Question," said Richard. "Who was this prisoner? What's so important about all this?"

As if in response, one by one the televisions on the far wall tuned to the same broadcast.

Dr. Know turned pale as he saw the screens.

In a dark room, three figures stood. One, Richard recognized from the battle in D.C. It was Sundancer, and she was holding the face of a bound man with a shaved head, pointing it toward the camera. The man's mouth was covered with duct tape, and his eyes darted nervously around the room. The third figure was a man dressed in a nice suit, with a green hood concealing his face.

"Greetings, Planet Earth," the hooded man said. "I'm Rex Monday. Welcome to an exciting new episode of Monday's Revelation. The man my attractive associate is presenting to you is named Anthony Wayne Walters. Two hours ago, he was sitting in an electric chair, sentenced to die for the tragic, pointless deaths of twelve children. Mr. Walters did the prosecution a tremendous favor by videotaping these murders for his own personal viewing pleasure. There is no question of his guilt. There was no last minute pardon. The switch was pulled at the appointed time. But, as you can see, Mr. Walters is very much alive."

"He's made a mistake," Dr. Know said, swiveling around in his chair to face Amelia. "They're in a television studio in Austin. They've killed two technicians, but a security guard is hiding in a closet, listening to them even now. I know where they are!"

"Yeah," said Richard. "They're in Texas."

"On my way!" said Amelia.

"Take Richard," said Dr. Know. "There's no time for your sister to get there."

"Whoa," said Richard. "Even in your jet, Texas is, what, four hours from here? They'll be long gone when we get there. What's the hurry?"

"I'm the hurry," said Amelia, as shards of metal materialized from thin air around her, wrapping her in armor. She thrust out her hand and grabbed Richard by the shirt. The flowing metal slithered from her hand, engulfing him in seconds.

There was an astonishing boom, then silence.

Richard was blind, deaf, and immobile. He couldn't breath, and his heart seemed ready to burst. His efforts to scream only led to a terrible pressure in his chest and head. He felt as if he weighed three thousand pounds.

Then as quickly as it had begun, it was over. The metal that encased him crumbled to dust, and he slumped to his knees, gasping for breath, coughing. He looked up.

He was in a television studio.

Rail Blade stood before him, soaked in sweat, the shards of the armor she had created dropping to the floor around her.

Just beyond her, the hooded man known as Rex Monday grasped at his throat, gurgling, blood pulsing between his fingers with every beat of his heart.

And just beyond him, a single blade, a foot long and razor sharp, hovered in the air, red and wet.

CHAPTER NINE

ROLLER COASTER

Sundancer looked pissed. She began to glow, and Anthony Wayne Walters screamed as his face started to sizzle. In the second it took for the spinning blade to reach her, Sundancer had turned white hot. The blade liquefied as it touched her, smearing sloppily against her neck before spinning off wildly across the room. Flesh melted from Anthony Wayne Walters and his scream died abruptly.

Nobody covered his eyes and crawled away from the terrible scene. Behind him, Rail Blade grunted as she parried Sundancer's plasma flare attacks with a mirrored shield.

The desk Nobody was hiding behind burst into flame. Sprinklers opened, drenching Nobody, and filling the air with steam. The desk continued to burn despite the water.

He scurried in the most direct route he could manage to put as much space between him and Sundancer as possible. He didn't know what he could do that would be of any use. The steam was burning his lungs. Running seemed practical. He looked around for doors, and found plenty of them. None were marked with a friendly exit sign. They all seemed to be offices or—

"Security guard in the closet," he said, snapping his fingers. On a hunch he grabbed at a drab beige door and jerked it open. The security guard inside yelped.

"Don't kill me!"

"I'm saving you, idiot!" said Nobody. Of course, the guy didn't hear him.

Fortunately, the guard took one look at the flame-engulfed room and the two battling women and decided to make a hasty retreat. Nobody followed the fleeing man through a glass door into a hallway, and outran him to reach the exit door in the lobby. He reached for the door bar and stumbled as his hand passed through it. He ghosted through the door, off balance.

Seconds later, the guard pushed open the door and ran through. Nobody regained his footing and chased after him.

Now safe, he looked back. A pillar of flame rose high in the sky, turning night into day. A steel rail spiraled into the air around the flame, as Rail Blade chased her fiery foe. Across the flat field that surrounded the studio, blue lights were flashing in their approach.

Nobody looked at his wrist, at the nice stainless steel diver's watch he'd picked up on one of his shopping trips. Not even three minutes had passed since the broadcast had begun.

The pillar of flame vanished. The roof of the studio was still ablaze, but the intensity of light dimmed, blending into the night. Looking up, Nobody saw Rail Blade plummeting from the sky, fragments of her red-hot armor sparking away, leaving a glowing comet's trail. She crashed into the roof, and, from the sound of things, through it.

Nobody ran back into the burning building. The smoke from the broadcast studio had yet to fill the front hall.

"Amelia!" he cried out, pushing open doors and staring into darkened rooms, searching for one with a hole in the roof. "Amelia!"

He found her sprawled on the carpet in some sort of meeting room. Her armor had fallen to red dust around her, and her body was covered with raw, red blisters. Though they were far from the center of the fire, the carpet she lay upon smoldered.

"Amelia," he said, running to her side. He slid to his knees beside her and turned her face toward him, flinching as he realized it was stupid to move her.

She groaned as she slowly opened her eyes.

"Amelia!" Nobody said. "You're alive. I'll get some help. Somehow. Just hang on."

She grinned feebly, then said, softly, "You're no good at this, Nobody. You're supposed to call me 'Rail Blade' out here."

"I'd rather call you an ambulance," said Nobody, looking around for a phone. Then he remembered the police cars on their way. Dialing 911 seemed redundant.

Rail Blade groaned as she grabbed the seat of a nearby chair and pulled herself into a sitting position. "I've lived through worse," she said, her voice quavering. "My training helps me block off the parts of my mind that feel the pain. We should leave before the police arrive."

"Are we going to do that metal prison teleporting thing again?" he asked. "I'd rather walk back to the island."

She shook her head. "Don't have the strength. Would have done better against Sundancer if I hadn't exhausted myself pulling that stunt."

"What did you do, anyway?"

"Earth's core is one big iron crystal," she said, gingerly picking carpet fibers from her wounds. "I can tune into it and trigger a magnetic quake, then surf the resulting shockwave. Takes me anywhere on Earth in seconds. I only use it in real emergencies. Father worries that frequent use might cause the magnetic poles to flip, which could be bad."

She grimaced as she rose, steadying herself against the seatback. "This chair has a steel frame. Sit."

Nobody sat.

The chair lurched upward, as a single steel rail materialized beneath it.

"Hold on."

The rail snaked upward through the hole in the roof and they began to rise along it. Nobody felt like he was on the front seat of a roller coaster, only there was no bar to hold him down. He clenched the seat edges with white knuckles.

The studio parking lot was filled with police cars and ambulances. Nobody coughed as Rail Blade steered them into the smoke.

"Sorry," she said, coughing. "Don't want them to see which way we're going. I can't make it far."

"Explain to me why we're running away?"

"I killed Rex Monday on live television," said Rail Blade. "I guess I should have gone for the cameras first, but I didn't want to give them time to exit. Monday has some kind of teleporting device. These guys can vanish in a blink. I did what I had to. But it's still going to be bad PR."

The rail slowly slinked into the tops of a nearby grove of trees. They had barely traveled two hundred yards, Nobody guessed. She sat them down in the middle of the grove. She leaned against a tree, panting.

"Take the chair," said Nobody.

She collapsed into it.

"Just need a minute to catch my breath," she said. "Left so fast, I don't have my radio. Can't call Father for help."

"I don't have mine, either," said Nobody. "Maybe we should turn ourselves in. Or you turn yourself in, at least. You need a doctor. You look like you're about to faint."

"No," she said, jumping out of the chair.

Then her eyes rolled up into her head.

He rushed and caught her before she hit the ground. She was surprisingly heavy. He struggled to place her back in the chair, worried about laying her on the ground with her open wounds.

Before he could decide what to do next, he heard the crunching sound of someone approaching over leaves. He pulled off the sweatshirt he wore and draped it over her. The sweats she had been wearing earlier were mostly burned away, leaving her wearing only a sports bra and tights. The beam of a flashlight glinted across the chair's metal legs. The crunching grew closer.

A tall, heavyset man entered the clearing. He looked like a former football player gone to pot but still physically formidable. He was dressed in a cheap blue suit with cowboy boots and a string tie. The guy looked around, then walked over to Rail Blade. He checked her pulse, then he took a small radio from his pocket, the type Dr. Know had given Nobody before his first mission.

"Dr. Knowbokov says that there's an invisible man here and that I should put this radio down then turn around if the little lady here couldn't talk," the man said and turned away.

Nobody grabbed the radio and held it to his ear.

"Hello?" he said.

"Richard," said Dr. Know. "Is my daughter alive?"

"Yes. I don't know how badly injured she is. She took a pretty bad beating, but was conscious a minute ago. I think she's gone into shock."

"The man who found you is named John Starkner. He's the warden at the nearby state prison. Keep close to him. He'll take Amelia to safety."

"OK," Starkner said. "Guess that's long enough. I'm going to turn around now."

As he did, Nobody feared the radio would slip from his grasp. It didn't. Apparently, Starkner no longer expected to see it.

Starkner gently lifted Rail Blade, and carried her through the woods, with his flashlight turned off. Nobody followed.

"How did you find us, Doc?" asked Nobody.

"There are still several dozen Soviet spy satellites in orbit over the U.S., most with infrared and a detail resolution of six inches. It was good fortune that one was passing over Texas."

"Why do you have access to Soviet spy satellites?"

"I have access to almost every satellite in orbit."

Starkner took Rail Blade to a huge SUV, then popped open the rear hatch with his remote. He gently laid her on a sheet he had spread out there, and covered her with a thick blanket. He went to the passenger side door and opened it.

"Wanna ride, Mr. Invisible?"

"The name's Nobody." He climbed into the seat, pulling in his left foot seconds before Starkner slammed the door.

STARKNER DROVE TO a plywood shack way out in the boondocks. Nobody stood by helplessly as Starkner carried Rail Blade's still body from the SUV, up the steps, and onto the rickety porch. The door opened on his approach.

An elderly woman, her hair pulled tight in a bun, stood in the doorway. She wore a white coat, with a stethoscope around her neck. Beyond her, the main room of the shack was brightly lit. As Nobody's eyes adjusted to the brightness, the room revealed itself to be a very clean and modern-looking surgical room. The woman wrung her hands and paced as Starkner placed Rail Blade on the table.

"I knew this would happen," the woman said, sounding frightened. "Did you see the TV? I saw the TV. It's out. The whole damn world knows Walters is alive."

"Was alive," said Starkner. "Old news. It's Knowbokov's roof to patch. Right now, this little lady needs your help, Summer."

"We're going to prison for this," said Summer, gently pulling aside the blanket that covered Rail Blade. "Every time we've turned a prisoner over to that man, I've gone cold in my stomach knowing it could come to this."

"But you did it anyway," said Starkner. "Can't look back now. We have to trust in the big guy to work things out."

"I don't believe in God," said Summer, checking Rail Blade's pulse.

"I was talking about Knowbokov," said Starkner.

"Pulse is good," said Summer, leaning over Rail Blade and pressing the stethoscope against her ribs. "Breathing is steady. Most of her burns are second degree. The best I can do now is clean and dress them. But she's going to have some serious pain. I'll start a morphine drip." She gently touched a bruised knot on Rail Blade's temple. "I'm more worried about this more than anything. We need to get her to facilities for a CAT scan or MRI."

"Knowbokov's sending a helicopter," said Starkner. "She'll get good medical treatment at home. You've been to the island. Do what you can for now."

As Summer worked, she continued to talk. "What will my husband say when he learns the truth? My kids?"

"Maybe it won't come to that. Knowbokov can pull a lot of strings. It happened so early in the morning, how many people saw it? How many people understood what they saw? I bet Knowbokov will have this buried and the sod patted down by lunch."

"Do you know what he does with the prisoners?" asked Summer.

"No," said Starkner. "What's it matter? How much worse can it be than being dead?"

"I worry about that sometimes," said Summer. "I went along with this because I wanted to save lives. But what if he's using them for some horrible experiments? What else would he need them for?"

"Not our cow to milk," said Starkner.

Silence followed, as Starkner slung his hefty frame into a chair and cradled his head in his hands. Summer continued to work, her lips pursed.

Nobody radioed Dr. Know. "Doc, we need to talk."

"Has Amelia's condition worsened?" asked Dr. Know.

"She's doing OK, I think. A doctor here named Summer is treating her. You know her?"

"Summer Pagent. Yes. She assists me in certain projects."

"These projects involve death-row inmates coming back to life?"

"No. Their deaths are faked. Summer merely declares them dead afterwards."

"Uh-huh. And why, pray tell, would you be doing something like this?"

"These are men whose lives have legally come to an end. They are society's waste. I recycle them."

"Doc, I doubt you have any idea how sinister that sounds to me. Am I fighting on the right side here? What kind of crazy game are you up to?"

"Richard, I have no intention or desire to keep you in the dark. There are many levels to this, as you put it, game. When you return to the island, we'll talk. There's no reason you shouldn't know the whole story."

CHAPTER TEN

THE SECRET ORIGIN OF DR. KNOW

Richard placed his hand against the warm glass. Before him, Amelia was suspended in a tube filled with translucent pink goo. She was awake but couldn't speak, as her lungs were filled with the fluid. She stared at him, her eyes gray and hard, her lips thin and tight. It wasn't a look of pain, so much as a look of contempt. Richard wasn't quite sure what to make of it.

He left the lab, unsure what to make of anything he had witnessed earlier that day. He tried imagining what good purpose Dr. Know could have for kidnapping death-row inmates, and was hard-pressed to find an explanation that seemed remotely ethical. What kind of man was he working for?

He went to the library, and found Katrina there. He didn't see her much these days, now that she had stopped attending dinners with her husband and daughters. He hadn't heard her speak to Paco or anyone else since the episode in the museum. She seemed a living ghost, just as he was. On the rare occasions he saw her outside the library, she seemed lost in her own thoughts, somnambulistic as she wandered through the halls. Presently, Katrina was reading a book written in an alphabet Richard didn't recognize. She stared at the text before her for what seemed an unnaturally long time before her trembling hand turned the page.

Kneeling before her, Richard said, "I feel so bad about all this. Like it's my fault. If Dr. Know hadn't tried to make you see me maybe you could have gone on in whatever passed for normal in your relationship with him. I'm sorry."

Of course, she didn't acknowledge this. With a sigh, Richard turned away, distracted by a noise from the lawn.

Richard walked out onto the balcony. A helicopter was landing. Something was familiar about it. Then he realized he had seen it in the background of dozens of news broadcasts. He wasn't surprised in the least when the President of the United States emerged from it.

He went back to the library.

"Your husband has powerful friends," said Richard.

Katrina continued her reading.

Richard left her, curious as to what the President might be doing here. After a brief search, he found not only the President, but also a dozen other men in suits seated around a large table. Some looked vaguely familiar, though no names sprang to mind. He wished he were more up-to-date on world affairs.

Dr. Know entered the room. The men rose from their seats.

"Gentlemen," he said. "Thank you for coming. I know you have many questions about the course of action that we will be taking to deal with recent events. Rest assured, your questions will be answered. Rex Monday's little stunt last night is far from a disaster for our cause. It is, in fact, a wonderful opportunity. But before we begin our discussion, I ask your patience. I have a brief matter to attend to."

As he said this, he looked across the room to Richard.

"Patience?" asked the President. "You have a lot of gall to ask for our patience. What's so important about this business of yours?"

"I merely wish to extend private thanks to someone who provided aid and comfort to my daughter in her time of need," said Dr. Know, walking toward Richard. "And we both know I have a surplus of gall."

He placed a hand on Richard's shoulder and led him from the room.

"Who are those people?" Richard asked.

"Heads of state, captains of industry. What the press might call world leaders."

"Might call? That's the President in there!"

"Yes. He's a vital member of my cabinet."

"Your cabinet? What's going on here? Who do you think you are?"

"Richard, I owe you a debt of gratitude. Amelia says you roused her from unconsciousness in the middle of a burning building. You may have saved her life."

"I don't even understand why her life was in danger. What are you doing kidnapping prisoners? Who was this Rex Monday and why did Amelia murder him? There's no way to justify that as an act of self-defense."

"Perhaps not. But it was a defensive act. It was a blow for the safety and security of the whole world. Alas, it was also a futile blow. The man beneath that hood has been identified. His name was Michael Winston, and he went missing from the campus of the University of North Carolina six months ago. He was far too young to be the true Rex Monday, though I have no doubt he was brainwashed to believe every word he said on television."

"So Amelia killed an innocent kid? This is supposed to reassure me that she was doing the right thing?"

"Richard, allow me to show you something."

As they spoke, they had walked back into the mansion's command center. Dr. Know went to his chair in the center of the room and pressed a button concealed under the armrest. The floor around the chair began to lower.

"You have a real fetish for this hydraulic stuff, huh?" said Richard.

They descended several hundred yards down a steel tube. Richard began to feel claustrophobic.

At last the walls of the tube gave way to open space. They were in a vast chamber, filled with the sort of pink goo tubes that Richard had seen in the infirmary. These tubes held dozens, perhaps hundreds, of men, all sleeping.

"By now," said Dr. Know, "I imagine Sarah has revealed to you my special ability."

"She says you can read people's minds," said Richard.

"This is accurate, to a point. On the subtlest level of consciousness, my mind touches the thoughts of nearly every other person in this world. I cannot focus on the direct thoughts of everyone at once, however. So the privacy of the vast majority of the world's citizens is in no danger. I have trained myself to pay attention to subtle anomalies in people's thoughts, so I'm aware when truly unusual events are occurring, and are being witnessed by someone my mind touches. This is how I found you. Henry and Martha truly believed they were seeing something supernatural. Scanning the area, I saw you on a television broadcast, dressed in your pink robe, and thought it strange that your presence failed to register in the minds of anyone who saw the broadcast. At first I thought you were perhaps one of Rex Monday's men, as my mind could not touch yours, and he has somehow perfected a way to shield his agents' thoughts from me. Only through careful analysis was I able to piece together the chain of events that led to your present existence."

"And this explains all these people in tubes how?"

"Richard, what I'm going to tell you next you might find morally objectionable. I ask that you approach this with an open mind."

"Sounds like you're an expert in open minds."

"Due to your no longer being fully in phase with our world, your mind is now closed to me, if it makes you feel any better."

"What might I find objectionable?" Richard asked.

"I have the ability to enter a person's mind so thoroughly, their entire personality is subverted. I control their thoughts."

"That isn't objectionable," said Richard. "That's flat out repulsive."

"It takes time," said Dr. Know. "Several weeks often, to suppress someone with a strong ego. But once this occurs, I control all areas of the brain devoted to conscious thought. I can't control their bodies, as muscular movement and balance requires more than the conscious mind. But, I can use the areas of the brain I do control to work on intellectual projects."

"So you take death row prisoners, fake their deaths, slap them into goo tubes, and turn them into external brain packs."

"Well summarized," said Dr. Know.

"That's just . . . monstrous. I mean, I don't support the death penalty, but death has to be preferable to this. What gives you the right?"

Dr. Know walked over to the nearest tube. The man within was small, thin, and bald, his skin covered with tattooed swastikas.

"This is Thomas Weilder. Twelve years ago, in celebration of his twentieth birthday, he took the .38 Special his friends had given him as a gift and tried it out by shooting the first black man he saw. His aim left something to by desired. He fired six shots at his victim, only two of which struck, both in the left thigh. In frustration, he beat the man unconscious with the butt of his pistol. Then, he locked the man in the trunk of his car, and kept him there for seven days. The man had stopped struggling and crying after two. But Thomas waited the extra five days to make sure."

"So the guy's a racist creep," said Richard. "It doesn't make what you're doing to him right."

"It's possible I could have stopped him," said Dr. Know. "My mind touched his. I also touched Marcus Jefferson, the man who died so horribly. I sensed the hatred, I sensed the pain and fear, and I paid it no attention because I always feel these things. Right now, you can't imagine all the hate-filled minds I am in contact with, all the fear and loneliness and despair I am witness to. I recoil at these emotions. I cannot focus on individuals, to bring peace and comfort to their lives. There is just too much pain in this world to handle on a person-by-person basis."

Richard was silent. The tortured tone of Dr. Know's voice revealed the true depth of his sorrow. But could mere sorrow justify this forest of tubes?

"All the evil in this world," said Dr. Know, "rests upon my shoulders."

"You aren't to blame for this guy being a Nazi," said Richard. "But I guess I can see where you're coming from. I can see why you want to change the world. But there must be a better way."

"Thomas Weilder's mind, once so filled with hate, now whirls ceaselessly as it processes the information flowing in from all the AIDS research centers that I fund. Within his head, I collate and analyze the data."

Dr. Know moved to the next tube. "Morgan Mathers. A tragic life, filled with abuse from his earliest childhood. He snapped one day, and seventeen people died before he turned the gun on himself. It was empty by then, to his dismay. He welcomed his death sentence, and fought every appeal on his behalf. Now, his head is filled with numbers. I use his brain to analyze financial data from around the globe. I create wealth with this knowledge, and use it to provide funding for dozens of charitable institutions. Through him, I feed the world."

He moved to the next tube. "Tyrone Adams. Rapist and thug. Murderer of a dozen men. Inside his skull I keep track of millions of endangered species and design plans for habitat protection."

The next. "Martin Banderas. Hitman for a drug cartel. Thanks to my use of his brain, the cure for most cancers has perhaps already been discovered. Even now, I am studying the test results he is receiving via electro-retinal stimulation."

"OK," said Richard. "OK. I get the idea. I still don't get what gives you the right. So you can't stand feeling people's pain and misery. Wouldn't it be simpler to just get out of everyone's heads? And what is it with your whole family anyway? How on Earth did you get such powers?"

Dr. Know faced him. He smiled gently, with the hint of a twinkle in his eye. "Perhaps when I say that I am to blame for evil in this world, you imagine that I speak metaphorically."

"You're not Satan," said Richard. "Wait. That would explain a lot."

"I'm not Satan," said Dr. Know. "But Satan didn't create evil."

"Then you're not God."

Dr. Know nodded. "I happen to know there is no God."

"*Really*," said Richard. "I'm not exactly religious, but blanket statements like that get me looking for lightning bolts. How can you be so certain God doesn't exist?"

"Because," said Dr. Know. "I was there when this universe was created. God was nowhere to be seen."

Richard studied the doctor, searching his face for some hint of a joke. "You mentioned that universe thing the day I met you. Sarah's also alluded to it. Does this have something to do with your time machine?"

"So much would have been different if my grandparents had never left Russia," said Dr. Know. "Because of my heritage, and because of my groundbreaking research on quantum mechanics, I was closely watched by the American military establishment during the late 1950s. Eventually, I learned to use their paranoia to my advantage. I made it known that the fruits of my research could be used to develop weaponry more powerful than even the H-bomb. This led to a long and intellectually profitable alliance with the American government. I was supplied with nearly limitless funds and equipment as I pursued my research into the energy potential of pure vacuum. The entire space race was concocted to mask the enormous expenditures the United States was making on the V-bomb."

"The V-bomb?" said Richard.

"The vacuum bomb."

"I feel inadequate," said Richard. "I know there's a joke here using the word 'suck,' but for the life of me I can't think of the punch line."

"I was, of course, disturbed by the prospect of the V-bomb actually being used in wartime. I deluded myself into believing that after one display of its potential, the world would shun its awful power and turn toward a path of peace. In truth, I didn't care about the consequences. All I wanted was proof of my theories."

"Which were?"

"One of the basic conclusions of quantum mechanics is that there is no such thing as a true vacuum. Particles and anti-particles constantly spring forth from pure nothingness, and annihilate each other. In theory, the vacuum is a source of infinite, inexhaustible energy. I felt certain I knew how to tap into this energy. It involves the fact that vacuum had undergone one phase transition shortly after the Big Bang, and still contains the potential for another."

"You're losing me," said Richard.

"At the time of the Big Bang, all of creation was confined in an infinitely tiny space. Yet, even then, there was vacuum. But the vacuum was, for all intents and purposes, solid. Only as the universe expanded did it melt."

"I'll take your word for it."

"In the summer of 1968, I went into a bunker three miles beneath the Nevada desert and made the worst mistake of my life. I proved my theory correct. With the power of twenty-two carefully focused H-bombs, we were able to shock a tiny, magnetically confined vacuum to reverse its phase transaction, for only a nanosecond. And when the vacuum melted back to its normal state . . . well, I found out just how 'infinite' infinite energy could be. I died instantly, of course. The vacuum phase shift had recreated the conditions present at the Big Bang. And there was no stopping it. A new Big Bang was happening, and in far less than a second, Earth, the sun, our entire solar system, were wiped out in the expansion of the new universe I'd given birth to."

"Tragic," said Richard, rapping his knuckles soundly against a nearby tank. "So what's all this we're standing in? Your story might be a tiny bit more plausible if the world no longer existed."

"I think I was Schrödinger's cat," said Dr. Know.

"Come again?"

"Surely you have heard of Schrödinger's cat. It's the most famous metaphor in all of quantum physics."

"Oh!" said Richard, slapping his forehead. "Schrödinger's cat! I thought you said Schlessinger."

"It's a famous thought experiment. You place a cat in a box along with a vial of poison. There is a fifty percent chance that the vial of poison has broken while the lid is closed. Without opening the box, we can't know if the cat is dead or alive. So, we must regard it as both alive and dead simultaneously, until an observation is made.

"This was perhaps the most controversial conclusion of quantum mechanics, the notion that particles exist in all possible states simultaneously until an observer makes a measurement, collapsing the possible states into one."

"Again," said Richard, "I'll take your word for it."

"I was alive after the Big Bang I had caused. I don't know how. I don't know why. I existed as consciousness unfettered by matter. And my condition, of course, panicked me. I was trapped in unbroken darkness and silence. I didn't yet comprehend what had happened. With no lungs to draw a breath, no throat to form sounds, and no tongue to shape syllables, I spoke: 'Will someone please turn on the lights?'"

"And there was light?" guessed Richard.

"And there was everything. I was standing in the observation room, in the presence of the nation's top military commanders. The room was exactly the same as it was before. Except my clothes were gone. I knew this not only from the touch of air on my skin, and from the evidence of my eyes, but from the evidence of the eyes of everyone in the room. Every thing they thought, felt, and saw, was in my head. The cacophony of sensory input was too much for me to bear. I began to scream, to shriek, to gibber. I was quickly confined and dragged away.

"I knew what had happened. The old universe truly did die that day. A new one was born. And I was the initial observer. There's no need to open the box to make an observation. There's already an observer present—the cat. I was the cat in the box. It was my consciousness that snapped the new reality into order, it was my knowledge of physics that gave the new universe its physical rules. But I didn't know all the rules. I understood the basic physical laws of nature better than any man, but my knowledge was still limited. The world was put together exactly the way I *understood* it to be. And it included certain 'improvements.' I had often fantasized about superhuman powers. I was a child during World War II, and drowned out worries about the war by reading a nearly limitless supply of comic books. The amazing things I read sparked my interest in science. I remember the sense of disappointment I felt as my knowledge of science increased. I understood why men could never fly just by jumping hard, or why no one could ever run faster than a mile in under three minutes, or why I would never be able to read other people's minds. But I still dreamed that such things might exist."

Richard was flabbergasted. "So, you're saying you and your daughters have superhuman powers because you put the universe back together wrong?"

"Precisely. And all the evil, all the darkness, all the pain and suffering in the world, exist because, in that brief instant of confusion, I wished for a world where such things existed. I had the power to create paradise. If I had understood the truth of what was happening, if I'd had had time to contemplate, imagine the world that could be! A world of peace and love, a world of beauty without flaw or blemish. I could have imagined Heaven. I didn't. I imagined . . . I imagined the world we now live in, with its poverty and hunger and violence. The dark brutal soul of a man who builds bombs cannot provide the template for a kind world. Now, if I wish for a world of peace, love, and beauty, I must build it from the materials at hand."

Richard shook his head. "This is crazy," he said, but didn't sound convinced.

"I hope that what you've learned today will change your mind about me, Richard. I am not a perfect man, and this is not a perfect world. But I am working to make a difference. Are you with me?"

Chapter Eleven

HI, HONEY, I'M HOME

Richard wandered from Sarah's room fumbling absent-mindedly with her lighter. His brain felt as blistered and tired as his feet had felt after running all over Washington. How was he supposed to deal with this? How was he supposed to judge right and wrong? A month ago the biggest test of his morality had been whether or not to cheat on his wife. Now he didn't have a wife, never *had* a wife, and he had to make decisions about life and death, good and evil. He had to decide if the man he worked for was the creator of the universe or just some mad genius with pitiful delusions. And creator or madman, Dr. Know did have a plan to change the world. Was it a good plan? Could making the world a better place justify the things Richard had seen? Who was he to decide such things? He was Nobody.

So Nobody sat on the front steps of the mansion, and tapped out a cigarette from the pack. He'd taken the cigarettes from Sarah's room. He'd never smoked before, but after about twenty seconds of practice he found the whole process surprisingly easy. He used to find the smell repelling. Now, the smell and taste reminded him of Sarah. He closed his eyes and thought of her.

Dr. Know was mad. The babble of V-bombs and recreated universes and living dead cats was all the proof Richard needed. He didn't believe a word of it, and consequentially thoroughly disbelieved all talk of time machines and erased realities. There must be some other explanation. Any minute now, it would come to him. *Any minute now.*

But, of course, as the mighty and powerful guests of Dr. Know left the mansion, they trod right through him as they descended the steps.

"You're Nobody," he said to himself. But it sounded false. It sounded like a surrender he wasn't ready to make.

"I am Richard Rogers," he said. And he was. This felt truthful. He was still the same man he'd always been.

"I might be reality impaired," he said. "But I'm still me."

He watched the visitors heading back to their helicopters.

"I need to get away from this craziness," he said, pausing to take another puff of the cigarette. "It's making me talk to myself. No it isn't. Yes it is."

THE PRESIDENT OF the United States came down the steps, grumbling to the black-suited Secret Service agent who accompanied him.

"This is going too far," the President said, but he didn't sound convinced. "That pig-headed son-of-a-bitch is going to ruin everything we've worked for."

The agent nodded.

Richard followed.

"You heard the way he talks to us," said the President. "He's getting cocky, and the whole thing's going to come down around our ears if we don't take steps to stop him."

Richard wondered if Dr. Know was listening to the President's thoughts at the moment. It would explain a lot, assuming it was true. If Dr. Know could be privy to every thought of every world leader, he would be in a position to demand almost anything. There wasn't a safe secret for anyone anywhere. No wonder Dr. Know acted as if he was king of the world.

Richard boarded the helicopter with the President and made himself comfortable. He lit another cigarette. He tried his first smoke ring. Sarah made it look so easy.

"Do you smell smoke?" the President asked as they rose into the air.

"No sir," said the Secret Service man.

THE WHITE HOUSE kitchen was just amazing. Dr. Know's mansion had been pretty well stocked, but Dr. Know and his family had unfortunately shown rigorous regard for their health. The White House had fresh fruits and vegetables, but even better, it was stocked with potato chips, cookies, ice cream and soft drinks. No wonder the President looked a little chubby. Richard pigged out without qualms. He was invisible. What did it matter if he put on a few pounds?

He gathered together a great big box of junk food and slinked off to one of the guest bedrooms. He clicked on the TV and kicked back, going through a box of chocolate chip cookies as his mind turned to mush watching cartoons.

He wondered if he would meet Abe Lincoln. He'd heard that Abe was supposed to haunt the White House. Of course, if Abe didn't turn up, maybe he could become Abe Lincoln. He could use his new abilities to spook guests at the White House, give them a good show, something to tell the friends back home about. He still had a bit of the show biz bug in him.

He sighed, and clicked aimlessly through the channels. So it had come to this. Vegging out in the White House with a new career of scaring vacationers as the only things he had to look forward to.

He ate the last cookie in the box.

He resolved, then and there, that he would kill himself.

The notion gripped him firmly for upward of seventeen seconds.

He sat up in the bed and cradled his head in his hands. "What am I going to do?" he said.

RICHARD HIT THE road the following morning. During the night, he'd come up with the perfect plan for how to spend the rest of his life. He'd used a computer at the White House to track down Veronica. She was living with her husband in Asheville, North Carolina, where she taught school. He had the printout with a map to her house stuck in his pocket. He would find her, and spend the rest of his life as her guardian angel.

The notion cheered him. He knew it would be difficult, being near her again, knowing she wouldn't know him or remember him even if she could see him. But there was something grand in the mission, something bigger than himself. Now that he'd found a purpose in life, the death flirtations he'd entertained the night before vanished.

It was Sunday morning. He snatched a paper from a newsstand near the Amtrak station. He was a little disappointed to find that Amtrak didn't go to Asheville. He hopped aboard a train bound for Charlotte, North Carolina, and decided he'd figure out what to do once he got there.

The train was nearly empty. He took a window seat in one of the nicer cars and turned to his paper while he waited for the train to depart.

On page four of the world news section, he found a story about Rail Blade and Rex Monday. The broadcast had been seen around the world, apparently, but the spin was that it had all been a hoax, a prank by some kid studying broadcast engineering out in California.

Of greater interest was an accompanying article entitled, "Who Is Rex Monday?" "Rex Monday," it turned
out, was a pun on Rex Mundi, Latin for "king of the
world." Apparently, U.S. intelligence forces believed
Rex Monday to be a wealthy Arab, intent on ending
Jewish occupation of Jerusalem and turning the city
into his home base for the advancement of a worldwide
jihad. Nobody read this news with interest, wondering
why Dr. Know had seemed unaware of this. Then he realized that this was most likely disinformation designed by Dr. Know to advance his agenda. The notion
chilled him. Most people would easily swallow this
story and would support whatever steps were needed
to put an end to Rex Monday. He'd long suspected that
most of the news put out by the media was fiction, but
seldom had he realized just how sinister this fiction
was. And what could he do to stop it? Write a letter to
the editor? He vowed to never read another newspaper.
Best to focus on the mission at hand. From now on, his
whole world would be Veronica.

Two TRAINS AND three buses later, Richard made it to
Asheville. It was before dawn, and very cold. He walked
until he found a convenience store, and looked over a
map while he sipped coffee. The clerk was talking to
somebody on the phone, and never even looked in his direction.

It turned out he was very close to her house, less than a
mile away. He left the convenience store and climbed up
the bank behind it, then made a dash across the highway.
It was around 6 A.M., and the traffic wasn't too bad. He
suspected that cars would pass right through him, but
why test these things? He descended the bank on the other
side of the highway and found himself in an older neighborhood filled with small wooden houses. He went to the
nearest street corner, then pulled out the map to orient
himself. Asheville's neighborhoods weren't exactly laid

out on a grid. It was a mountain town, and the roads looped around like a drunken man's scribbles.

He resumed walking once he had a good feel for where he was and where he was going. The sun had risen now, and people were starting to leave their houses. The neighborhood was a step down from where he had lived with Veronica. The houses were packed together tightly on small lots, and many of them were in poor repair.

At last, he reached the street she lived on. Heading down it, he could see a school bus at the far end, moving slowly up the street, stopping every few houses.

He studied the numbers on the doors and mailboxes: 412, 414 . . . 416 Courtland Street. He had arrived. As if in welcome, the door to the house swung open.

Veronica stood in the doorway shouting, "The bus is here."

He stood, glued to the sidewalk, as the bus pulled up behind him.

Veronica was lovelier than he'd remembered. Her hair was still the same bright red, her face still had the same cute freckles. She was heavier now, curvier, but she carried her weight well. She wore no makeup. She was wearing a robe with fuzzy slippers and seemed very unconcerned that she was standing in an open door where everyone could see her. This was so unlike the fussy, vain woman who used to drive him crazy.

Her kids ran out the door. The little boy was about seven, the girl about nine, and both had their mother's freckles and red hair. They ran through him and leapt onto the steps of the bus.

He took a step forward. Behind Veronica, he could see someone else approaching, a man. Richard looked on with a mix of jealousy, horror, and fascination as the man kissed Veronica. He was a large, rough-looking man, wearing blue coveralls with his name on a patch. He looked like some kind of mechanic. His hair was thin and poorly cut, and his complexion very pale.

"I don't believe it," said Richard.

The man passed by, heading for the beat-up pickup truck in the tiny driveway. His name-badge said "Earl."

Richard went up the front steps as Veronica closed the door. He stepped inside, ghosting through the door while her hand was still on it, and said, "Hi honey, I'm home."

She walked across the living room into the kitchen and poured herself a morning cup of coffee. The house smelled of coffee and laundry detergent. It was tiny, half the size of the house they had shared together. Richard leaned against the counter and studied the woman who had once been at the center of his life.

"I don't believe it," he said again. "You look so . . . domestic. And so broke. Something sure did change your priorities."

She picked up the phone and made a call. Richard wandered through the house. There were clothes on the floor. There were dishes in the living room. The only reading material was a *TV Guide*. It wasn't as bad as Henry and Martha's house. When he checked the shower tiles, they were squeaky clean. But this was a far cry from the home he had shared with his former wife.

No matter where he went in the house, he could hear her phone conversation. She was talking to her mother. It was bizarre to hear her talking, because she sounded happy and relaxed. Veronica hated her mother. But now, even after three minutes of talking, they hadn't started shouting at each other. Weird.

"Yeah, we've got a bike on layaway down at Kmart for Billy's birthday," she was saying. "He's going to be thrilled."

"Sandy's doing better," she said, after a pause. "I think that thing on her back has finally healed up."

Nobody dropped onto the couch. On the table beside it were a half dozen picture frames. He picked up a family photo, a few years old, of Veronica, Earl, Sandy, and Billy.

Billy was still a toddler in the photo. He noted that Earl wasn't wearing a tie.

One frame held a montage of photos, mostly of the children, many taken at the beach. One showed Veronica holding Sandy. Veronica wore a two-piece bathing suit, and the way she was standing made her her belly look pudgy and lumpy. Her thighs were a little on the lumpy side as well. She wasn't fat, exactly, but Nobody could tell that Veronica no longer did aerobics. He studied the pictures and noticed that all of the ones of Veronica had something in common. She was smiling. She was smiling like . . . like nothing he'd ever seen before.

"Great," he said. "There it is. Proof. She's happy. Happier than she ever was with me. And all because I've never been born."

He felt like he was trapped in a horrible parody of *It's a Wonderful Life*. He imagined he would find Veronica and her life would be a mess and he'd work invisibly to make it better. Ten minutes into it, his plan to be a guardian angel seemed less clear-cut. His own guardian angel wasn't proving to be much of a role model.

Veronica finished her phone call and went into the bathroom. She left the door open as she used the toilet.

"Well," he said, sighing. "This has certainly proven to be a mistake."

He got up from the couch and headed for the back door. She came out from the bathroom and went back into the kitchen, swinging open some doors to reveal a washer and dryer. He went over and kissed her on the cheek.

"Bye," he said.

He ghosted out the back door.

That's when he found out about her dog.

The dog was a big, black, stocky one, who growled the second Richard's foot hit the back porch. He froze as the dog lunged toward him. The chain jerked the dog to a rapid, slobber-spattering halt. The dog continued to bark maniacally.

"Christ," he said, his heart thumping. "Of course I'd still be real to mean-tempered dogs."

Only the dog wasn't really facing him. It seemed to be barking at something to the side of the house.

Richard peeked around the corner.

Inside the house, something crashed.

Veronica began to scream.

He ran back to the door. Unfortunately, no one was near enough to it now for him to ghost through it. He turned the knob. Nothing. He slammed his shoulder into it. It popped open. He stumbled into the house, moving in the direction of the screams.

In the living room, holding Veronica, were the Panic and Pit Geek.

CHAPTER TWELVE

HALL OF MIRRORS

Veronica kept screaming. Something in her throat had torn from the force of air, and her screams now ended with wet gurgles as she sucked in air to scream again. Blood dripped from the corners of her mouth.

The Panic kept hold of her arms, pulling her to him, forcing his face inches from hers. "You here, Nobody?" Panic called into the air, while Nobody grabbed at his shoulders, uselessly.

Pit Geek sat on the couch, his feet kicked up on the coffee table. He chewed idly on a pencil, working it down to just a nub with an eraser, as he watched the Panic. He flicked away the eraser like the butt of a cigarette.

"Wonder if we got his attention yet?" said Pit Geek.

The Panic spun Veronica around and clamped a hand over her mouth to silence her.

"Hey, Nobody!" the Panic called out. "You hear me?"

"Yes," said Nobody, his voice cracking with frustration. "What do you want?"

The Panic gave no indication that he heard.

"Maybe you should use the mask," said Pit Geek.

"Hold her," said the Panic, shoving Veronica in the direction of his partner. Pit Geek grabbed Veronica, pulling her into his lap. He began to run his filthy fingers through her hair. She clamped her eyes tight and grew silent, unable to even draw a breath.

The Panic pulled what looked like a sock knitted from silver thread from his pocket. He tugged it over his head, masking his face, then looked around the room.

"Well what do you know," he said, as his gaze fell on Nobody. "There really is an invisible man here."

"You see me?" said Nobody.

"Oh, yeah," said the Panic.

Nobody leapt forward. His hands clamped around the Panic's throat, and he used his momentum to slam the Panic into the wall. The Panic was just a kid, a foot shorter, and a good fifty pounds lighter than Nobody. He struggled, pulling at Nobody's arms, but Nobody couldn't be stopped. With sudden clarity, Nobody realized that he was going to kill the Panic. All he needed to do was continue squeezing, and keep slamming the Panic's head against the wall. He gritted his teeth and growled with rage.

"Nobody!" shouted Pit Geek. "Back off!"

Nobody looked over his shoulder. Pit Geek had Veronica by the hair, pulling her head back. Pit Geek opened his mouth, preparing to sink his yellow teeth into her exposed throat.

Nobody jerked the Panic from the wall and threw him toward the coffee table. The Panic toppled over the table, landing on his chin on the carpet.

"Let her go," said Nobody.

Pit Geek paid him no attention, watching the Panic instead as he stumbled back to his feet.

"Jesus, kid," said Pit Geek. "You're getting your ass whipped by a ghost."

"Screw the boss," said the Panic, staggering backwards until he came to rest against the far wall, steadying himself. His right hand slipped into his waistband and came back holding a small black pistol.

"You're dead meat, Nobody," he said, taking aim.

He pulled the trigger.

Nobody closed his eyes as the crack of the shot deafened him. He flinched, expecting the impact. It didn't come.

He opened his eyes.

The bullet hung in mid air before him, a silvery cylinder frozen in time.

Next to the Panic, the window crashed inward, glass shards flying around the room as a white-clad figure smashed into the scene. It was the Thrill. She spun around in the air, pointing to Pit Geek.

"Let her go!" she demanded.

Without the slightest hesitation, Pit Geek closed his mouth around Veronica's throat. He raised his head, grinning red, as blood spurted into the air.

The pistol flew from the Panic's hand and landed near Nobody's feet. Rail Blade slid through the shattered window, glancing toward the Panic. The silver hood flew from his head as if jerked by an unseen hand and landed near the pistol.

Nobody dodged around the frozen bullet and reached for the gun, grabbing the hood in the same motion. He fired at Pit Geek. If the bullet struck, Pit Geek didn't react. Tears in his eyes, Nobody leapt at the grinning bum.

"Ex—" said the Panic.

Nobody reached Pit Geek, and watched as his hands passed through him.

The room vanished.

Nobody found himself staring into a reflection of his reflection. The world had become an infinite hall of mirrors, twisting and spinning. He found himself staring at the bottom of his feet, the back of his head, into his nostrils.

Before he could comprehend what he was seeing, he landed on a rubbery, pinkish floor.

"—it," said the Panic.

Pit Geek fell on his ass, flailing around in the same physical space as Nobody. Veronica was gone, as were the Thrill and Rail Blade. Nobody looked around, unable to figure out what was happening. He was in a pink, rubbery chamber, much smaller than Veronica's living room. The walls were curved and roiling with a wave-like motion. Large phosphorescent patches on the floor and ceiling gave the room a dim, eerie light.

"Great," said Pit Geek. "We're in Baby Gun."

"Boss?" said the Panic.

"Could the two of you have screwed that up any worse?" asked a disembodied voice. For an instant, Nobody thought it was the voice of Dr. Know. But the voice had a harder, rougher edge to it. The unseen speaker continued: "You were supposed to bring me the target, not kill him. What part of this didn't you get?"

"He almost killed me," said the Panic. "Besides, I don't think the bullet hit him. I think Rail Blade stopped it just before she yanked off my hood. Why aren't we back at the cabin?"

"I've had a bit of a mood swing. I'm sending Baby Gun to stomp the hell out of Jerusalem. Rail Blade used her magnetic quake to get to you so fast she'll be too wiped out to bother us now. With her on the other side of the planet, we should have several hours to kick up a real nice war. Your powers will add to the general confusion."

"Take over Jerusalem?" said the Panic. "Since when do we care about Jerusalem? That's the bullshit Knowbokov's been feeding the media."

"That's part of what makes this sweet. He'll hate himself when he realizes he gave me the idea."

"Let's get up to the head," the Panic said to Pit Geek. They moved to a tube at one end of the room and half-crawled, half-climbed into it, ascending its convoluted walls. Nobody followed, shoving the gun and the mask into his pocket. The tube had a peculiar smell, like a hot plastic baby doll, and had the same hard yet yielding solidity of a fully inflated waterbed. At least the dry surface provided easy traction.

After a very long climb they reached a larger chamber, in the center of which was a sickening sight. A body was suspended from the ceiling by a web of pink, worm-like cords that pulsed and writhed. The body resembled a male fetus, pale and wet, but huge, perhaps three hundred pounds.

"Yo," said the Panic, tapping his knuckles against the fetus's huge, distorted skull. "How 'bout a window?"

In response to the Panic's action, the wall near Nobody began to melt and swirl, turning into a thin, smoky, mostly transparent film. Outside this window, and just above it, Baby Gun's surreal, gun barrel face loomed. Looking down, Nobody at first thought they were still in Asheville. The landscape was mountainous. But he quickly realized the hills were covered with olive trees instead of pines. Instead of the closely packed factory houses, the city below was built of white stone, with box-like houses stacked on top of one another and narrow streets that twisted and turned like a dusty maze. Wherever he was, the buildings were crunching to rubble beneath Baby Gun's enormous feet. People fled in panicked streams as his huge doll feet rose and fell.

"Jesus," said Nobody. He was halfway around the world, trapped in the body of an enormous baby doll, and the only thing he could think about was Veronica.

Was she dead? Everything had happened so fast he couldn't be sure. He knew she'd been bleeding. He knew there was a terrible wound to her throat. Could Amelia and Sarah save her?

He looked at Pit Geek. Veronica's blood still stained his chin, and red smears marked the back of his hands where he had wiped his mouth.

Nobody pulled the gun from his pocket.

He had fired at Pit Geek only moments before. Had he missed? Was the gun useless in his ghost state? Or was Pit Geek just impervious to pain, and impossible to kill? He remembered his first encounter with the foul bum, and the bullet that had struck Pit Geek between the eyes. Pit Geek still had a hole there, half concealed by a crusty scab. So, even though Pit Geek was directly responsible for Veronica's death, attacking him seemed pointless.

On the other hand, throttling the Panic had been surprisingly easy and effective, at least when he'd been wearing the silver hood.

Nobody pulled the hood from his pocket and studied it. It was made of a fine silver mesh, with the texture and thickness of nylon. Touching it made his fingers tingle.

Suddenly, a deafening roar staggered him, and the floor beneath him lurched sideways. Outside the window, a trio of fighter jets sped away from Baby Gun.

Baby Gun returned fire, with an explosive motion that knocked Nobody from his feet. Pit Geek and the Panic also were thrown to the floor. One of the jets exploded into a fireball.

"Dammit, ya weird bastard," grumbled Pit Geek. "Give us a warning, will ya?"

"Better yet," said the disembodied voice that Nobody had heard earlier, "Let's get you into the action."

Before Pit Geek and the Panic could rise, holes swirled open beneath them. Pit Geek let out a muffled curse as the floor swallowed him.

Nobody was now alone with the gigantic fetus that seemed to be the control center of Baby Gun. He wondered, was this the source of the disembodied voice? Was this strange being Rex Monday? No one really knew what the über-terrorist looked like. Could this *thing* be the source of so much misery and evil? Was it responsible for Veronica's possible death?

The hood seemed very stretchy. Nobody pulled the opening wide and slipped it over the hideous fetal head. The creature opened its eyes—huge, black circles, faintly visible through the thin silver web.

It cast its gaze upon Nobody and made a soft mewing sound as its slobbery mouth slid open. Its proportionally tiny hands clenched and unclenched, and the pink worm tubes that supported its body began to coil and kink.

Nobody placed the gun against its head, and pulled the trigger. The silver sock exploded like a paint-filled balloon. The floor began to shift. Very quickly, the floor became the wall, and Nobody was sliding up it, the rubbery surface now slick with blood. Through the window, the buildings of old Jerusalem grew rapidly closer as Baby Gun toppled.

A shower of brick and stone burst through the thin membrane of the window, smashing into Nobody. He blacked out. He opened his eyes briefly. He could smell smoke somewhere close. He could barely breathe. He seemed caught in a sticky tangle of rubber bands. Dim firelight flickered in the distance. Far away, he heard a series of explosions. Then he lost consciousness once more.

WHEN NOBODY WOKE, his surroundings had once again changed. He was in a soft bed, in a large room. A breeze stirred the white linen curtains by the window. He sat up, his body aching. He sported several clean, white bandages on his left arm and shoulder.

Sarah sat next to him, dozing peacefully in a large wicker chair. He reached out and touched her thigh gently. Her eyes fluttered open. Her peaceful expression turned into a slight frown.

"Hey," he said.

"Hey yourself," she said, a bit grumpy.

"What?"

"You didn't even leave a note."

"Oh," he said. "Sorry. I did leave pretty quickly."

"And you took my favorite lighter, you bastard."

"Sorry. You can have it back."

Sarah held up her hand, showing him the lighter. "Found it in your pants. Dad told you about being God, didn't he?"

Nobody sank back onto his pillow. "He actively denied the existence of God, as I remember it. He did claim to have created the world. He did admit to body snatching prisoners and turning them into memory banks for his brain. I don't know, Sarah. These things kind of bother me."

"I know. My father's insane. I don't believe he really created the world. I think he's some kind of evolutionary next step or something, some kind of super-telepath, and he's built this whole God fantasy to cope with it. I can't explain how or why he has such fantastic powers, or why Amelia and I have the abilities we do. But I've learned to deal with it, more or less. I think, I hope, that in the balance, my father does more good than harm."

"Oh my God," said Nobody, draping his good arm over his eyes. "Veronica's dead, isn't she?"

"That woman you were with? The one Pit Geek killed?"

"She *is* dead."

"Yes. Who was she?"

"She used to be my wife. In another lifetime. Literally. Oh, God. She's dead because of me."

"No. And she's not dead because I flew through the window and tried to use my powers on someone I suspected was immune. She's dead because Pit Geek tore her throat out."

"But it's because of—"

"Don't," said Sarah. "Don't go down this path. We can wonder what would have happened if we'd acted differently, but we'll never know. Dwelling on it will make you as loony as my father."

Nobody felt numb. He said, "She's not the only blood on my hands. I killed that . . . thing. I think . . . I think maybe it was Rex Monday."

"Baby Gun? He wasn't Monday. Baby Gun was some freak who controlled silicon the way Amelia controls iron. Only he was like completely insane, and saw himself as that horrible monster, and his powers made that real. You did him and the world a huge favor by putting him out of his misery."

"I don't feel like I've done anyone any favors. Christ, I wish I'd never been born. Oh, wait. That's right."

"I'm glad you were born, at least once upon a time, Richard," said Sarah.

"Richard. Richard Rogers. That name's meaningless now. Who was Richard Rogers? Just some nobody."

"Look," said Sarah, rising from her chair, her voice hinting at anger. "You want to wallow in self pity? Fine. I can't stop you. I just want to know one thing. You going to run away again?"

"I don't know. I'll have to think about it."

Sarah turned away. She walked to the window, and said, "I understand. But, for what it's worth, I liked having you around."

Nobody nodded. "I liked being around you. But, please don't take this wrong, I don't feel terribly romantic right now. I've watched a woman I devoted my whole life to die and I think it's going to take a while to get my head wrapped around that. I wish I'd met you under different circumstances."

"Well, we get what we get. In the end everything is pointless, but that doesn't mean we can't have fun along the way."

"I like your attitude toward life," Nobody said. "It's a kind of happy pessimism."

She shrugged, grinned, and headed for the door.

"I think of it as fatalistic optimism. Look me up if you decide to stick around," she said, pulling the door shut.

The curtains flowed inward as a cool sea breeze filled the room with fresh air. Nobody lay back and looked at the streaks of light that played against the ceiling.

"Fatalistic optimism," he said. "Maybe things will be better when I'm dead."

CHAPTER THIRTEEN

TRIGGER OF THE APOCALYPSE

Richard found Amelia in the gym again. Sweat rolled down her bare legs and arms as she ran on a treadmill. The evidence of the terrible burns she had received weeks before had vanished.

"Looks like that pink goo does pretty good work," said Richard.

"My work gives Father frequent opportunities to expand the frontier of medical trauma treatment," said Amelia, continuing to run.

"You saved my life, stopping that bullet," said Richard. "Thanks. But, uh, aren't bullets lead? How'd you grab it?"

"I've been practicing with bullets since I was eight," said Amelia. "A lot of bullets these days have steel jackets, which makes it easier. The trick is to wrap all of the lead in a thin shell of steel before stopping them."

"Good trick," said Richard.

"Sarah says the woman who died was important to you," Amelia said. "She says you blame yourself."

"Yes."

"Sarah probably told you it wasn't your fault."

Richard leaned against the doorway. "Yeah. I don't know. Maybe she's right."

"Don't listen to her," said Amelia.

"What?"

"There are a million things you could have done differently that would have changed things. You're right to blame yourself."

"Christ," said Richard, walking into the hall, running his hands through his hair. "Is this some kind of reverse psychology? Or are you just wanting me to kill myself?"

Amelia smacked the stop button on the treadmill and stepped off, panting. She walked toward him, locking her eyes on his.

"Make no mistake. I'm also to blame. Much more than you."

"Look, now I know you're playing head games. Sarah's right, the one who's really to blame is Pit Geek."

"I could have been quicker to analyze the situation," said Amelia. "I have a tendency to focus on weapons. I had my attention on the gun, and that high-tech mask the Panic was wearing. If I could do it over, I wouldn't just stop the bullet. I would have kept its momentum, but changed its trajectory, and put it straight into Pit Geek's head."

"I'm not sure how effective that would have been," said Nobody. "You know what happened in Washington."

"If it had only stunned him for half a second, I could have done something to save the woman. I could have sealed his head inside a steel mask, if I'd thought fast enough."

Nobody shook his head. "This is perverse. I know why I feel bad. If I hadn't found Veronica, Rex Monday would probably never have known she was important to me.

She'd still be alive. For you to blame yourself, though, is just plain unhealthy. You did save my life, after all. You can't focus on everything at once."

"Then I'm not trying hard enough," said Amelia. "Every time I hesitate, people die."

"You didn't hesitate down in Texas. You killed that guy who said he was Monday without blinking an eye. Yet he was just a brainwashed victim. Maybe there's something to be said for a slow approach."

"His death is just one of hundreds I have to live with," said Amelia.

"You take this stuff seriously," said Richard.

"Unlike Sarah, I believe in my father's mission. We can make the world a better place, if we devote our minds and bodies to the task."

"You're being a little unfair to Sarah," said Richard. "She's fighting beside you, putting her life on the line. How can you say she doesn't take it seriously?"

"Did she tell you she thinks Father is insane?"

"Yeah. Not a bad theory."

"But she continues to do his bidding."

"So do you."

"I believe him," said Amelia. Her gray eyes continued to stare at him.

Nobody turned away. The punching bag was nearby, and he jabbed out at it, not very hard, but enough so that his knuckles stung.

"Have you considered my offer to train you to fight?" asked Amelia.

"I don't know," he said, tapping the bag again. "I have to admit, you scare me. You might even be scarier than your old man. You are a very angry person, Amelia."

"Anger is a tremendous source of power," said Amelia. "Anger, fear, guilt, shame . . . if you embrace these things, they can make you better. They can light a fire within you that burns away your weakness and doubt. If you feel guilty over Veronica's death, you can push that guilt down and let it haunt you, or you can keep it always in the front of your mind. You can let it drive you to train and prepare to do the right thing the next time you're in a tough situation."

Richard hit the bag again, then once more, harder, making his fist throb. He turned to face Amelia.

"OK," he said. "Train me."

Amelia punched him in the stomach, dropping him to his knees, barely able to breathe.

"Rule one. Never let your guard down."

"Noted," he wheezed.

DR. KNOW WATCHED the banks of monitors before him, barely listening to Nobody's words.

"Funny," said Nobody. "I thought you'd be happy I decided to stick around."

"These are not cheerful times for me, Richard. My years of hard work seem to be unraveling before my eyes. The Middle East is on the brink of self-destruction. The more effort I place on securing peace, the more the people clamor for war. Baby Gun's attack on Jerusalem has taken on some sort of prophetic significance, I fear. He's being seen as an avenging angel, martyred by Israeli jets. There's no rationale, no logic behind what is happening there. To bring peace, I have channeled enormous resources to provide all citizens of the area with a strong economy, with good health and fair laws. Our dome project for Palestine will transform desert into cropland, and allow people to live in a modern paradise. Yet everyone seems ready to throw these things away, all in the name of religion. The mention of the word Jerusalem seems to destroy all reason among residents of the area."

"It's been that way forever," said Nobody. "Don't blame yourself. Oh, wait, I bet Amelia gets her blame philosophy directly from you. You like blaming yourself for all of this don't you?"

"Don't be absurd," said Dr. Know. "I don't like blaming myself. But as long as we are discussing blame, I want to find out how you feel about my role in Veronica's death."

"Your role? What role did you play?"

"After you left, I placed Veronica and your parents under surveillance, guessing you might attempt to contact them. Rex Monday seems to be aware of your existence, and I feared he might try to use them to manipulate you."

"How does he know about me? He seemed aware of me from the very first mission."

"I don't know. I can only speculate he has some method of spying upon my electronic communications."

"That was a pretty clever gadget he cooked up to see me, that hood. Why don't you fix me up with something like that, maybe in reverse? A suit I wear that lets people see me?"

"The hood's circuitry was too damaged to reconstruct. But I can work to develop something comparable."

"So maybe Rex Monday is another mad scientist with super-telepathy?" Nobody said. "That would explain a lot."

"It would," said Dr. Know. "But while I'm perfectly aware of the many absurdities of my existence, I'm not quite prepared to accept that I have an evil twin."

"I guess that is a stretch," said Nobody. "But here's what I'm prepared to believe. I believe you want to make things better. So I'm signing on. I know you have projects all around the world. But if you need an invisible man on the ground anywhere, you can put me on a plane tomorrow."

"Yes," said Dr. Know. "Yes, I can make use of you. Get some rest. You'll accompany Sarah to Jerusalem tomorrow. She is overseeing an important development."

"Oh?"

"I'm taking the Old City of Jerusalem away from Israel. I'm making it a world city, under the protection of the United Nations. It will be ruled by a triumvirate of clerics, one Jew, one Christian, and one Muslim."

"I can't imagine many people are going to be happy about that," said Nobody.

"I'm not searching for happiness. Only fairness, and peace."

"And you think people will go along with this?"

"Sarah can be very persuasive," said Dr. Know.

"True," said Nobody.

JERUSALEM TURNED OUT to be many cities. Nobody wandered the streets, amazed at the contrast between the different cultures and eras. In the space of an hour, he could walk from modern shopping districts almost indistinguishable from an American city to the Old City, where narrow, sunken streets formed labyrinths through stone buildings unchanged for centuries. The whole city, old and new, was a trip back to the stone age. The rocks quarried from the land had a distinctive whiteness, and all buildings, old and new, were built using this stone. Nobody guessed it must be a law that the stone be used.

The other continuity was guns. Every shop, every intersection had guards, now wearing the baby blue helmets of UN peacekeepers. Nobody hung out in the restaurants, getting a feel for how people felt about this. Not many people spoke English, although many of the signs and menus sported it. He picked up enough to know that the average citizen, both Jew and Arab, viewed the UN troops with a feeling of dread. It was only a matter of time before the peacekeepers were tested for readiness by a suicide bomber.

Still, Dr. Know seemed on top of this. Nobody had been run ragged for a month, invisibly thwarting the plans of terrorists Dr. Know found with his telepathy. There had been a lot of bombs that failed to explode lately, and a lot of vehicles prepared for suicide runs that had mysteriously developed slashed radiator hoses and ruptured fuel lines.

Only this morning he had managed to put a stop to a situation in a hospital on the edge of Jerusalem. This time it had been an Israeli settler that had taken hostages on the third floor of the hospital, saying he would kill one person per hour until the Peacekeepers withdrew from the city and returned it to the sovereign rule of Israel. Nobody had reached the scene before Sarah, who was on the other side of town when the crisis broke out. He had infiltrated the third floor and discovered, to his great relief, that the hostages were already being released as the UN negotiator demanded. Then the gunman threw his guns out the window, and Nobody felt like his work there was done.

Then he saw the gunman set the timer on the bomb vest he wore under his coat.

"I'm coming out with my hands in the air," said the gunman. "Don't shoot."

Nobody studied the bomb. The timer read ninety seconds. Just enough time to ride the elevator to the ground floor and be surrounded by a dozen UN Peacekeepers.

Nobody walked backwards as the gunman walked toward the elevator. Nobody ran his ghostly fingers along the wiring, searching for some pattern in the multicolored spaghetti. It was possible he might be able to pull a wire while the gunman was distracted, but which one?

Just then the elevator door slid open, the Thrill stepped out, looked at the gunman, and said, "Sleep."

The gunman smiled as his eyes rolled up into his head. He swayed backward on his feet. A sickening hollow formed in Nobody's stomach as he realized he was suddenly solid again, in the absence of any observers other than Sarah. Worse, he'd materialized in such a way that a green wire from the bomb was actually looped through the buttonhole on the sleeve of his shirt. He tried to keep the gunman from falling backwards, to no avail. The man slipped from his grasp and the wire popped out of the bomb with a barely audible snap. The timer froze at seventy-three.

The Thrill looked at the timer, then patted Nobody on the back. "Good work on the bomb," she said. "How'd you know which wire to pull?"

"I always knew one day I'd sell my soul to the devil," said Nobody.

The Israelis had once asked for a week without bombings. Thanks to Nobody, they'd had a month.

And what a whirlwind month it had been. The agreement had been announced shortly after he arrived. As far as the world knew, the agreement had been hammered out over long weeks of negotiations by the American President, the Israeli Prime Minister, and representatives from several Arab nations. Nobody knew the reality involved very little arm-twisting. The Thrill had just told those concerned what needed to be done, and they did it, with smiles on their faces.

Sitting in a street café on the edge of the Old City, eating falafel and humus, Nobody listened in on those conversations he could follow. Dr. Know's scheme was accepted by most people. Or, if not accepted, tolerated. People here were used to the world's meddling.

The deployment of United Nations troops in the Old City was almost complete. A ceremony was planned at the square edged by the Wailing Wall. The three ruling clerics were to sign a treaty and take command of the city. Nobody rubbed his tired shins. It had been a long while since he'd had a day off. But he wasn't complaining. He finally felt he was on the right team, that he could make a difference in the world. It was a good feeling.

RAIL BLADE JOINED the Thrill and Nobody the day before the ceremony.

"It's been quiet," said Nobody. "People seem to have accepted this world city idea."

Rail Blade looked at him like he was a foolish child. "Rex Monday has something planned. He'll do whatever it takes to stop this ceremony."

"I can't imagine how we can be any better prepared," the Thrill said. "We've got UN troops everywhere. Everyone who enters the square to witness the signing will be checked for weapons. And of course, we have you scanning for weapons as well. If there's going to be trouble, it won't be coming from the crowd."

"I still think something bad will happen," said Rail Blade.

"We'll be careful," said Nobody. "Trust me, we aren't complacent about this."

"Good," said Rail Blade. "Because these are the most serious stakes you can imagine. If something does go wrong, it could plunge the whole region into war, and drag the rest of the world with it. One false move, and we could trigger the Apocalypse."

Nobody started to tell her to lighten up. But he wasn't in the mood for another punch in the stomach, so he kept quiet.

A CIRCULAR PLATFORM was erected in the middle of the square. Nobody stood at the foot of the Wailing Wall, staring at all the slips of paper stuck into the cracks. Studying it, he finally understood something about the sacredness of this place. He was cynical enough to doubt that the world truly held sacred spaces, especially now that he'd met the man who claimed to have assembled the world. But maybe it all came down to what people believed. He believed he was real, and so he lingered on despite the time accident. People believed this ground sacred, and that was enough to make it so. He felt once more that he was grappling with things his mind hadn't been fully prepared for, concepts too large to fit neatly inside his skull. No wonder Dr. Know used spares.

The signing was scheduled to take place at noon. Blue UN peacekeepers helmets were everywhere. A half dozen television cameras were set up to record the ceremony, with feeds available to all networks and news media. Ten thousand citizens of Jerusalem—Muslim, Jew, and Christian—had won tickets in a lottery to witness the signing, and the square was packed. Nobody walked through the crowd, keeping an eye out for anything that looked suspicious. Too many people were wearing loose clothes for his comfort. He kept imagining dynamite beneath every burqa or plastique in every suit. But Rail Blade would sense anything if there was trouble, and Dr. Know was on the lookout for minds shut to him, a sure sign of Rex Monday's involvement. For the most part, people seemed excited and happy. Had Sarah talked to every resident of the city individually?

"Things look good here on the ground," he said into his radio. "How's the sky look?"

"All clear here," said the Thrill. She was stationed nearly a mile overhead. The sky above the city had been declared a no-fly zone, and the Thrill was there to enforce it. "How you doing, Rail Blade?"

"I detect no unusual magnetic movement," Rail Blade answered. She was hidden just outside the walls of the city, spreading her iron awareness to its limits. If anyone other than the UN troops tried to bring in a weapon, she would know it.

"Looks like the show is getting underway," said Nobody, moving to the front of the crowd.

The three clerics solemnly strode onto the stage. The cameras recorded them as they took their seats at the large round table.

And then, without a noise of warning, the three clerics vanished. Their seats were empty. The crowd murmured in confusion.

"Something's wrong," said Rail Blade.

"What just happened?" said the Thrill.

Nobody ran toward the stage.

With a silent flicker, the three clerics reappeared.

Only, on second glance, Nobody saw the clerics weren't the ones who had reappeared. They had been re-placed.

By a skinny, scab-faced old man.

By a flame-haired woman whose chair was smoldering.

And by a teenage boy in jeans and a tee shirt, who knocked his chair backwards as he jumped on the table, faced the crowd, and shouted, "Boo!"

Chapter Fourteen

THE GREAT, BIG, FINAL SMACKDOWN!

"Live from the Apocalypse!" said the Panic, facing the camera. "Citizens of Earth! Rise up! It's time to riot in the streets! It's time to take what's yours! It's the End Time, Armageddon, the Great, Big, Final Smackdown! Waaaaa-hooooooo!"

Nobody's stomach twisted in knots. All around him, panicked people were stampeding, trampling those too young or too old to move out of the way. Sundancer rose into the air, flinging glowing balls of plasma at the United Nation guards, who screamed as their weapons melted in their grasps. Pit Geek belched, bringing up a buckle to his lips. He tugged on the buckle, and dragged out a bandolier of hand grenades.

"Crap," said the Thrill, her voice crackling over the radio. "Trouble. A dozen helicopters just popped up from nowhere. They—shit! Missiles fired! Missiles fired!"

"On it," said Rail Blade.

In the distance, loud explosions could be heard.

"Sarah, get down here and calm the crowd," said Nobody. "People are dying."

"Oh no," said the Thrill. "Tanks. We have tanks moving in on the edges of the Old City."

"Do what you can with the crowd," said Rail Blade. "I'll stop the hardware."

High overhead, a glimmer of light, a daytime star, grew brighter and larger. In seconds, the image had resolved itself into the Thrill, clad in mirror armor, wielding her glowing sword.

The Panic looked up.

"Ex—" he said, and vanished, just as the Thrill reached him, slashing the air where he had stood. With grim satisfaction, Nobody noted a stream of blood whip from the sword as the Thrill pulled from her dive and shot back into the sky. Apparently, the Panic had been a little slow.

"Think I got him," the Thrill said, her voice strained. "Felt like I got a solid hit."

"Watch out!" said Nobody.

Sundancer blazed a trail behind the Thrill, slamming into her back with a hard tackle. The Thrill went into a spin, but pulled up before hitting the ground.

"Monday's pulled out all the stops," Rail Blade complained over the radio. "Every tank I tear apart, two more pop up. I've never seen him use his teleporter so aggressively."

Nobody wasn't exactly focused on her words. Even with the Panic gone, the crowd was still going crazy. By now, Pit Geek had strapped on the bandolier and stood on the edge of the stage, lobbing grenades into the mob, laughing.

Nobody raced onto the stage, banging his fists on the treaty table to get Pit Geek's attention. It didn't work.

He noticed the treaty on the table. The formal, gold-rimmed parchment had vanished. In its place was a sheet torn from a notebook, with words written in red marker: "Ah, screw it. Let's just fight." Beneath it were three neat signatures.

"Doc," said Nobody. "The clerics. When Monday teleported them, could you follow them? Can you track them?"

"They reappeared beneath the ocean," said Dr. Know. "They died in seconds."

The platform shook as though an earthquake had struck. Nobody was thrown from his feet. The Thrill lay beside him, among shattered boards, shaking her head. She still had her shield, but had lost her sword.

"I'm so sick of this bitch," she grumbled.

Nobody rolled aside as a ball of flame smashed into the Thrill's shield. The Thrill flew into the air, deflecting another ball of flame, then buzzed over a UN guard who was trying to carry a wounded child to safety.

"A little help here," she yelled. "Shoot her."

The guard dropped the child and placed his rifle to his shoulder, unleashing a stream of bullets toward Sundancer. Sundancer motioned toward the gun, melting its barrel, causing it to explode in the guard's hand.

The Thrill swooped in, using the momentary distraction, screaming her best kung fu yell as she delivered a powerful kick to Sundancer's head. The burning woman spun backward, looking surprised and disoriented. The Thrill pressed forward with her attack, continuing to deliver savage kicks with her metal boots. The boots glowed red hot, but if the Thrill felt any pain, she didn't show it. Instead, her features locked in an angry grimace as she struck Sundancer again and again.

"Come on, Sunny," Pit Geek screamed. "Take her! You're making us look bad."

Sundancer didn't have anything witty to say in response. Instead, she crashed to the ground, hard, rolling to a stop on the pavement stones. The Thrill swooped down, continuing her assault.

Pit Geek pulled a pin on a grenade and lobbed it toward the fighting women. It bounced on the stones, and burst open in a loud flash. Nobody ducked and covered his eyes as shrapnel ricocheted around him.

He blinked, trying to make sense of the smoking aftermath. The Thrill had been thrown back, lying still against the pavement, though her armor appeared to be intact. Sundancer was screaming. Her left leg was gone from the knee down, and jets of flame spurted from her wounds with each heartbeat.

"Oops," said Pit Geek.

Nobody spun around, running toward the filthy bum. Pit Geek didn't notice him. Nobody passed through him, and turned around. There were grenades on the back of the bandolier as well. Gritting his teeth, he pulled one, two, three pins, then ran. He was knocked to the ground by the explosion seconds later. Pit Geek's head bounced to the ground in front of him, his eyes blinking wide, his lips mouthing words that Nobody couldn't make out.

Then, the head vanished.

Looking back, Sundancer was gone as well.

Nobody raced over to the Thrill, who had risen to her hands and knees.

"You all right?" he said. "Are you hurt? Burned?"

She shook her head. "Amelia makes good armor. Plus, I'm wearing asbestos long johns."

He helped her to her feet.

"No rest for the weary," she said. She rose into the air, two dozen yards over the platform.

"Listen up!" she said. "Yo! Look at me!"

In unison, the hundreds of people within the sound of her voice stopped their panicked flight and looked to her.

"We've got a lot of wounded people here. I don't know how long it will be until help gets here. I want everyone who knows anything about first aid to stay and help those too hurt to walk out under their own power. Every one else, I want you to leave, slowly! Stay calm, don't step on anyone, and get to safety. Let's move it, people."

A pleased murmur came from the crowd, a chorus of "Great idea," and, "She's so clever!"

"Ground zero's locked down," the Thrill said, dropping down to grab Nobody. "Let's see if Amelia needs a hand."

It quickly became evident that things were even more chaotic outside the plaza. Everyone in the streets appeared to be armed, and firefights were blazing from every window and doorway. A millennia's worth of frustrations and anger had apparently boiled over, and the ancient buildings of the Old City were slowly being chipped to gravel by the relentless spray of bullets.

"Stop shooting," the Thrill said, flying low and slow over the streets. "Go home! Be nice!"

She left a small wake of peace and quiet, but the sound of gunfire was still omnipresent.

"It's hopeless," she said. "We're never going to put a lid on this."

"Don't say that," said Nobody. "I signed on as one of the good guys. We don't give up."

Ahead of them, a tank flew into the air and disassembled itself, sending its astonished crew screaming toward the ground.

The Thrill darted forward, placing a free hand on one of the falling men, and lowered him to the ground. He stood, staring at her, his eyes wide.

"You're welcome," she said.

Then he pulled a pistol and thrust it into her stomach.

He pulled the trigger. His hand dissolved into red mist as the gun disintegrated. The bullet flashed backwards with a loud crack, punching a jagged hole through the man's chest. With a gurgle, he toppled.

"Don't show them mercy," said Rail Blade, sliding up behind them on her gleaming steel beam. "Everyone signed on for this intending to kill or be killed. I say we don't disappoint them."

"How many more tanks?" the Thrill asked.

"None. I've taken apart over fifty of them. All the helicopters are down. I've detonated all the missiles."

"Then all that's left are the small weapons," said Nobody. "It's down to people shooting people now."

Rail Blade's track crumbled to rust, dropping her to the dusty street. "You have no idea how tired I am," she said.

Nobody knelt beside her, placing a hand on her shoulder. "You've done good work. You've saved a lot of lives. Maybe we should go. The peacekeepers can get all this under control. Eventually."

"No," said Rail Blade. She sucked in a deep, long breath. "No. I'm the only one who can stop it. I just need to catch my breath. Just need to think."

"What—" Nobody cut his question short as Rail Blade closed her eyes. Her body trembled, as if about to explode.

Suddenly, the cacophony of nearby gunfire dimmed.

"I can feel them," Rail Blade whispered, opening her eyes. "All around me. The guns. I can feel the atoms, agitated and hot. They're singing to me. Can't you hear the singing?"

"Um," said Nobody.

"And I can silence them."

She breathed deeply once more.

"Triggers snap," she whispered.

The gunfire lessened further.

"Barrels snake into knots," she said, sweat beading on her brow. The gunfire grew even dimmer. Angry and confused shouts could be heard.

"Bullet jackets rust," she said. And all the gunfire stopped. But the shouting continued.

"They . . . they pull their knives," she moaned. "So many knives."

Nobody placed his arms around her as she tried to sit up. She slumped against him, her eyes focused somewhere he would never be able to see.

"And the knives crumble to dust," she whispered.

Suddenly, even the shouting began to calm. Nobody could see men stepping from their hiding places, looking down at their empty hands, their faces confused.

Rail Blade went limp, her face falling against his shoulder. "It's over," she said, quietly. "That's all I have. It's over."

He stroked her hair. "You did fine," he whispered. "You stopped it. You just stopped the Apocalypse."

"Wow, Sis," said the Thrill. "You kicked butt."

One by one, the confused men in the streets looked at one another, bewildered. Then, with growls, they lunged at each other, fists flying. They lifted paving stones and hurled them with angry curses.

"No," whispered Rail Blade. "No."

"Don't sweat it," said Nobody. "They can only do so much damage. You've stopped the killing."

"I haven't stopped the hate," said Rail Blade, pushing him away. She rose on wobbling legs. "I'm too tired now. I could slap everyone in handcuffs, I guess, but I'm beaten. I don't care anymore. Let them kill themselves. I've done all I can."

Nobody nodded.

"Don't beat yourself up," said the Thrill. "What you did was amazing. You did good."

Rail Blade's shoulders drooped. "I'm so tired."

Nobody looked at the fighting in the streets. In a way, it was comical—the flabby, middle-aged men kicking and cursing, slapping each other like children on a playground.

From the crowd of men, an actual child appeared. He looked to be about ten years old. His features were dark, his eyes red, as if he had been crying. He wore torn, tattered, dirty clothing, and he walked slowly toward them, his eyes focused on the two colorfully garbed women.

Nobody started to point the boy out to Rail Blade, to let her see that her work had possibly saved this boy's life. Perhaps that would make her feel better. But something about the boy's eyes made him think differently. They were too hard, too full of hate. The madness that had infected the adults also seemed to be gripping him, though he was too small and powerless for his anger to find any outlet.

He kept walking, until he was only a few yards away.

He reached into his coat and pulled out a hand grenade.

Nobody's mouth dropped open as the boy pulled the pin.

CHAPTER FIFTEEN

A WHITE FLASH

The pin fell to the dusty ground. The boy ran forward, passing through Nobody. Nobody swung around, screaming, "Rail Blade!"

Rail Blade turned her head.

A white flash cast the boy's shadow in a long arrow back to Nobody.

A red spray painted the white cloth of the Thrill's costume.

The boy slumped to the ground.

In the air where the boy had stood, a black cloud of grenade fragments hung motionless, spread out like a dense swarm of flies.

Rail Blade's lips were pressed tight, her face white, her eyes narrow, as the swarm condensed and coalesced back into a grenade. The grenade dropped to the ground, landing in the red pool that grew around the boy.

"Get away," said Rail Blade.

"My God," said Nobody. "He couldn't have been ten years old."

"Get away," said Rail Blade, through clenched teeth. She dug her fingers into the dust. The air began to smell of ozone. Lightning crackled overhead. Nobody's watch began to spark. He fumbled to unclasp it, then threw it to the ground. But it didn't hit the ground. It hung motionless in the air, glowing with static.

"Amelia," said the Thrill. "Calm down."

Rail Blade grabbed the Thrill by the shoulders and stared into her eyes.

"Leave this place!" she shouted. "Get far from this place as fast as you can. Don't. Look. Back."

Nobody put his hand on Rail Blade's shoulder. "Amelia," he said.

His hand went numb. He pulled it away. Thin lines of blood bubbled across his palm and fingers. Rail Blade's uniform shredded as razor sharp spikes grew from her back and shoulders.

"Go," said Rail Blade, releasing the Thrill with a backward shove.

The men who had been fighting nearby began to shriek in agony. Nobody looked at them. One by one, they were rising from the Earth, levitating like his wristwatch. The looks of agony that twisted their faces were nightmarish.

"Amelia," said the Thrill. "Stop this now!"

"What's she doing," said Nobody. "What's going on?"

"She's lifting them by their blood," said the Thrill. "It can kill people, cause strokes, rupture vessels. Stop it Amelia!"

The screaming men were lifted higher now, moving faster, being carried away from Rail Blade. Rail Blade's sweat had turned to liquid steel, running down her face like beads of mercury.

"Amelia, please," said Nobody, kneeling before her.

Then he couldn't breathe. His heart was stopped mid-beat as he was lifted into the air. The pain was indescribable, like being lifted on the points of a billion sharp needles resting against his heart, his lungs, his liver. The pain stopped suddenly as Sarah placed her hands on him.

"I'm touching Earth's core," said Rail Blade, her voice calm and cold. "My power is limitless. Leave . . . this . . . place."

"We're going," said the Thrill.

They rose into the air, giving Nobody a better view. All over the city countless thousands of people were flying, in a vast dark circle, as Rail Blade evicted every last citizen of Jerusalem.

"Father," the Thrill said into her radio. "Amelia's losing it. Talk to her."

Dr. Know didn't answer.

Nobody looked down. Rail Blade had risen now. She stood in the eye of an expanding circle of spinning blades, a cloud of dust fleeing their approach. Lightning spiked from the ground around her, passing through her, and the blades whirled faster. The blades reached the wall of the nearest building, and rasped it to gravel in seconds. Rail Blade tilted her face upward, spreading her arms. Her face was angelic and peaceful. The storm of blades continued to build. Within a dozen yards of her, the ground was now flat and featureless, carved smooth by flashing steel.

The Thrill pulled them higher into the air, still vainly shouting for her father to answer.

"She's losing it! She's losing control!" said the Thrill.

Nobody didn't think so. Below him, the blades whirled in perfect symmetry, multiplying and pushing outward like bright shards of a kaleidoscope. There was nothing out of control about it. It was perfect grace, perfect geometry, as wheels of razors rolled within wheels, grinding outward, leaving polished land for a hundred yards in all directions. Where ancient walls once stood, there was now a gleaming white floor of packed dust. Mountains vanished before the dance of the blades.

"Take us back down," said Nobody.

"No," said the Thrill.

"We have to talk to her. We have to—"

"She'll kill us. She's snapped. Only Father can stop her now. Why won't he answer?"

Nobody knew. Nobody knew why Dr. Know wasn't going to answer. Rail Blade was fulfilling his wish. She was solving the problem. She was wiping Jerusalem from the face of the Earth.

He could still see her, though they had now risen half a mile. Rail Blade was a tiny shape, a dark dot in the center of a circle of white. Nobody realized what he was witnessing. Baby Gun had been seen as an angel of prophecy, the spirit of war given shape and substance, a harbinger of the coming Apocalypse.

Rail Blade was the fulfillment of prophecy.

Rail Blade was the Angel of Death.

And she danced, with the pool of the boy's blood as her pinhead. Her body flowed in fluid arcs, forming the letters of a new language, spelling out her message with every graceful motion of her arms and legs.

Jerusalem vanished from the face of the Earth as Nobody watched in awe. All of the impossible, horrible, wonderful things he'd witnessed in recent months paled before what he was now seeing. This was like watching the fall of a comet, like witnessing a volcano's eruption. He'd never seen such power. He'd never seen anything so chilling, so perfectly terrible, and so perfectly beautiful.

THEY RODE A jet back to the island. They watched what television channels they could tune into in silence. This wasn't something that could be covered up, like the

Texas prisoner incident. Every channel they could find kept showing weather satellite photos of the area. Jerusalem was gone. In its place was a ten-mile circle, polished and gleaming like a mirror.

Most of the residents had been safely deposited beyond the range of the destruction. But when the news anchors spoke of casualties, the numbers they used were grim ones. Hundreds of people had died of heart failure. Hundreds of thousands homeless. The religious shrines of three major religions had vanished. Nobody had been to the homes of the people who lived in the city. He'd seen the children's rooms painted with flowers and smiling clowns. All of those rooms were gone now. All of the restaurants he'd enjoyed, gone. He knew what it felt like to have your world stripped away. He felt he should weep for all that was lost. But he didn't have any tears left.

World leaders issued condolences and called for calm. The Pope openly wept as he offered a prayer for the lost souls. Rail Blade was mentioned only in passing, her role in stopping the tanks. At least in these early reports, no one yet was pointing fingers at Amelia.

"Dad could have stopped this," said Sarah, quietly.

"No one could have stopped her," said Nobody. "Your sister was like some force of nature. Stopping her would have been like stopping a hurricane."

"My father has worked out the science to stop hurricanes," said Sarah. "He keeps it secret because he fears environmental damage if nations start shutting down every storm that heads their way."

"You're joking," said Nobody.

"I'm in no mood to joke right now. My sister has just killed uncounted innocent people. My father allowed it. It's possible he put the idea into her head."

"Christ," said Nobody. "Your sister has always seemed so cold. I knew she could kill without blinking an eye. But this . . ."

"There's something you've never been told about her," said Sarah. "It's a family secret. It's something that drove her crazy."

"Yes?"

"We used to have a brother."

"That is a well-kept secret. There are no photographs or anything around the mansion."

"He was the middle child, a year younger than Amelia, a year older than I. His name was Alexander. He also had strange powers. He could breathe water. He would spend hours in the ocean. He loved to swim like I love to fly."

"Did something happen to him?"

Sarah shifted uncomfortably in her seat. "Amelia killed him."

"Oh," said Nobody.

"She was thirteen. Her powers were starting to grow strong. She'd been able to move steel with her mind from birth, but it wasn't until puberty that she was able to create it from thin air, and make it flow like water. Alex was jealous of her, I think. Dad had always devoted a tremendous amount of attention to him, but as Amelia's powers started to develop, Dad focused on her. Alex began to torment Amelia, teasing her and stuff. Normal sibling rivalry, I guess, but he really seemed to want to make her look bad in front of Dad. And one day, he just pushed the wrong button. She lashed out, forming a blade with her mind, and cut him very badly. She wasn't trying to kill him, just scare him by shooting a blade near him, but he moved. He died in her arms."

"Holy cow," said Nobody. "No wonder she's crazy. That's quite a burden of guilt for a thirteen year old."

"You would think so, yeah. But then Dad used that incident to twist Amelia into his own personal weapon. Amelia didn't want to use her powers ever again after she killed Alex. Dad insisted that she learn martial arts for discipline, that she hone her powers to insure that the next time she aimed a blade at someone, she would have complete control. Since Alex's memory seemed to make Amelia afraid of her powers, he was erased from our family history. Father destroyed photos of him. The walls of his bedroom were knocked down and the library was expanded into the space. Alex has a gravestone in the rose garden, but it's featureless. His name was never carved into it."

"That's awful," said Nobody.

"It hurt Mother worst of all. She's like a shadow of the woman I remember from my childhood. I haven't seen her smile in over ten years."

"How about you? How did his death make you feel? Weren't you afraid of Amelia?"

"No. Not really. We fight, but not the way she and Alex did. Our relationship is strange. In some ways, she's the person I'm closest to in the whole world. In other ways, she's a complete stranger."

"She's very protective of you," said Nobody.

"I think that's likely to change very soon," said Sarah.

"Why?"

"She's completely loyal to father. And once she hears what I have to say to him, she's going to hate me forever."

DR. KNOW LOOKED pale and weary. The lights in the nerve center were off, save for the illumination from the wall of televisions. The volume was barely audible, forming a background murmur from which words and phrases like "destruction" and "death" and "Apocalypse" bubbled forth.

If he had heard Sarah's words, he did not acknowledge them.

Nobody positioned himself between Dr. Know and the televisions.

"Well?" asked Nobody.

Dr. Know looked at Nobody, then glanced at Sarah. He opened his mouth, but no words came out. He lowered his head, shaking it.

When he finally spoke, his words were quiet and calm. "I have dedicated all of my life to the elimination of such senseless tragedy. It hurts me that you would believe I condoned this, let alone provoked it, Sarah."

"Then why didn't you say anything?"

"It happened very quickly," Dr. Know said. "Even now, I cannot imagine what I could have said to her to calm her."

"Has she contacted you?" asked Nobody.

"No. I don't know where she is. No one whose mind I can touch has seen her. But no one has undertaken a thorough inspection of the zone of destruction. Perhaps the strain of her actions killed her. Perhaps she took her own life. We will learn when we learn."

Dr. Know straightened his shoulders and looked at Sarah. "What matters now is our reaction to this. The world is still in shock, but soon the accusations will start. This is a tremendously important moment in the history of mankind. The next twenty-four hours may well decide if the world unites in common cause, or splinters into chaos and war. I will need your help to manage this, Sarah."

Sarah turned her back to him. "You won't have it."

"Please don't allow your grief over what you've witnessed to cloud your judgment. You have a responsibility to the world to—"

"Fuck responsibility," she said, throwing up her hands. "It's over. It's time for you to quit. Every scheme you've ever hatched leads to greater and greater grief. The more you try to control the world, the more damage you do. I'm quitting. You should do the same."

"Quitting?"

"I'm leaving. I'm going away, someplace you won't be able to find me. I'm through being a pawn in your game."

"Please consider the ramifications of what you are saying," said Dr. Know.

"Goodbye, Father," she said, floating away.

Nobody followed her, outside the mansion into the bright sunlight. She hovered a foot in the air, looking back at the mansion, then looking at him.

"You want to come with me?" she asked.

"Yes," said Nobody. "But . . ."

"But what?"

"I'm staying for now. I feel as though I should, I don't know, keep a watch on your father. Stick around and make sure he doesn't do anything stupid."

"You don't have to worry about that. He never does anything stupid. He screws things up with every ounce of genius he can muster."

"I can meet you later," said Nobody.

"I don't know if you'll be able to find me. I don't know where I'm going." She pulled the small radio from her ear and threw it to the ground. "I envy you, being invisible. All I want right now is to vanish from the planet. I don't want to be the Thrill anymore. And I don't want to be Sarah Knowbokov."

"I understand," he said. "Good luck."

"I'll miss you," she said, swooping down and planting a kiss on his cheek. There were tears in her eyes as she pulled away, and floated off on the wind.

Nobody wiped his cheek.

"Take care," he whispered.

Chapter Sixteen

PERHAPS YOU
DO LEARN FROM
YOUR MISTAKES

Katrina sat in the library, lost in the book she held. Nobody sat across from her and studied her face. She looked very old, far older than Dr. Know, too old to be Amelia and Sarah's mother.

"I wish we could talk," said Nobody. "I wish you could tell me how you feel, being caught in these circumstances, with every member of your family so powerful. Do you question your sanity? What parts of yourself have you been forced to put aside just to make it through your day?"

The questions weren't that difficult to come up with. They were the same questions he was asking himself.

Katrina continued reading. Nobody rose, and wandered back to the nerve center. Dr. Know was in animated conversation with a video display showing the President.

"What caused this disaster is irrelevant," Dr. Know said. "I think it is best treated as an act of God. Perhaps a meteor struck. If people start laying blame, war could erupt throughout the world."

The President shook his head. "The world is demanding answers. I have every intention of throwing my weight behind the UN's investigation. And if it's discovered that you are behind this, so be it. Not everything can be spun away."

"Look for all the evidence you wish," said Dr. Know. "I want to know the truth as much as you. But some truths may be too difficult for the general public to accept. I could mention one you feel the same way about, for example. I say you lay the groundwork now for a story the world can accept that will lead us away from war."

The President looked as if he were about to unleash a string of expletives. Instead he said, "I'll take your advice under consideration. Now, if you'll excuse me, I have other calls to take."

"Of course," said Dr. Know. The screen went dark. "Hard-headed fool," he grumbled.

"Doc," said Nobody. "We should talk."

"I see you decided to stay," said Dr. Know. "When Sarah left, I assumed you had gone as well."

"Sarah has a lot of reason to mistrust you."

"And you don't?"

"I think you're a scheming, manipulative son-of-a-bitch. You're playing God, and people have died because of it. But I haven't made up my mind if you're doing more harm than good. For a while there in Jerusalem, before it all spun out of control, I felt like we might be doing something important. I guess my decision depends on what you do next."

"I see. I'm curious. What do you think I'm going to do?"

"I know what I would do," said Nobody.

"Which is?"

"I'd use my damn time machine. I'd erase this. Shouldn't be difficult. You just need to stop the boy from pulling that pin. If Rail Blade had seen him five seconds earlier, this wouldn't have happened."

"An interesting theory."

"Let's test it."

"No."

"Why not?"

"When I designed my time machine, I did so purely with the intention of gathering information. My plan was to discover Rex Monday's identity in the past, but I would never have tried to stop him from doing the things he was fated to do. I knew the consequences would be unpredictable and chaotic. As it was, even the act of gathering information changed the world with terrible consequences, for you, at least. If I use my time machine to save Jerusalem, why not use it to stop all tragedies? No plane that has ever crashed would need to take off. Every murder could be prevented. But the consequences of such actions are unimaginable. I could do irreparable damage with such meddling."

"I think I have a fair understanding of the consequences," said Nobody. "But this is something you, in a way, contributed to. Rail Blade was in Jerusalem because of you."

"My decision on this matter is final," said Dr. Know. "You waste precious time in attempting to persuade me."

"Fine," said Nobody. "And for what it's worth, I'm a little relieved."

"Oh?"

"Perhaps you do learn from your mistakes."

"I try," said Dr. Know.

"Then let's talk about Alex."

"My son? Why? What possible purpose could be served?"

"Sarah told me how you tried to erase all memory of him. I'm wondering, if Amelia is dead, will she also be placed aside? I don't think your wife could survive it. I think Amelia deserves better."

"When did you decide to become my spiritual advisor, Richard? Who are you to tell me how to deal with my grief, or with my wife, or my daughters?"

"I'm a man who's lost everything. I'm a man who knows what it's like to have the memory of his life erased. Crazy as it sounds, I would like to keep you from this fate."

"So that your life will have some meaning?" asked Dr. Know. "You get to pass on the precious bit of wisdom you've gleaned from your suffering, and hope that gives your experiences some importance? Is that it?"

"More or less."

"Then here's some of my wisdom: The dead are a waste of time. It is pointless to regret the words never spoken, or the opportunities lost, or the feelings never shared. The past should not be changed. The future is the only time worth any concern or energy. You can take my word for this—after all, I'm the one with the time machine."

"You are one hard-headed, hard-hearted bastard," said Nobody. "Maybe you don't learn from your mistakes, after all."

"If you are finished questioning my emotional capacity, I have a mission for you, should you still desire to work for me."

"Go on."

"Since Amelia hasn't returned, I must assume the worst. The UN is sending a team to investigate the ruins of Jerusalem, to try to discover what happened. My greatest fear is that they will find Amelia's body and link her to what happened. I would like to send you along to sabotage such a mission in anyway you can."

Before Nobody could give an answer, there was a clang of metal striking metal from behind him. He looked toward the sound.

Rail Blade stood near, stepping forward in her heavy steel boots.

"They won't find my body," she said. "Though I signed my work just the same."

Dried blood and dust caked Rail Blade's face. Her clothes were ripped and ragged, her body emaciated but strong. She smelled strongly of stale sweat.

"Daughter," said Dr. Know. "You are still alive."

"You say that so coldly," said Rail Blade. "A simple observation. There's no joy in your words, Father."

"I didn't think I would see you again," said Dr. Know.

"Was that a fear? Or a hope?"

"You look exhausted," said Nobody. "Maybe you should sit down."

"Your concern is touching. But I've passed beyond exhaustion. I've discovered resources within me I've never imagined. I have no need for food, or rest. I've become . . . something more than I was. I don't know that I can explain."

"There is nothing to explain," said Dr. Know. His voice was no longer cold and calm. Now, an edge of anger was evident. "There is no explanation possible. You have done something unforgivable."

Rail Blade wiped her cheek, and sighed deeply.

"I have no hope of forgiveness," she said. "I have no need for it. Does one forgive the hurricane? Does an earthquake ask for grace? You destroyed an entire universe, Father, and created a new one in its place. Who is there to judge you?"

"Daughter," said Dr. Know. "I believe you are ill."

Rail Blade stared at him. Her lips were quivering.

Nobody stepped backward slowly, removing himself from the path that separated Rail Blade and Dr. Know.

"Ill?" she asked, softly.

"You killed hundreds of people, perhaps thousands. You've done economic damage beyond calculation. You endangered the peace and stability of the world. You've done more damage to my plans than Rex Monday could have dreamed."

"Oh," said Rail Blade, her eyes narrowing. "Of course. Your plans. I forgot whose planet I was on."

"My work . . . our work was, is, important. You have always been my most trusted ally in my struggle. But this—"

"Ally?" asked Rail Blade. "What a strange word to use for your own daughter."

"You know what I mean," said Dr. Know.

"You need not fear for your . . . our plan, Father. I have learned much from you. There will be no war. Soon, people from all over the Earth will find the message I've left at ground zero."

"Message?"

"I signed my work, Father. I forged a plaque on the spot where the boy fell. The iron from his blood, and the shards of the grenade, have been melded together in this work. I give the world a warning. Jerusalem will not be the last city to feel my touch. Any place that men kill other men over ancient, pointless prejudice, wherever the Earth seems cursed with unhealing hatred, I will cast my judgment. The Balkans, Northern Ireland, throughout Africa, the violence must stop. I've given the world one year. Then, in the places where the Earth is still stained by blood, I will scour it clean."

"My God," said Nobody. "You're serious."

Dr. Know stared at Rail Blade. He seemed lost in thought.

"Very well," he said.

"What?" said Nobody.

"One year," said Dr. Know. "Who can say what a year will bring? Perhaps I've been a fool all along. Perhaps I've worked too long behind the scenes at peace, and have been blind to the obvious truth. People respect power. They comprehend violence. And perhaps war can only end if another, more horrible threat forces it to end."

"You're both insane," said Nobody.

"Your opinions are duly noted," said Dr. Know.

"Your opinions are completely irrelevant," said Rail Blade.

"Amelia," said Dr. Know. "Richard was correct about one thing. You do seem very tired. I don't pretend to like what you've done. But you are still my daughter, and it bothers me to see you in such a state of obvious exhaustion."

"I . . . am weary," said Amelia. As she said this, her thick steel boots crumbled to dust and she stumbled forward on her bare feet.

"Let me help you, child," said Dr. Know, extending his hand toward her.

She reached out to him, a single tear trickling down her cheek. She placed her hand in his. As he looked into her eyes, he turned her arm forearm up, and stroked it gently. Then, with a smooth, subtle motion that Nobody almost missed, Dr. Know slipped his hand into his pocket. When he pulled it out, he held a syringe.

Rail Blade gasped as he slid the needle into her vein with a rapid, precise stroke. He pushed the plunger, and released her arm.

She stumbled backward, then collapsed, motionless.

"I'm sorry," said Dr. Know.

"Oh my God!" said Nobody, dropping to her side. "What did you just do to her?"

"I gave her an injection of pentobarbital," said Dr. Know. "She felt no pain. She was dead within a heartbeat."

"I can't believe it! I can't believe you just murdered your own daughter!"

"You saw what she had become. You saw what she was capable of. I prepared for this contingency. Perhaps the world will amend its ways in one brief year. But I doubt it. No doubt, in a year, she would have carried out her threats. I couldn't risk it. Who knows how powerful she would have been in a year? Since puberty, her power has increased at an accelerating rate. I believe this contributed to her mental breakdown."

169

Nobody swallowed hard. Looking down at Rail Blade's pale, still form, he felt an immense sorrow.

"She tried so hard to please you," said Nobody, choking up. "You were the center of everything for her. And you murdered her."

"I did what I had to do." Dr. Know also sounded on the verge of tears.

Nobody reached out, and placed his hand on Rail Blade's cheek, and wiped away the tear that still glistened there.

And her eyes fluttered open.

CHAPTER SEVENTEEN

TERRIFY IS A BETTER WORD

Dr. Know pulled his gas gun from his lab coat with one hand, and a small mask for his nose with the other. He turned a dial on the handle as he stepped toward Rail Blade, who was raising herself on her hands, looking groggy.

"Step back, Richard," said Dr. Know, placing the barrel of the gun near his daughter's mouth. "This is Sarin. Not as painless as the pentobarbital, I fear."

Richard staggered backward. Dr. Know pulled the trigger before Rail Blade even seemed to realize what was happening. The pistol gave a small click. Dr. Know's brow wrinkled in bewilderment.

Rail Blade turned her face toward him, the faintest hint of a smile on her lips. "There's a small steel spring," she said, through labored breaths, "just inside the trigger."

Dr. Know stepped back as Rail Blade sat up. She nearly toppled backward, like a toddler surprised by the momentum her body possessed. She steadied herself, and brushed her hair back from her face. "You'll also find the taser in your watch has malfunctioned," she said. "The syringe in your other pocket—the needle just knotted itself."

Dr. Know nodded. Then, fluidly, he flew forward, delivering a savage kick to her throat. She fell, arms flying limp. He leapt into the air, almost faster than Nobody could follow, and thrust his foot down with his full weight aimed at the side of his daughter's head. Just before he made contact, a crown of gleaming spikes materialized around Rail Blade's brow. He landed with a cry of pain, as four inches of slender red steel punched through the tops of his fine leather shoes.

He pulled himself free, hopping backward until he reached his command chair. He leaned against it for support, then cried out once more as the chair came to life. Steel belts snaked out and encircled his waist, pulling him sharply into the seat. Bands of metal snapped from the armrests, pinning his arms. A rake of iron that dug into his scalp and forced his head back jerked at his head.

Rail Blade placed a hand against the wall, her limbs wobbling as she tried to rise. Instinctively, Nobody reached out to steady her, placing one hand on her arm, another on her waist. He felt cold as he realized how stupidly dangerous this was.

But Rail Blade didn't respond with aggression. She leaned her weight into his arms, and pulled herself to her feet, her breath coming in labored, ragged heaves.

"Thank you," she whispered, turning to look into his eyes.

"Um," he answered.

"You," she said, turning her gaze to her father.

"Finish it," said Dr. Know, grimacing as he fought against his bonds. "Finish it!"

"You killed me," she said softly. "You killed me."

"You killed uncounted innocent people! Now you'll murder me! Finish it!"

Rail Blade's weight shifted from Richard's arms. The air hummed with energy as a second skin of iron seeped from her pores, bringing solidity and strength to her trembling limbs.

A whining wail like a singing saw pierced the room as a steel rail whipped into the air in front of her. She leapt onto it, wheels springing into existence as she moved.

She skated toward her father with a gentle kick, gliding slowly and smoothly, her arms stretched to her sides in beautiful balance.

Dr. Know writhed in the chair, blood streaming down his face as his scalp tore against the metal fingers that held him.

Rail Blade traced a graceful circle around the chair, then drew to a halt before him. Razor sharp swords as long as she was tall materialized at her sides as she drew her arms upward.

"Rail Blade," said Nobody. "Don't."

"Do it," said Dr. Know. "Finish it."

"Please," said Nobody.

"Finish it!" said Dr. Know.

"But," said Rail Blade, tilting her head to the side, "I haven't even begun."

"Let him go, Amelia," said Nobody. "There's been enough death already." Her "thank you" wasn't much to go on, but the look in her eyes a second ago hadn't been the look of someone out to kill him. This wasn't a hurricane or a volcano before him. This was Amelia, a person, a friend. He could still talk her out of this.

"Enough death?" Rail Blade said with a coy tilt of her head. "I know that better than you'll ever understand. My heart stopped beating the second his poison entered my veins."

"Doesn't seem to have slowed you down much," said Nobody, cautiously moving around her to get within her line of sight.

"Blood is iron," she said. "I don't need a heart to move it through my veins. But I still feel the pain. There's a cold, dead lump in the center of my chest. How could you, Father?"

"You'll never believe me," said Dr. Know.

"Try me."

"I did it because I love you, Amelia."

Amelia snorted with brief laughter.

"You could have sent flowers, Doc," said Nobody.

"You're in such pain," said Dr. Know. "Before I ever acted, there was a poison eating at your heart. You've fought the evil of the world for too long, been too often witness to violence and hate, and it's twisted you, corrupted you. You've become a mad animal, with pain erasing all reason. You lash out at the guilty and the innocent alike. My needle was an act of mercy."

Rail Blade chuckled.

Nobody ducked as the blades at her side began to carom wildly around the room. Monitors erupted in showers of sparks as the blades smashed through them. Arcs of current zapped through the air as the blades sliced through power cables. The hum of information flowing into the computer bank grew still, replaced by the screech of metal jagging through metal.

Rail Blade bowed to her father's face, and kissed him on the forehead. She stood, her chin wet with his blood.

"It has only begun," she said.

Rail Blade pirouetted about, turning her back to her father. She kicked, moving back along her rail, as blades grew from the axles of the wheels, reaching out to scrape and score the walls.

Nobody jumped over the whirling blades, running to Dr. Know. He pulled at the bonds that held him, to no avail.

"Don't worry about me," Dr. Know said. "Stop her. Any way you can."

By now, Rail Blade had left the lab, her wheel blades tearing through the doorframe. Down the hall she skated, ripping plaster, smashing through wood and wire. The paintings of masters that hung along the walls were cut in twain as she passed. The blade shattered a Ming vase on an elegant ebony table, spilling flowers to the hardwood floor.

Nobody chased after her, mindful of the torn wires that crackled on the floor. Plaster fell from the ceiling in great chunks. The walls creaked and moaned as their supporting beams were severed.

Now she was in the front entryway. This was an enormous room, bathed in light from the tall windows. In the center of the room was a huge staircase covered with red carpet. Rail Blade rode her silvery beam down the middle of the stairs, turning her gaze to the crystal chandelier high overhead. The chain that supported it snapped, and it fell before her, covering the floor of the entryway with a million sparkling prisms. She waved her hands before her and a stream of darts sprayed forth, shattering the windows. Nobody hung back, covering his eyes, as shards of glass rained down. She skated through the gleaming storm of glass without harm, the fragments shattering further against her steely skin.

She passed through the front door, her blades cutting across the entire length of the front of the house. Nobody ran for the door as fast as he could, as the walls began to cave. He passed through to the relative safety of the outside as the entire front wall of the house crumpled and collapsed, revealing rooms in every story of the house, like a giant dollhouse, with a cherry red rocket ship in the attic. Katrina Knowbokov, with almost comic calm, looked up from her book to where the wall had been seconds before.

Nobody followed Rail Blade as she glided along above the stone pathway that led to the garden mazes beside the house. She had withdrawn the wheel blades, and the metal skin that coated her began to melt away. She passed through a corridor of hedges until she reached a large circle of rich green grass, in the center of which was a fountain. Around the circle were dozens of rose bushes supported by trellises. Nobody had seen this garden before, but only from the library balcony.

The rail he followed crumbled to red dust. Rail Blade walked around the fountain, balanced on the marble lip of the pool. She moved carefully, slowly, her arms held slightly away from her body for balance.

She reached the far side of the fountain and hopped down onto the grass. Nobody saw she was looking at a granite slab that was set into the ground.

He walked around the fountain, and noticed a small stone bench. He took a seat, only a few yards from Rail Blade. No, not Rail Blade, from Amelia. He had to be careful how he thought of her. No doubt when Dr. Know had said to stop her any way possible, he'd been envisioning some violent struggle, some surprise sneak attack. Nobody had other plans. The key to stopping Rail Blade was simple. He had to turn her back into Amelia. Forces of nature were beyond his control. But as for the Knowbokov sisters . . . he had a certain flair at dealing with them.

Amelia glanced at him, but said nothing. He pulled a cigarette from the case in his front pocket, and lit it. She seemed to relax a bit and sat down on the edge of the fountain. She supported herself with her arms, as she still seemed a bit wobbly. She continued to look at him.

He stared back. All the steel that had covered her was gone. Only the tatters of her uniform remained. He shifted uncomfortably on the bench as he realized that he could see her right nipple through a rip in her jacket.

"Nobody," she said.

"Amelia," he said. He took another drag on the cigarette, his eyes returning to her nipple, and to the gentle curving shadows that lay near it.

"Rough day," he said.

She nodded, smiling coyly.

"The way you're looking at me," she said. "How strange."

"You're a beautiful woman," said Nobody. "People are going to look at you."

"I've never liked people looking at me," said Amelia. "Not like my sister. She's the pretty one."

"Huh," said Nobody. "I mean, Sarah is pretty. But you, you know, aren't exactly hard on the eyes. And there's something about you . . . a complexity, shall we say, that Sarah can't even touch."

She smiled, and glanced down at her tattered clothes.

"I think you're looking at my breasts," she said.

"Yeah," he said, sheepishly, but continuing to look. "You're, uh, kind of hanging out. Sorry."

She moved her hand to the strips of cloth that covered her right breast and shifted them, concealing the nipple but revealing more of the breast, with its pale curves. He could see the beads of sweat that rolled across her skin.

"You find me attractive?" she said.

"Very," he said.

"Have you . . . ever thought about me?"

"Sexually?" he asked.

She blushed, and turned her gaze from him.

"Yeah," he said, taking another puff of his cigarette.

She looked back at him, her eyes narrow, but the corners of her lips curved into a smile. "Don't I scare you?"

"Terrify is a better word."

She nodded. Her smile faded. She said, "Terrify is a much better word."

"Do I scare you?" he asked.

"Maybe," she said.

"You've never even been kissed, I bet," he said.

She looked hurt. He got up, flicked his cigarette away, and strolled toward her. He sat next to her. She watched him from the corner of her eye.

He reached out, and placed his hand on her chin, and turned her face toward his. He looked at her face, at the sweat, and the dust, the dried blood, the trails of tears. And her lips. Her lips were dry and pale and thin, but possessed an appealing shape. He wiped the blood from her chin. He kissed her, lightly, tenderly. She didn't close her eyes.

He pulled back, and stared into her eyes. They were unearthly, with gray irises that seemed to be forged from steel.

"You have the most extraordinary eyes," he said.

Her eyes grew moister.

"Don't cry," he said. "They'll rust."

She closed her eyes. He kissed her once more, and placed his hand around her waist. She kissed him back this time, awkwardly, as if unsure of what to do. He stroked her hair gently. She placed her hand on his leg.

He pulled his lips from hers, and moved them to her ear. He kissed her lightly on the curve of her neck. She gave a soft moan of pleasure.

He whispered, "You just keep making that noise when I do something right."

She put a hand on his chin and turned his head, looking into his eyes. Her eyes were wet, shedding tears as she blinked.

"How did you know I've never been kissed?" she asked.

He smiled, and pulled her closer to him. He ran his hand beneath the ruins of her clothes, stroking her back as he pulled her closer.

"Didn't I tell you my other superpower?" he said, lowering his lips to her neck.

She groaned once more.

"Show me," she said.

CHAPTER EIGHTEEN

THE WOMAN WITH THE DEAD HEART

He lowered her to the soft green grass, pulling away the remains of her jacket. He dropped his mouth to her breast. She arched her back and gasped.

He ran his hand along her leg. Her skin was hot and soft, slick with sweat. He reached the edge of her skirt and explored beneath it. Her breathing quickened.

She smelled so alive. Her odor was intoxicating, full of musk and mystery. Blood, sweat, tears, the dust of Jerusalem, all blended together into some alchemical potion of desire. The perfume of the nearby roses paled in comparison to the rush he got breathing in the air that flowed across her moist skin.

Her panties were drenched, more with sweat than excitement, he guessed. He ran his finger along the inside of the elastic band. She was burning hot, and trembled at his touch. She shifted her legs wider as her hands clenched into fists in his hair.

"I didn't know," she groaned. "I didn't know it would feel this good. I don't want it to stop."

He cocked his head to one side, in an echo of her earlier gesture. "It's only begun," he said, lowering his mouth to her skin once more.

THE NIGHT BROUGHT a bright, full moon. They lay together on the granite slab, on his spread out shirt. His jacket was pulled over them. He cradled her as she lay her head against his chest.

"I understand now," she said.

"What?"

"Why they call it 'making love.'"

He ran his fingers lightly across her back.

"I've never been in love before," she said.

With his other hand, he traced the gentle arc of her lower lip. She kissed his fingers.

"Do you love me?" she asked.

"Hmmm," he said.

She tensed, ever so slightly.

"I don't want to lie to you," he whispered. "I don't know. I don't know if what I'm feeling is love, or just bliss."

Amelia nodded against his chest.

"It feels wonderful, whatever it is," he said.

"Do you love Sarah?" asked Amelia.

"I don't know. I don't think so. If I did, I wouldn't be here with you."

"No one has ever loved me," she said, in a matter-of-fact, unemotional tone.

"Don't say that."

She rolled away from him and sat up.

"Do you know where we are?" she asked.

"Um . . . in a garden?"

"This is my brother's grave."

"Oh." He sat up, looking down at the granite slab they had been lying on. He felt the hair rise on the back of his neck as the realization of where they'd been making love sank in.

"This bothers you," she said.

"No," he said. "It's just . . . slightly spooky. But I'm cool."

"I killed him," she said.

"I know. Sarah told me it was an accident."

"I don't remember," she said. "I've heard the story of what happened so many times, it seems like a memory, but I don't know. I've blanked it out. My father weaves so many lies. There are no photos of Alexander. What I remember of him is so hazy, more like imagination than memory. I sometimes wonder if there's anything under this slab at all."

"Sarah remembers him. Your mother does too."

"Father did everything to make me forget," she said. "He didn't want me to feel any guilt when I used my powers."

She clasped her knees with her arms, and rested her chin on them. "So," she said. "Eventually I stopped feeling anything."

Her face wrinkled, as she clenched her eyes shut. "Oh God," she said. "I wish I could stop now."

He placed his arms around her, holding her tightly.

"He said I was a monster," she sobbed. "But I'm so much worse than that."

"No," he whispered. "No, don't say this. Don't think it."

"I'm evil," she said, tears streaming down her cheeks. "I'm death. My heart is dead. I kill women and children and men, young and old, and I never feel a thing."

"You aren't evil," he said, rocking her gently in his arms. "You're just a girl. You're just a girl who's made a terrible mistake."

"Oh God," she cried, her voice cracking. She pressed her head to his chest and wept. "Oh God, oh God, oh God!"

"Shh," he whispered, his own voice choking. "Shh."

"I've done . . . such bad . . . things," she gasped. "And I . . . I think it might have been different . . ."

"It's OK," he said, stroking her hair. "Shh. It's OK."

"If only I could remember him," she said. "If I could remember what he looked like. If I could remember his voice, or . . . he's gone. I'll never see him again. And all those people in Jerusalem. Gone. The people who love them will never hear their voices, or see their smiles, and it's so awful. So awful."

"Yes," he whispered. "It is. But you aren't. You've been carrying the weight of the world. Your father told you the whole damn world was your responsibility, and no one is strong enough to carry that. You've made a horrible mistake. The worst ever, maybe. I watched you do it. And I saw something beautiful as I watched you. I can't explain it. But I think maybe this isn't bliss. Bliss doesn't ache like this. I think I do love you, Amelia. And you shouldn't hate yourself for what you've done."

"Everyone dead because of me," she whispered, her voice hoarse. "My heart stops, and I keep moving. It feels so wrong."

"Sarah ran away," said Nobody. "She felt like your father was to blame for what happened. She wants to go lose herself in the real world, live like a normal person, who doesn't fly, or mess with minds. I think you should do it too."

"I don't know what normal is," she said.

"You can be normal anytime you want," he said. "Normal is only a state of mind."

"I don't know how."

"You can learn it. You've got to get away from your father, with his schemes and plans for the world. You've got to stop worrying about the wars that won't end and the hatreds that won't die. You've got to let it all go, and take care of yourself."

"I can't even imagine it," she said. "Normal."

"Maybe you'll like it," he said.

She ran her fingers across the granite slab.

"His name," she said, "was Alexander."

The stone seemed to bubble as she spoke, in thin lines spaced closely together. Iron letters formed, spelling his name, and the dates of his death and birth. Beneath this, a rose of black iron formed, its petals delicately and artfully formed.

"I'm so sorry," she said, wiping her cheeks. "I'm so sorry I lived and you died."

"Amelia," said Nobody. "You're a beautiful person. You have a beautiful soul. Please live. For me."

She stood up, staring at the moon.

"I've been there, you know."

"Where?"

"The moon."

"Get out."

"Three years ago. Rex Monday was building a missile base there, to hold the ultimate upper hand against the world. Father built a space ship in a little under six hours once he figured out what was happening. I went up and tore the base apart. Mindo went along also."

"You're making this up," said Nobody, though why this was so hard to swallow he couldn't say, having actually seen the space ship. But, still, the moon?

"I've been there," she said. "And I've seen Earth, all at once, like a little shining Christmas ornament just beyond my grasp."

"Wow."

"It didn't look so heavy," she said. "And I thought, looking up at it, that I could actually save it."

"You've done what you could," said Nobody. "You just had some bad guidance."

"I'm sorry I hit you those times in the gym, Richard."

"Eh," he said. "Don't sweat it. I'm tougher than I look."

"Will you come with me?" she asked.

"Just did," he said, grinning.

"You can help me learn to be normal," she said.

"It's best that I don't," he said. "You should leave now. Before I change my mind."

"So change it."

"Get out of here," he said, waving his hand. "I'll find you. When it's time."

"Promise?"

"Promise."

"Very well," she said, leaning down to kiss him once again. Then she sent a rail toward the moon, and rose along it, nude in the night sky.

Nobody gathered up his clothes and began to dress. Not that it mattered, really. He still didn't exist. A girl who could fly might learn to walk among normal people, and a woman with a dead heart might learn to live like everyone else, but for him there was no everyday left to go back to. Now and forever, Richard Rogers was Nobody.

THE NEXT DAY, boats and planes began to arrive, and dozens of workers descended on the mansion, beginning the repair work. Nobody slipped aboard one of the outbound planes and a few hours later found himself in Atlanta.

By now, he was starting to stink. He hadn't showered since his encounter with Amelia, and the aromas that had been a pleasant reminder of their lovemaking in the few hours after her departure had now soured. He stole a cab ride with a pair of flight attendants and accompanied them to their hotel room. He engaged in a bit of voyeurism as he shared a shower with one of them.

"I sure am seeing a lot of naked women lately," he said, making small talk as she toweled herself off afterward. He sat on the toilet and studied her body in minute detail. It was interesting, her posture, her movements. In the cab Tonya had been talkative, a little too perky for his taste, really, with a face that seemed permanently set to smile. But now she was "off," her face sagging, her make-up washed away. In the cab she had seemed much younger than he was, but now he was pretty certain she was at least ten years older than him. The lines on her face were deeper, now that the make-up was gone, and her stomach had a bit of a middle-aged pooch to it. Her breasts sagged more than most women he'd been with, and her skin seemed a little leathery. She looked as if she'd spent a little too much time in the sun in younger days.

Curious, how he found himself studying her flaws. He realized that he'd never spent so much time near a naked person whose guard was so completely down. She wasn't trying to hide anything from him. She used the toilet, raising the lid despite the fact that he was sitting on it. He found himself sharing her body. He couldn't feel her, but when he looked down it was her body he saw, her breasts and legs. The tinkle of water in the toilet was curiously arousing.

Perhaps, he thought, this would be how he spent his life. Instead of being a poltergeist, or a guardian angel, he could become a voyeur ghost, eternally seeking truth and beauty, jerking off when he found it.

There were worse ways to pass time, he supposed.

HE READ IN the paper the next morning that the Israelis and Palestinians had formed a joint security alliance to defend themselves against a common enemy. The UN investigation was still under way, and it was cautioned it would be months, possibly years before any conclusions were reached. Less cautious commentators were throwing out theories as diverse as meteor strikes and alien invasions. Now governments of the world were opening lines of communication with one another, sharing information, and watching the skies.

He assumed this was Dr. Know's spin on things, and it wasn't a bad one. He wondered if Amelia had seen the same story, and if it made her feel any better.

Later that day, in the supermarket, he saw in the *Weekly World Star* that Rail Blade and the Thrill had been discovered to be aliens. Their photos had been airbrushed to reveal their antennas, and their ears had a definite sinister slant to them.

He wondered if that was also the work of Dr. Know.

THE FOLLOWING MONTHS, he discovered that airbrushing was a more common practice than he realized. He'd decided to haunt famous supermodels. All proved to be disappointments. For a little while, he had stalked Charity, the cute lead singer for the Famous Five. She stayed cute even when the cameras weren't around. She had an interesting love life, sleeping with two members of her band and her publicist, and she was fun to listen to as she talked. And she talked all the time, more even than Paco had. She talked over breakfast, with whomever she woke up with. She talked in the shower on a cell phone. She continued the conversation on the toilet, often switching between conversations with call waiting. Then she would talk with a dozen people at once at lunch, then spend all afternoon talking with members of her band, and then spend all night talking with strangers at a club, until she finally was dragged back to the bed of whoever she was sleeping with that night, where, of course, she talked in her sleep. A week of this was enough, and Nobody moved on.

After months of wandering in and out of the lives of the famous and not-so-famous, he found himself at the Pulpit, Chicago's most famous comedy club, one he'd always dreamed of playing back in his amateur days. Now, he got to sit in the audience and listen to a string of great comedians while he swiped cigarettes and stole drinks. Eventually, the last comedian left the stage and the bar closed. There were only a handful of people remaining in the bar. He looked around for an attractive woman, and found one quickly. She was a redhead, very well built. He had a sneaking feeling that he recognized her, maybe from the week he'd spent hanging around at Heff's. He followed her out. She was a bit tipsy and was hanging on the arm of a middle-aged man, who led her to a shiny new convertible.

He watched them as they drove off. He'd changed his mind. Following around beautiful women was beginning to lose its charm. He kicked at a piece of gravel in the parking lot, sending it skipping off across the pavement. What to do, what to do?

He turned around and went back into the club.

He felt funny.

CHAPTER NINETEEN

IS THIS THING ON?

Long ago, the Pulpit had actually been a church, a small-ish one. For decades the old building had stood as the congregation grew. Eventually they had built a gleaming new church in the suburbs, and the little church at the dead end of the street had been abandoned, put up for sale for years before the present owner had turned it into a bar. Much of the original stained glass and woodwork had been preserved, though the pews had been replaced with tables, and a bar ran the length of one wall.

The man who stepped before the microphone was dressed in an expensive silk suit. He wore a fedora, and sported gold and diamonds on his fingers, his wrists, and his tiepin. His shoes were Italian leather. Everything revealed him to be a man of success, wealth, and good, if a bit flamboyant, taste.

The bar before him was nearly empty. The lights were off on the stage, the candles on the tables extinguished, the chairs turned upside down on the tabletops. Far across the room, two men sat. He knew their names. They were Tony and Jake. Tony was the barkeeper, Jake was his friend. It wasn't unusual for them to hang around the empty bar and watch the little television that hung over it, chatting into the wee hours of the night.

The man on the stage took the microphone in his hands.

"Hi," he said. "I'm Richard Rogers, but my friends call me Nobody."

He started to wander around the stage, trailing the mike cord. "There's kind of a funny story behind that. It involves a time machine and a condom that didn't break."

He looked out over the empty tables and listened to the silence that greeted his opening material.

"Oh," he said. "Guess you've heard it."

He pushed his hat back. He took out a cigarette and placed the tip in the corner of his mouth. "But that's OK. That's OK. I've got all kinds of material. I mean to tell you, I've seen some crazy shit in my time. I've slept in the Lincoln Bedroom. I've traveled all over the world. I was there when Jerusalem bit the dust. I mean, the stuff I could tell you about, it would make your head explode."

He paused to light his cigarette. "Oh, yeah. Oh, yeah, and I've seen that. I've seen heads explode."

Across the room, Jake chuckled at something Tony said.

Encouraged, Nobody pressed on. "So, the long and short of it is, I'm invisible. I mean, really, no one can see me. And this has its advantages. Like, you see my watch? It's a Rolex. You know what it cost me? Nothing! 'Cause I'm fucking invisible, man!"

He sat the mike back into its stand. He was starting to feel warmed up.

"This tie. You know how much they wanted for this tie? Six hundred dollars! I mean, come on! I saw this thing in a shop downtown and I thought, 'Hey, that's a nice tie.' And then I saw the price! Yow! I mean, what kind of idiot drops six hundred bucks on a tie? Not me! 'Cause I'm fucking invisible, baby!"

"Heh," he said, smoothing his tie back down. "Yeah. And you guys. Come on, guys, tell me what you'd do if you were invisible. Come on, admit it. You'd use your newfound talents to look at naked chicks. Yeah. Yeah, I've done that."

Tony and Jake continued to chat, oblivious to the act on stage. They were watching some beer commercial that prominently featured women in bathing suits.

"Those women in that commercial. I've seen 'em. Probably. They all sort of run together after a while. I mean, I've hung out at the freakin' Playboy mansion. I've seen my share of nekkid women. No kidding."

He loosened his tie. He felt like he was buzzing now. He had no script; he had nothing practiced. He didn't need it now. He just talked and people thought he was funny. And if he got into trouble, there was always a silly walk.

"And women, good God, women say the raunchiest things when men aren't around. I swear, you ever turn invisible, you go hang out in a women's restroom for an hour. You'll hear things that make your hair fall out. When the men aren't around, women are just downright crude. I heard these two girls once, they were riding in a car, and this one was talking about her boyfriend's penis. I'm not kidding. A twenty-minute drive, and the whole way she keeps talking about this penis, talking about what kind of veins it has, talking about, I swear, what kind of *moods* it has. I mean, come on! Men could never carry on a conversation for twenty minutes about the physical attributes of their girlfriends. They need, what, three words, tops,"—he lowered his voice and swaggered into his he-man stance—"Hooters. Big ones."

He chuckled deeply, doing his macho man slow laugh.

He straightened up, wiping his brow. He took a long drag off his cigarette, then blew a perfect smoke ring. How come he could only do this when no one was watching?

He looked at Jake and Tony, shaking their heads about something. He felt some of the energy drain from him.

He tapped the mike with his finger. "This thing on?"

It wasn't.

He looked at his watch. Four in the morning.

"I wonder where my children are," he said.

He flicked his cigarette into the huge potted tree at the edge of the stage. He dropped down from the stage and made his way over to the bar. While Tony and Jake watched the television, he snagged a bottle of tequila and a shot glass.

He did a shot, then took a suck of a bar lime. He shuddered as it took hold.

"You believe this?" said Jake, pointing at the television.

It was Rail Blade he was pointing at. Rail Blade was on TV. Nobody perked up. Had it been a year already?

He realized quickly that this was old footage. They were watching some tabloid TV show about the sinister alien origins of Rail Blade and the Thrill.

"What's to believe?" said Tony.

"That they're aliens. I mean, come on, look at this woman. She's not no damn alien."

"Jake, she has steel spikes shooting out of her ankles. There's a clue."

"I dunno," said Jake. "I mean, spikes or no, you gotta admit she's one hot babe."

"Did her," said Nobody.

"I just think she's spooky," said Tony. "She weirds me out."

"Brother, you don't know the half of it," said Nobody, doing another shot. He wiped his mouth, then stuck in another cigarette.

"How 'bout her sister?" said Jake.

"Who? The Thrill? She's pretty hot I guess."

"Had her," said Nobody, lighting his cigarette with his diamond studded gold lighter.

"But," said Tony, "I hear she's got some kind of mind control powers. I mean, you know I don't like women who mess with my head."

"Oh brother, preach it!" said Nobody. "Amen."

"I saw them once," said Jake.

"Get out."

"Really. I was in D.C. for the dome celebration. There was some kind of attack by this huge baby doll—don't look at me like that, it was a damn ten-story baby doll with a gun for a head—and everyone was panicking when all of a sudden the Thrill flew over our heads and yelled, 'Stay calm! Keep down!'" Jake looked dreamily into the distance as he spoke of her.

"So what did you do?" asked Tony.

"I stayed calm. I kept down. But it didn't feel like mind control. It was something that just seemed like a really good idea. Still does."

"Huh," said Tony. He glanced down to the end of the bar. His eyes locked where Nobody was sitting.

"What?" said Jake.

Tony walked toward Nobody. "How'd this bottle of tequila get down here?"

Nobody grabbed at the bottle as Tony took it, his fingers passing though as if it were made of smoke.

"Excuse me," Nobody said. "I'm not done."

"Maybe you got mice," said Jake, chuckling.

"Damn big mice," said Tony.

Nobody leaned back in his stool and blew a perfect smoke ring. He blew a lot of perfect smoke rings these days.

As Jake and Tony returned their gaze to the television, Nobody ventured behind the bar once more for the tequila. Behind the booze was a large mirror, and he revealed his face as he took the bottle into his grasp.

He studied himself, in this $300 fedora, with his gold tie clasp. He didn't look bad, he thought. He needed a haircut, sure. But living on the road had been good to him. He'd aged well over the months, his face growing a little tanner, a little more rugged. He looked like a mature, seasoned man of the world. If only his eyes weren't so bloodshot and wet.

"Yeah," he said. "Kind of a funny story behind that."

NOBODY SWIRLED THE ice in his margarita with the wedge of lime. He scooped the lime across the rim of the glass, gathering up salt, then licked it. He contemplated the lime, with its withered brownish edges. Why did bar limes always look like they'd been cut two weeks before?

By now, the bar was completely empty. The barkeep and his friend had turned off the television and gone home. It was five-thirty in the morning, and Nobody had sampled a little of everything in the bar. Sadly, the bar didn't have a jukebox.

"Strike up the steel guitar, boys," said Nobody, his voice slurred. "I've lost my woman, my house, my car, my job, everything that used to be me has gone and died. All I've got left to live for is booze and cheap thrills. I'm living in a goddamn country song."

He stared down at the margarita. "OK. So maybe the margarita is more a Jimmy Buffet thing. Gotta have the right props."

He rose drunkenly from the stool and crept his way behind the bar, looking for a bottle of whiskey.

"*Whiskey river, take my lime,*" he sang softly. "*It's done turned all brown and dry . . .*"

He returned to his stool with the whiskey. He tilted the bottle up, filling his mouth, then spat out the contents.

"Whoa, let's not do that again," he giggled.

Behind him, he heard footsteps.

He looked over his shoulder. There was a man standing in the shadows, looking at him.

"Howdy, partner," said Nobody.

"Partner," said the man in the shadows, with a nod of his head.

"Wait a second . . . you heard me," said Nobody, scratching his head.

"Hear you, see you. Smell you from over here. You drinking that stuff or just wallowing in it?"

"Wallowing mostly," said Nobody, sighing. "Wallowing in booze and misery. How come you can hear me? Wait, don't tell me, I've drunk myself dead. You're the devil, come for me at last."

"Good guess," said the stranger. He stepped forward, into the dim light of the single candle Nobody had lit on the bar.

"Well, well, well," said Nobody, recognizing his guest. "If it ain't my old buddy Dr. Know."

"It ain't," said Dr. Know, sitting down next to him. He looked different somehow. His hair was longer, his face was thinner, and he was wearing blue jeans and a black leather jacket. But what was really different, Nobody realized, was the way he carried himself, loose and relaxed. He looked as if the weight of the world had been lifted from his shoulders.

"Doc, I gotta admit, I never thought I'd see you again."

"You aren't seeing me again," said Doctor Know. "This is our first meeting."

"Holy crap," said Nobody, his eyes widening. "You've done messed things up with your time machine again. Jesus Christ. When I go outside, I'm going to find a world run by apes, aren't I?"

"The world's been run by apes for quite a while now," said Dr. Know.

"So," said Nobody. "I guess you're feeling pretty smug these days, huh? Looks like the world's starting to get its act together. Everybody rallying together in defense of Earth. And I saw in the paper that Hong Kong's decided to build one of your dome thingies. Guess everything's going according to plan."

"So it would seem," said Dr. Know. "But not my plan."

"What do you mean?"

"I would never cage in humanity beneath plastic skies. I would never subvert the liberties of people, forcing them to live under an authoritarian scheme managed by a shadow king only a handful of élites even know exists. All my life I've fought for free will, free skies, and free love. By the way, I gotta admit I admire you. Boffing both the Thrill and Rail Blade. Sweet."

"You sick fuck," said Nobody. "No wonder they both hate you."

"They hate me because they've been trained to hate me. But I think you're trying to imply that they hate their father. You still haven't figured out who I am, have you?"

"You're Dr. Know," said Nobody. "What, you having an identity crisis or something?"

"I know exactly who I am," he answered. "I'm Nikolas Knowbokov."

"A.K.A. Dr. Know," said Nobody.

"A.K.A. Rex Monday."

Nobody stared at the man next to him. He reached for the whiskey, and took a sip.

"I'm a little drunk," Nobody admitted. "So maybe I'm not catching this. You mean all this time, you've been Rex Monday?"

"Yep. I've been Rex Monday. But I haven't been Dr. Know."

Nobody lowered his head and shook it. "Who's on first," he mumbled.

"So I've heard," said Rex Monday.

"And Dr. Know and Rex Monday are the same person," said Nobody.

"No, not really."

"You are one mean bastard, messing with me while I'm this drunk."

"I'm a mean bastard most of the time. I have a lot of things to feel mean about. Like the fact that the world is presently being run by my goddamn evil twin and I'm starting to think he's actually going to get away with it."

"Evil twin," said Nobody, chuckling. Why hadn't he thought of that? It seemed so obvious now. He nodded slowly, and said it again. "Evil twin."

"I like to think of him as such, yes."

"My head hurts."

"Did he tell you he destroyed the universe in 1968?"

"Yeah."

"He lied," said Monday, tapping his chest. "I destroyed the universe in 1968. I was the one whose mind provided the template for its re-genesis. I imagined myself in the world, and so someone very much like myself filled that role. But I was still outside. I wasn't the cat in the box, I was still the one who had opened the box. I watched, ghostlike, in horror as someone who looked, sounded, and seemingly thought just like me carried on with what should have been my life. And for years, that was all I could do. Watch, while he gathered up wealth and power, watch while he fucked my wife and fathered her children. I hated him. I despised him. And I swore that one day I would kill him."

"I've either drunk too much or not nearly enough," said Nobody. "I believe every word you just said."

"On December 16, 1974, I broke back through. It was as if my hatred for him built up to a point that it twisted the very fabric of reality, tearing a hole. I stepped through, and found myself real once more. I was naked, starving, cold, and lost. On one side of the hole I had been watching him play with his baby daughter. And when I stepped through the hole to strangle him, I was on a snowy tundra, with no one around. I willed myself to walk for three days before I found a small cabin, inhabited by a wild-eyed, shaggy-bearded recluse. He pulled a shotgun on me and told me to get off his property. I informed him this was my planet, tore the gun from his grasp, and beat him to death with it. I took his clothes. I ate his flesh. I stayed in his cabin for three weeks while I figured out what to do."

"You ate his flesh . . . ?"

"Don't judge me. You can't imagine the state of mind I was in, after being trapped so long outside of reality."

"I can imagine better than you might think."

"Perhaps you can. During my stay in the cabin, I realized how much Dr. Know had the upper hand. He was the one with the wealth and the power. He was the one with the ability to read minds. I thought of confronting him directly, but feared the consequences. I think he is the anti-matter to my matter . . . should we ever meet, I believe it will destroy us both. His life I wouldn't mourn, but my death would be just one goddamn bummer."

"I hear ya."

"But, eventually, I learned I had special abilities of my own. I couldn't read minds, but I could close them off, prevent him from reading them. I began to father children, and was pleased to learn they displayed strange powers and abilities, just as his did."

"The Panic and Sundancer I can see," said Nobody. "But Pit Geek was, like, fifty."

"I can't explain Pit Geek. I just sort of found him, and worked him into my little army. For years, I've worked behind the scenes in opposition to my dark half's sinister schemes. Where he tried to oppress indigenous people beneath the thumbs of colonial invaders, I provided the arms to fan the flames of revolution. Where he tried to disarm those nations that might oppose him, I worked to keep them one step ahead on chemical and biological weapons. But now, it seems my hard work and dedication are coming to naught. With the destruction of Jerusalem, he seems to have stoked the fears of the world sufficiently to provide the leverage he needs to carry out his mad plans."

"Dude," said Nobody. "You can't really think you were doing the right thing by starting wars, can you?"

"I wasn't starting wars. I was just trying to ensure they run their natural course. Where natural hostilities are repressed by outside forces, the hate festers and grows until the war that finally comes when the outside forces vanish is far worse than what would have come before. The lessons of history are harsh, but irrefutable. True peace only comes when one side becomes powerful enough that the other side is no longer a threat. Then guilt sets in, the side with the power throws the side that lost a few crumbs, and all is right with the world. That's how the west was won."

"Forget the forces of history," said Nobody, feeling increasingly sober. "You were going to blow up school buses filled with children."

"Hard choices must be made when fighting a foe as powerful and nearly omniscient as Dr. Know. I can't pretend I'm proud of the things I've done. But perhaps you can understand a little of the desperation and fear I felt, knowing that every lie on the evening news bore the stamp of his plotting."

"Well," said Nobody. "He's no saint, that's for sure."

"I want you to help me stop him," said Monday.

"How?"

"I'm thinking a bullet in the head will do the trick."

"Ah."

"His island is wired. If one of my agents stepped foot on the sand there he would know it. But you've been there as his guest. You could still get close enough to deliver a fatal blow."

"Rex, if I may call you Rex . . ."

"Feel free."

"Rex, go screw yourself. I'm not a murderer."

"You killed Baby Gun, my own flesh and blood. I know you're capable of murder."

"Baby Gun was kind of stomping through Jerusalem at the time, under your orders, and innocent people were getting hurt."

"You didn't kill Rail Blade when she was polishing off Jerusalem."

"Because of you," said Nobody, stabbing a finger toward Monday's chest, "Veronica's dead."

"An unfortunate misunderstanding. I wanted them to use her to contact you. There was never an order from me to harm her."

"Just get away from me," said Nobody, throwing up his hands. "Jesus, you're both a couple of sick bastards."

"You could still have her back, you know," said Monday.

"Who?"

"Veronica. Once you kill Dr. Know, we'll have access to his time machine."

"You're freaking crazy."

"You could go back in time and kill Dr. Know just before he leaves on the trip that led to your present condition."

"Don't be stupid," said Nobody. "I've watched *Star Trek*. If I go back in time and kill him, then I would never even meet him, which means I'd never have a reason to kill him. Oh, Jesus, that kind of stuff makes my head hurt. Or maybe it's mixing all this liquor."

Rex Monday grabbed a bar napkin and took out a pen. He drew a line to the midpoint of the napkin, then looped the line into a circle, returning to the line once more, continuing on straight, so that he'd drawn a circle intersecting a line at one point only.

"This is your time line," said Monday.

"And this is your time line on drugs," said Nobody.

"Follow me," said Monday. "This line veers off into a circle, but returns to continue its path. The same would be true of your personal timeline. All the events that would have occurred in your life since the morning you woke up unborn would still exist, here, in this loop. The existence of the line isn't disturbed by the existence of the loop. You would wake up in bed, next to your wife, with full memory of everything that happened. But your life would be normal again. You'd be free of this strange curse."

"But Dr. Know would be alive again."

"In your timeline, sure. Not in mine. I'd finally have what I want most."

"I think this is the stupidest thing I've ever heard. No. No. I mean, everything would be back? Like it was? Oh, forget it. I'm not going to kill him. You're more deserving of a bullet in the head than he is."

"Maybe you'd give me a chance to change your mind."

"I can't think of a damn thing you could say to change my mind."

"There are things I could show you," said Monday. "Let's take a little trip."

Nobody opened his mouth to speak, but no sound came out. The bar vanished.

CHAPTER TWENTY

TALKING ABOUT
WEATHER

Once more, there was no up. Nobody watched with nauseated fascination as his body fractured and folded, smearing out over numerous flat and fragmented dimensions.

When he snapped back into a cohesive whole, he dropped to his hands and knees on rock-hard frozen ground, and retched.

"Yeah," said Rex Monday, watching. "I thought it would be best not to take you directly inside."

"Aauugh," moaned Nobody, drool dripping from his lips. "Ooooh, Christ. Give me some warning next time you . . . you . . . you do whatever the hell it is you just did."

"Dr. Know built a time machine," said Monday. "I built a space machine."

"Space machine?"

"Some of my less-educated colleagues insist on calling it a teleporter. But a teleporter would imply the transition of matter into information into matter again. Possible I suppose, but only with absurd levels of computing power and raw energy. My machine exploits the fractal math that underlies the fabric of space, allowing the spontaneous transposition of points along a curve. I built it out of a pocket calculator and a microwave oven. Simple and obvious, at least if you were there to watch the Big Bang."

"Nothing absurd about that," said Nobody, wiping his mouth on his sleeve. The cold wind made him aware of the beads of sweat dripping down his face. "Oh, God, I don't feel so good."

"Come on inside," said Monday, motioning toward a small, crude cabin nearby. "I'll put on some coffee."

BY HIS SECOND cup of coffee, the aspirin Rex Monday had given him started to kick in. Nobody still felt like he was going to die, but he no longer craved the relief death would bring the way he had earlier.

Monday stood by the cabin's single small window, watching the sunrise. The cabin was lit by oil lamps, and the coffee pot was still simmering on the wood stove. The cabin was one large room, with a single, small cot, a small table made from an upturned barrel, two folding chairs and a very out of place metal and glass office desk, on top of which was a laptop computer.

"Beautiful morning," said Monday. "Pink sky. Might be a storm on the way later. Last big storm we had, snow got higher than the roof."

"You didn't bring me here to talk about the weather," said Nobody.

"Didn't I? I like talking about weather. Weather is uncontrollable, unpredictable, something big that gives man a little philosophical perspective."

Nobody rubbed his temples. "Sorry, but I'm not really in the mood to discuss philosophy."

"We're not talking philosophy. We're talking about weather."

"My bad."

"Dr. Know threatens this, you know."

"What? Weather?"

"You been to D.C. since they finished the dome?"

"Briefly," said Nobody.

"It's always the same now. It's always seventy degrees. There's fake rain three times a week to keep the trees growing, and wind on demand to keep the air fresh. In D.C. now, talk about weather is a thing of the past. They've done something about it."

"Sure. But, really, is it any different than this cabin? I doubt you like weather enough to keep the door and window open during snowstorms. Just think of the D.C. Dome as a great big cabin."

Monday nodded and took a sip of his coffee. After a pause, he said, "He can stop hurricanes, you know."

Nobody nodded. "Yeah. Yeah, now that you mention it, I heard that."

"He's trying not to abuse it. But the temptation must always be there. I know how he thinks. He thinks like I used to think. He can save lives and property by stopping hurricanes. Of course, hurricanes play important ecological roles in the grand scheme of things. So, he'll look for ways to create new hurricanes, ones he'll control, that stay below dangerous levels, and make landfall where he thinks they're most needed. He's already running tests."

"How do you know that?"

Monday sat down at the desk and powered up the laptop. "Remember," he said. "I spent years as a ghost, just like you are now. I was able to watch him while he was putting together his laboratory in his mansion. He's made some significant upgrades to his systems over the years, but underneath it all, he's still running slapped-together code he jammed out way back when. Getting into his systems is a breeze. That's how I found out about your existence. I was listening in on your encrypted radio transmissions."

Nobody thought of something that struck him as important. "You built that hood the Panic was wearing. The one that let him see me."

"Yes. I had worked out the design in my head ages ago when I was trapped outside of reality."

"You could build more for me."

"Don't need to," said Monday, pulling open the center desk drawer. He pulled out another hood, and tossed it to Nobody. "My compliments."

"This will let anyone see me?"

"Yes."

Nobody held the hood, running his fingers across the fine mesh, imagining the possibilities. For the briefest instant, he imagined himself leading a normal life again. But, of course, that was absurd. The hood would only let one person at a time see him. It was unlikely he would be able to convince six billion people to wear hoods all the time just so he'd be real once more. If anything, holding the hood made his situation seem more hopeless than ever.

"Look at this," said Monday, tapping the laptop screen. "I can get into all of his files from here. I can pull up information on his weather control experiments. I can pull up live feeds of his agents who are negotiating with cities around the world to put up domes. His goal is to have two-thirds of the Earth's population under artificial skies by the year 2050. And even that is just the midpoint of his plan. Eventually, he plans to build floating super-cities in the middle of the ocean. He's designed them to comfortably support ten billion people."

"That's quite a crowd."

"Most of the time the citizens will be stacked up like firewood, existing in life-supporting wombs, participating in a virtual reality. This is his ultimate plan to save the Earth. Hitler had a final solution, and so does Dr. Know. By 2150, he intends for the continents to be devoid of permanent human habitation. Then he will begin to reforest and repopulate the vanished species of Earth."

He tapped some keys. A list of endangered species began to scroll up, a very, very long list.

"He's got a gene bank containing all these species, and is pretty far along in developing the process he'll need to clone them."

"Sounds pretty noble to me," said Nobody.

"People with noble intentions do the greatest harm," said Monday. "And no one has ever had greater intentions."

"OK. I won't deny he's got some pretty ambitious schemes, and I've seen some of the bad things that can result from them. But the stuff you're talking about is pretty far-fetched. I don't think the people of the world are likely to go along with it."

"He's working on that." Again, Monday's fingers flew across the keyboards, now bringing up a list of names. "He controls the world's media. Not all of it, of course, not yet, but one by one he's taking over newspapers, networks, Internet outlets. Do you know what this list of names is?"

"You send them Christmas cards."

"These are reporters who've stumbled onto parts of his master plan." He began to scroll through the list. Most of the names were green, some were red, and some were black. "The green ones are dismissed as conspiracy nuts. The information they put out isn't very well-documented, and they also get fed enough disinformation to render them harmless, no matter what they say. They're the lucky ones. The red names are reporters who've had the bad luck to stumble onto something more solid."

He tapped a name on the screen.

"This one, Christina Garamond, she's been to Dr. Know's island. She was a journalism student working summers with her father's construction company. She helped install some of those fancy goo tubes Dr. Know keeps his victims in. Most of the workers just put the stuff where they're told and don't ask questions. Christina asked lots. She took a lot of pictures and swiped whole reams of documents and blueprints. She wrote a truly devastating book about her discoveries, and mailed it off to publishers. A lot of the editors she sent it to are also on this list as red names. One by one, the manuscripts have been destroyed. Many of these people have lost their homes in fires. A few of these people have landed in jail on trumped up charges. Christina is presently in a hospital, her intelligence reduced to that of an eight-year-old, thanks to a head injury she received in an 'accident.'"

Nobody quietly stared at the list. There were a lot of red names. And more than a few black ones.

"The black ones are dead now," said Monday.

"You're saying he killed these people."

"Yes."

"To keep his secret."

"Yes."

Nobody rubbed his throbbing temples with his fingers. "I don't believe you."

"I know. It's tough to swallow. If you'd like, we can visit some of the red names. You can hear their stories directly, judge for yourself. Although, I have to warn you. They talk too much, they wind up a black name."

"Doesn't matter. You could take me to people you've planted. They could say anything you want them to."

Monday grinned. "Ah. A skeptic. I admire you for maintaining your skepticism after receiving unquestionable first-hand proof of time travel, mind control, and women who aren't bound by laws of gravity."

"Even if I believed, it doesn't matter. I mean, when it comes right down to it, I'll give you the benefit of the doubt. Maybe Dr. Know is up to his eyeballs in this conspiracy junk. Maybe you see yourself as some kind of noble freedom fighter in opposing him. But you said it yourself—people with noble intentions do the worst things. And you've done some fairly vile things, placing children in danger."

"I won't stand by idly while Dr. Know twists the world to conform to his warped vision."

"I will. Because, you know, it just doesn't matter. Dr. Know and you, you're like, what, sixty? Sixty-five? He's making plans for the world in 2050, and 2150, but he's not going to be around to see them come to fruition. Whatever damage he's doing will be undone, eventually. One man, even as powerful as he is, only gets so many years to mess things up."

"You must not have been paying attention," said Monday. "Didn't I mention his cloning program?"

"Fine. So he clones himself. It's not like his clones will really be him. They'll have their own experiences, their own lives."

"No. His ability to use other minds to house his consciousness will be greatly enhanced with his clones. He will be able to effect a complete transfer, with total control of a new host body, if his theories are correct. He'll be able to move from body to body, should such a thing even be needed. His medical research leads him to believe that with proper diet and genetic repair therapy, he may be able to extend his own healthy life to well over one hundred and twenty years. And who knows what meddling he'll be able to accomplish in another six decades?"

"And who knows how many busses full of children you'll blow up, huh?"

"I do. None. You go back in time and stop Dr. Know, and I stop my war against him. You kill him, and I'll take his place, and stop his mad schemes. I'll turn the world free of his grasp, and mine as well. And you, you'll get to go back to the life you knew. You'll be happy and free of your curse."

Nobody looked at the silver hood he held.

"It still doesn't make sense," he said. "He'll be alive when I go back."

"He'll be dead in my world. You have your time line, I have mine. There are infinite worlds. It's only the limitations of our minds that make us think there's one. In my world, he'll be dead. You have the power to grant my wish. I have the power to grant yours."

Nobody wadded up the hood and shoved it into his pocket. This was too much to think about. But maybe it was time to stop thinking. Maybe it was time to follow his gut instinct. He wanted off this roller coaster.

"Fine," he said. "Give me a gun. Send me back to the island. I'll put a bullet in his head. All I want is to go home."

CHAPTER TWENTY-ONE

I'M NOT REALLY
YOUR FRIEND

Monday handed him the pistol. Light played over its smooth black surface. It weighed heavily in his hand, the most solid thing Nobody had ever touched.

"If I use the space machine to take us to the island, he will know instantly," said Monday. "It's important that you approach in a fashion that he won't find suspicious."

"I guess I could dress as a pizza boy."

Monday took a large graphing calculator from his shirt pocket. "How's your stomach?"

"Um . . . a little better. Not much. Is that your space machine? I thought you weren't going to use that thing to get to the island."

Rex Monday leaned over his laptop, pulling up a scheduling program. "Hmm. Looks like Mindo is at the Miami airport even as we speak. That'll do."

"For—"

Monday clicked the equal key on the calculator.

The world twisted as Nobody blinked. His eyelids felt dry as they slipped across his toes.

"—what," finished Nobody. There was a blast of heat, and he raised his hands to shield his eyes from the bright sunlight.

"Welcome to Miami," said Monday, though he could barely be heard. Overhead, a giant jet was climbing into the sky.

"You did it again, you bastard," said Nobody, clutching his stomach.

"No time to waste," said Monday. Mindo is heading for Dr. Know's jet right now. You need to sneak onto the jet, and get back to the island."

"What's Mindo doing here?"

"Buying beer and cigarettes? Does it matter? You've got about thirty seconds before they close the door. That's his jet over there."

Nobody recognized it.

"Go," said Monday.

Nobody loped across the airfield, reaching the steps and racing up them to get inside just before the door closed.

He felt the weight of the gun in his pocket, shifting as he took a seat. The plane taxied down the runway. From the window, he watched the ground slip away.

"Next stop," he said, "Murderville."

HE WALKED SLOWLY from the airstrip to the mansion. Mindo had gone ahead, taking a golf cart, but Nobody felt the need to walk. He had a few stops to make before meeting Dr. Know again.

He went to the rose garden, to the fountain, and to Alexander's grave. But the grave was gone. Where the stone slab had stood, there was only a carpet of green grass. He walked around the fountain to be sure. It was true. Dr. Know had either moved the gravestone, or destroyed it.

"Oh, Doc," said Nobody, with a sigh. "Why do you have to make this so easy?"

He walked up to the main house. The repairs had been completed, and the house looked as if it had never been chopped in half. The newness of the paint gave it a brighter, happier look than it had the last time he'd seen it. But when he stepped inside, he could sense a change in the atmosphere of the place. The portrait of the family that had once hung above the giant fireplace was gone, replaced by a gilded mirror.

He walked up the staircase, listening to the silence of the house. Not that the house had ever been the home of raucous parties, but usually it hadn't been this quiet. Gone were the sounds of Rail Blade exercising in the gym, vanished were the rap songs that the Thrill would play at top volume from her stereo.

And yet, as he walked down the hall and came to the library, he found one thing unchanged. Katrina Know-bokov still sat in the library reading, in her padded leather chair, her glasses perched at the end of her nose. Nobody approached her.

He pulled the silver hood from his pocket. He carefully, gently, pulled it over her head. The second it slipped over her eyes, she jumped, sending her glasses falling to the floor.

"Aah," she cried, kicking his legs as she scrambled backwards, knocking over her chair.

"Whoa!" said Nobody. "It's OK! It's OK. I won't hurt you. I won't hurt you."

"Who . . . who are you?"

"Remember about a year ago? Dinner with an invisible man? I'm him."

"You . . . you're real?"

"Define real," said Nobody, shrugging. "No, don't bother. I'm real enough."

Katrina cautiously touched the hood. "What's this thing you've pulled over my eyes?"

"It's . . . I don't know what it's called. But it lets you see into my reality. Allows you to hear me," he said, raising his leg and rubbing his shin where she'd kicked him. "And you can touch me, too."

"You frightened me," she said.

"Sorry. I just wanted to talk."

"I don't know that I want to talk to you," Katrina said, picking up her chair. "You certainly have approached me rudely."

"I guess," said Nobody. "But, I've been wanting to talk to you for a long time. I was there the day you tried to talk Paco into poisoning your husband. I've watched you withdraw into yourself ever since then. I wanted to say something, though I still don't know what I can say that might help."

"You've spied on me?" she said, taking her seat once more.

"Occasionally. But I swear to God I don't follow you into the bathroom or anything sick. Mostly I just see you here in the library. You seem very . . . studious."

"How is it that you are invisible?" she asked.

"Your husband's time machine—"

"Stop," she said, holding up her hand.

"Don't believe in the time machine?" asked Richard.

"I have a daughter who flies," said Katrina. "Another destroys cities with a wave of her hands. I can believe in a time machine. But I don't want to."

"It wears you out, doesn't it," said Nobody.

She stared him thoughtfully, then nodded.

"Wears me out too," said Nobody. "Why haven't you ever left?"

"There is no place on Earth I could go. Were I to leave, Niko would notice, and with but a thought, he would find me and dispatch his emissaries to bring me home. I choose to retain what few shreds of dignity I have left rather than find myself carted home slung over Mindo's shoulders."

"But if you could leave, would you?"

She looked toward the floor, and sat silent for a moment.

"I don't know," she whispered. "I don't know if it's possible to run anywhere untouched by Niko. His handiwork is evident throughout all the world."

"Have you ever talked to him about leaving?"

She looked at him with her eyes wide, as if shocked by the question. "What's the point of conversation with a man who knows your every thought? The only time my thoughts are safe is when I'm reading. Then the words in my head are not my own. I'm beyond him then. My only hope now is that I'll outlive him. He's ten years older than me, and seems under great stress. Do you think it horrible of me that I daydream about his funeral?"

"Not in the least," said Nobody. Then he realized that Dr. Know was probably reading her thoughts right now. He'd best cut this short before he said anything suspicious. "Thanks for talking to me. If you don't mind, I'd like the hood back."

She pulled it off, and looked where he stood, her eyes straining. With a gasp, she dropped the hood, then stood and walked from the room.

He took the hood and put it in his pocket once more.

"Yeah," he said, taking out his gun. "Yeah, this will be easier than I imagined."

He walked out of the room. Somewhere in the distance was a strange noise, like an elephant farting.

NOBODY FOUND DR. Know in his command center, facing him as he entered the door.

"Hello, Richard," said Dr. Know.

"Good-bye," said Nobody, raising the gun to fire.

Dr. Know crossed the ten-yard gap between them before Nobody even extended his arm. He kicked the gun away, then delivered a tremendous punch to Nobody's groin. Nobody hit the floor unable to breathe.

"How decidedly amateurish," said Dr. Know. "I knew the second you snuck aboard my plane. Sensors detected the gun. Then, when my wife's thoughts momentarily vanished, I was able to listen in through microphones in the library. Since you are in possession of one of his thought-blocking hoods, I assume you've been brainwashed by Rex Monday."

"No," said Nobody, reaching out and grabbing at the doctor's legs. The doctor nimbly evaded him. "I pretty well hated you before I ever spoke to Monday."

"Hmm," said Dr. Know. "You admit to speaking with him. Although, given his history, it's far more likely you spoke with one of his agents."

Nobody managed to get on his hands and knees, wincing. "Oooh. No. No, I'm pretty certain it was him."

"Really. And what makes you so sure?"

Nobody swiveled his head around. The gun had fallen back in the hallway.

"Go for the gun and I'll paralyze you," said Dr. Know. "You know I'm not bluffing."

"Yeah," said Nobody, looking at the doctor. "Yeah, I don't think you're bluffing."

"Get up," said Dr. Know. "Now that we have quashed any absurd notions of assassination, I think we should have a serious talk."

"I'm not very talkative, all of a sudden," said Nobody. "And I bet that frustrates you. I bet it drives you crazy, not being able to get inside my head."

"You think very highly of your thoughts," said Dr. Know. "I have far better things to go crazy over, believe me."

"I see you destroyed Alexander's grave."

"I had him interred elsewhere," said Dr. Know. "Amelia had defaced the original stone."

"Defaced?" said Nobody. "She put his name on it!"

"Let's talk about Rex Monday," said Dr. Know.

Nobody noticed something on one of the monitors behind Dr. Know. He stepped past him for a closer look. On a grainy black and white camera, Amelia could be seen in a sandy, stony landscape. It reminded Richard somewhat of the Middle East. She was sitting cross-legged, in a lotus-position meditation, her back to the camera.

"Oh my God," he said. "That's Amelia. Is she working for you again?"

"My hiring standards aren't that low," said Dr. Know, turning toward the monitor. "Amelia returned and stole a vehicle from me shortly after we parted ways. I keep tabs on her now, in case she becomes irrational again. For the time being, she doesn't seem to be a danger to Earth."

"Doc, I've got to say that setting up spy-cams on your own daughter seems a little sick," said Nobody.

"It's for the world's safety," said Dr. Know, turning toward the monitors. "You heard her threats."

"I bet you know where Sarah is, too. She didn't threaten anyone."

"Sarah continues to abuse and waste her powers," said Dr. Know. "She's living in Dallas, in a mansion she's secured with her powers and furnished with theft. She's a potential threat in that her selfish behavior may make her easy prey for Rex Monday, but, for now, she's not endangering anyone."

"Ah, yes, Rex Monday. I've met him. I know who he is. Would you like to learn his true identity?"

"I believe you know the answer to that."

Nobody faced him. Behind him, in the hall, Katrina watched, the silver hood pulled over her face. But if she had the hood, what was this lump wadded up in his pocket?

Remaining casual as Katrina aimed the pistol she carried, Nobody said, "Rex Monday's real name is Nicolas Knowbokov."

"Is this a joke?" asked Dr. Know.

Then the shot rang out.

Dr. Know fell forward, a stunned look in his eyes. Nobody caught him in his arms.

Katrina dropped the gun and fled, her hands over her mouth.

For the briefest of seconds, Dr. Know's eyes locked on Richard's. They were full of confusion. Then, they lost their focus. His body went limp. Richard lowered him gently to the floor. There was surprisingly little blood. The bullet had entered the Doctor's back, just behind his heart. It hadn't come through the other side.

"Kind of anticlimactic, isn't it?" said a familiar voice.

Nobody looked up. Rex Monday walked toward him, slipping the calculator back into his shirt pocket.

Nobody said, "I told him who you were. I think he was so bewildered he never knew she was behind him."

"Pretty clever, giving her that hood. I don't remember telling you it would block her thoughts."

"Pretty lucky. It's not like I planned it."

Then Nobody furrowed his brow. He stuck his hand into his pocket. The hood was still there. Something was wrong here.

Monday held up a pocket calculator, bigger and more elaborate than the one he used for his space machine. He turned it on.

"Of course," he said, after studying it for about thirty seconds. "I can't believe it. This is so freaking obvious, I can't believe I didn't make my own. Then again, it helps if you have your own fusion reactor in the basement to power this thing."

From somewhere in the distance, there was another long farting noise.

"Simplicity," said Monday, handing him the calculator. "You key in the time, date and year, hit the memory key. Here's your ticket home, friend."

"I'm not really your friend," said Nobody, watching himself, wet with blood, leaning down to pick up the gun Katrina had dropped. He watched himself stealthily walk up behind Rex Monday.

Rex Monday's breath caught in his throat as the gun barrel was placed to the back of his neck. Blood splashed over the front of Nobody's shirt, drenching him. Nobody's ears rang from the shot.

"Guns make us all superheroes," said the Nobody holding the still smoking weapon. "Here's the plan: Go to the library and set the time machine coordinates for five minutes ago, then give the hood to Katrina once more. Tell her Dr. Know can't read her thoughts and show her the gun. She'll volunteer to pull the trigger. Then pop ahead three minutes and pick up the gun from where she drops it. You know the rest."

"OK," said Nobody, as his duplicate handed him the gun. "Sounds like I've got it all figured out."

"Go," said the older, wiser Nobody. He watched himself leave the room and head for the library. He took a seat in Dr. Know's command chair, the time machine in one hand, the space machine in the other.

"Nobody, Master of Time and Space," he said with a deep voice, then giggled nervously. His body slackened as he sank into the chair. His blood-soaked shirt clung to his body. He was too tired to care. It was finally over.

He looked at the row of monitors, at broadcasts from around the world.

"You're free," he whispered, addressing the whole damn world.

CHAPTER TWENTY-TWO

SEE, THIS IS WHY
I LIKE YOU

Nobody found Sarah sunning herself by the pool of the biggest mansion in Dallas, Texas. The house made her father's island residence look quaint and homey. He took a moment to steady himself as his stomach unknotted from the trip. By now he'd used the space machine a dozen times and was getting used to it.

She was reclining in a lounge chair, looking more relaxed than he'd ever seen her, and Sarah was someone who knew how to relax. She'd dyed her hair black, but somehow this didn't change her appearance much.

She still hadn't seen him. The space machine worked with eerie silence. He tried to figure out how he was going to say what he needed to say. The possible scripts kept getting tangled up in his head. What was the funny, clever way to say, "Hi, I've killed your father?"

So, at last, he just said, "Hi."

Sarah tilted her head toward him, raising a hand to adjust her sunglasses.

"Richard?" she said.

"How you doing?" said Richard, looking back toward the house. "Pretty nice digs you got here."

"Oh my God, it is you," she said, sitting up.

"Is this a good 'oh my God' or a bad 'oh my God?'" asked Richard.

"What are you doing here?" said Sarah.

"There's a long story behind that," said Richard. "But not a funny one."

"Come on into the house," said Sarah. "I'll have Irwin fix us something to eat."

Richard followed her, stealthily staring at her lithe, seductive body as she walked. She seemed more naked now in her bikini than she had when she actually was naked, lying beside him in the huge bed back at her father's house. Did she ever think about those days, he wondered. It seemed like a lifetime ago.

They entered through the dining room, a huge open space framed by windows rather than walls. "Irwin!" Sarah yelled out.

A young man appeared in the doorway, dressed in a white butler's uniform. Something about the puppy-dog look in his eyes as he looked at Sarah made Richard deeply uncomfortable.

"We have a visitor, Irwin. Fix us some sandwiches and lemonade," said Sarah.

"Yes ma'am!" said Irwin.

"Oh, and Irwin?" said Sarah. "My guest is standing right next to me. You see him don't you?"

"Of course!" said Leroy, who then turned and left.

"Huh," said Richard. "I wish I'd known you could do that."

"If he's telling the truth," said Sarah. "People lie to me to make me happy with astonishing frequency."

"No surprise there," said Richard. "You're a hot babe. Plenty of men would lie to you even if you didn't have your mind control powers."

"I told you I don't like the term 'mind control,'" said Sarah. "My power is nothing like Dad's. I don't get inside people's heads."

"You're right. I've read your father's files on you. He believed that you have a vibration in your voice that stimulates human pleasure centers. Obeying your words is like a dose of heroin to most people."

"Great. Now I'm a drug."

"I didn't say that."

"Irwin is addicted," said Sarah. "I caught him trying to steal my Porsche about six months ago. I could have turned him over to the police, but I figured I'd turn him into an honest citizen. Now he hangs on my every word even when I'm not using my powers on him."

"That's funny that you say he was stealing your Porsche," said Richard, aware he was about to start a fight. "Didn't you kind of steal it from the guy who used to own this house?"

"I see that my father's file on me is complete. No surprise there. Yeah, I had Vincent Kay sign over the titles to his house and cars and boat to me. Why not? The man was the worst sleaze-bag CEO in America. If I hadn't taken his toys he would have lost them all anyway after his stock bubble burst."

"I suppose there's a sort of Robin Hood justice there," said Richard. "Taking from the rich to give to the, uh, to you."

"Don't judge me," Sarah snapped. "I was homeless, OK? I didn't have anywhere to go. My father has made my life almost as isolated and lonely as yours, Nobody."

"That's all the more reason to judge you," said Richard. "You really think this is the best way to live your life? Hiding out here in this mansion, with your only companion a toady butler?"

"I call it my Batman plan," said Sarah. "Minus the part where I put on a cape and fight crime."

Richard grinned. "You've got a smart mouth on you, kid. I've missed you."

"I'll let you know whether I've missed you or not after you tell me why you're here. You've been reading my father's files. I assume he sent you."

"Your father's dead," said Richard.

"Oh," said Sarah. She sat down at the end of the long dining room table. "Oh," she said, softly.

"So you're free," said Richard. "He's not peeking into the thoughts of potential boyfriends any more. You can make friends with anyone in the whole world. I suggest you start with your mother."

As he said this, he dug into his pocket and pulled out two small disks the size of pencil erasers. He sat them on the table in front of Sarah.

"What are these?" she asked. "Pills?"

"Hearing aids. Sort of. Hearing blockers, I guess would be more accurate. Rex Monday had whipped them up for his henchmen to wear when they fought you. It blocks the frequency in your voice that activates pleasure centers. I think you should give these to your mother. I think the two of you could really benefit from talking to one another without her being scared of you."

"These really block my powers?" she said, picking them up.

"According to Rex Monday's notes."

"How have you been reading Rex Monday's notes? What does he have to do with any of this?"

"Now, see, this is where it turns into a long story. The executive summary is that Rex Monday convinced me to help him kill your father. But I had my own agenda during this, and I managed to kill Rex Monday as well. Oh, and Rex Monday was your father's evil twin."

"You killed my father?"

"In the broad sense, yes. Your mother pulled the trigger, but it was my plan."

"My mother kill . . . how? Why?"

"You know what you said about a life of loneliness and isolation? I think it went ever deeper with your mother. She felt trapped in a world she had no control over. When I put the gun into her hands, I think she realized she had a way to take control back."

"Oh my God," said Sarah, placing her elbows on the table, dropping her head into her hands. "Oh my God."

"These are not good 'oh my Gods,'" said Richard.

"How did you expect me to react? Did you want me to be happy? To be grateful? I can't believe this."

"I didn't know how you'd react. I could have kept it secret. You could have lived your life here and never found out. But that didn't seem fair."

Sarah sagged into her chair. She wasn't crying. She didn't look angry. She looked drained, stunned.

"I know this is a shock," said Richard. "I hope you can forgive me one day. But, more importantly, I hope you can forgive your mother. She was caught up in something she couldn't control for a very long time. Please don't hate her."

"I can't believe it," said Sarah. "My mother? She was so quiet and harmless. She was just a little statue in the library. How could she have done this? How?"

"You can ask her," said Richard. "This might sound crazy, but, with those earplugs, and with your father out of the picture, this might be a good time to get back in touch with her."

"That does sound crazy," said Sarah.

"Look," said Richard. "I'm more to blame for this than she is. And I think I might have a little insight into this. You have a chance to do something that is forever lost to me. You can still talk with your mother. This is a second chance for you."

Sarah toyed with the tiny hearing blockers.

"You know, it's funny," she said. "But I don't hate you for this. I don't hate you for killing my father, for coming here and judging me, for telling me how I should treat my mother. But . . ."

"But?"

"But I've hated you for a long time now for not coming to find me. I haven't exactly been keeping myself secret. I've been mentioned in news stories as Vincent Kay's 'mistress.' They've run photos of me in tabloids. And I always thought you'd find me. But it took this to make you come here?"

"I've been a little unfocused for the last year," said Nobody. "Sorry."

"Do you still love me?" asked Sarah.

"No."

"Oh."

"Not romantically," said Richard. "But I hope we'll be friends. This isn't some kind of bullshit. I really enjoy your company."

"So what changed?"

"You'll kill me when I tell you."

"How bad can it be compared to your killing my dad?"

"I might be in love with your sister. I was hoping you'd help me find her."

Sarah cut him a glance that twisted his stomach worse than the space machine. He knew he'd gone too far in revealing this.

Then Sarah started to laugh.

"Wow," she said. "I mean, wow. You have a lot of nerve, Nobody."

"What do I have to lose?" he asked.

THEY CONTINUED TO talk for the next few hours. Richard was relieved to discover he'd done the right thing. With everything out in the open, Sarah seemed more curious than angry about what had happened. He told her about the fight between Rail Blade and Dr. Know, about the mansion being cut in half, what had happened in the garden, about his lost year wandering the country, and everything he knew about Rex Monday up to and including how he died.

"It makes perfect sense," said Sarah, after hearing about the time loop that had put the gun back into his hands.

"See, this is why I like you," said Richard.

LATER THAT NIGHT, Richard demonstrated his space machine. One moment they were standing on the patio outside the dining room of the mansion, the next they were standing in Dr. Know's museum, and Sarah was throwing up onto the metal toes of a two-story-tall robotic ostrich.

"Don't . . . do that again," said Sarah. "Jesus, that has to be the worst way to travel ever."

"I rode a bus across North Carolina once," said Richard. "The space machine just takes getting used to."

Sarah wiped her mouth as she looked around the museum. "I never thought I'd admit it, but I've missed this place."

"I guess it's home again for you, if you want. It's got to be less lonely than that mansion. Use those earplugs. Talk to your mother."

"OK. Is Paco still here?"

"Paco? The chef?"

"Yeah."

"I think so."

"Good. Irwin could barely make toast."

"I'm glad you can see the upside to this. Especially so soon after throwing up."

"So what's next for you?" said Sarah.

"I'll keep looking for Amelia. She needs to know that the war between your father and Rex Monday is over. And, of course, I want to find out if she ever thinks about me."

"That's it. Rub it in," said Sarah. "I'm still having a hard time getting my head around this. On my brother's grave? Ew."

"I didn't pick the spot," Richard said, apologetically.

"And you have no clue where she is now? It's not in my father's files?"

"All I have is those weird videos of her in a desert, and a map with an X on it I can't even begin to figure out."

"Let me have a look," said Sarah.

As they moved toward the door, Sarah looked overhead.

Richard looked up to the empty ceiling.

"Huh," she said. "I wonder what Dad did with the spaceship?"

CHAPTER TWENTY-THREE

MOONSLIGHT

And so it was that Nobody went to Mars.

It took a little while to piece together. Sarah's contacts at NASA needed a few weeks to match the map up to satellite photos. Then a generous grant from Katrina Knowbokov set the entire Cambridge University math department working on extrapolating Rex Monday's co-ordinate system for the space machine to a number sequence appropriate for another planet. Richard spent the time testing the spacesuit Dr. Know had whipped together for Mindo on her trip to the moon. It was comically large on him, but airtight.

On Christmas morning, when the air was still and silent, Richard tapped in the coordinates, hit enter, and took the biggest leap of faith he had ever taken.

On Earth, the transposition of points on the curvature of space felt close to instantaneous. The swap of information occurred at the speed of light, and there were no two points on Earth where this took more than a fraction of a second.

Given the relative positions of the two planets on that Christmas morning, it took twenty minutes for the transit.

Richard went insane. There was no way of comprehending the realms he passed through. It was a void of unending darkness where everything glowed with a blinding light. It was a blast furnace that blistered his skin and yet left his teeth chattering beneath a casing of ice. Only he didn't always have teeth and skin. Sometimes his skin would just vaporize away, at other times his individual teeth danced before him in a delicate pearly arc. His mind snapped at this, shattering into a thousand jagged shards. Part of him stood, dispassionate, distant, watching his twisting body against the pure white screen of the unspace. He nodded slowly, coolly, contemplating the painful things happening before him, but no longer truly aware of the pain of his head being forced through the track of his own intestines.

Even without a mouth, Richard said, "Get your head out of your ass."

The world stopped dancing. His teeth flew back into his mouth. His eyes tugged back into their sockets with disgusting wet plops. The blank white screen before him became blowing red sand as he fell to his knees, which were now, thankfully, where they should be, and not glued on backwards.

And then he went sane, staring at his gloved hand in the red sand. At least he thought he was sane. "I am sane," he said. It didn't sound crazy to say this.

He had fallen down. Immediately before him was the glass of his visor, and beyond this were sand and pebbles and his glove. He had an excellent view of them. His stomach was oddly quiet. The anti-nausea medicine he had taken had worked.

He lay there for a moment, fascinated by the sand six inches from his face. This was Mars. He was laying face down on Mars. Why had this seemed like a good idea?

Then he remembered why he was here. He grew vaguely aware of his arms and legs, and managed to move them. He flailed about, unsure which way was up, until finally he realized he had achieved a sitting position. No longer limited to the view six inches from his face, Richard looked around the rocky landscape of Mars. He was near a red cliff, with a wall as straight as if it had been measured off with a chalk line. The seamless barricade gleamed like red glass in the feeble sunlight. Perhaps a football field in height, it stretched as far as he could see in both directions. As he looked around, he could see a second wall opposite him, perhaps a mile away, a crisp, dark line running parallel to the wall he was near.

And above that, shimmering in the sun like a mirage, was a steel dome. He let out a long, slow whistle.

He began to walk. It was oddly difficult, given how light he felt. The sand beneath him was frequently very fine; it was like walking on talcum powder. He tried jumping. He could launch himself twenty feet across the landscape with little effort, but the many brick-size stones that jutted up from the sand made landings tricky. Only luck kept him from breaking a leg or an ankle the few times he tried.

He was worried about what would happen when he reached the far wall. He had no idea how he would climb such a smooth, featureless surface. Programming the space machine on an alien planet to use as a shortcut might be rash. And, low-gravity or no, he would never be able to jump such heights.

Closer to the wall, a particularly odd-shaped boulder caught his attention. It was smooth and polished, tall as a house, and an odd color for the landscape, a brilliant Earth-sky blue. He was struck by how much it resembled a boat lying on its side. It even had a rudder, and on what would have been the deck, there were openings like hatches that revealed a hollow interior.

Fifty feet away, Richard stopped and blinked. This wasn't a rock that looked like a boat. This was a boat. He rushed forward, stumbling over rocks, slipping in dust, until he reached the deck. He ran his hand along the glazed translucent surface. The boat seemed to have been molded as a single piece; he couldn't find a seam or a joint anywhere. The deck was tilted too steeply for him to climb to one of the hatches, but he had no doubt now that he was looking at an artificial construction.

Had Amelia built this? Why would she have built a boat on a desert world? He swallowed, trying to make sense of it.

He stepped back for a better view. His back ran into something hard. He spun around to find iron bars. In a whirl, iron bars thrust from the soil around him, in seconds joining over his head to trap him in a man-sized birdcage. The bars kicked up dust as they rose, and for a moment the dust cloud blinded him.

As the dust settled, he could see a shining steel rail arcing through the air from the top of the cliff down toward the boat. Sliding toward him along the rail, Amelia drew nearer. She was encased entirely in a shell of steel that mirrored perfectly her nude body beneath. She raced toward the cage at a speed that made Richard flinch, until she halted, instantly, inches beyond the bars. She reached her hand through the cage, and placed her slender steel fingers upon his visor. Her face gave no clue as to what she might be thinking.

Then the small speaker near his ear buzzed, the noise rising and falling until it formed a robotic, mechanical voice.

"Oh," she said. "It's you."

The cage crumbled to rust. She wrapped her arms around him, not in a hug of greeting, but in the manner one might embrace a particularly bulky rolled up rug. With a lurch of motion the dusty red soil was left behind and they rose into the sky as the rail whipped around, back toward the top of the cliff. For a moment, he could see the landscape clearly, and it seemed to him that thin dusty roads radiated out from the steel dome. The valley he'd landed in was revealed to stretch straight as a mile-wide highway toward both horizons. Then his focus shifted to the steel dome, which was several hundred yards around and dotted with semi-transparent ruby panels. Just before they smacked into the wall of the dome, the metal split open like a giant mouth, and swallowed them.

Within the dome, the light was brighter than Richard would have guessed, and not as red as the outside windows would have indicated. A fountain bubbled with water in the center, and grass grew across the floor. Flowering plants bloomed everywhere in neat rows, next to blue walls crafted from the same material as the boat. Near the fountain was the husk of the spaceship Richard had seen in the museum, now disassembled into several cylinders that looked like little buildings.

Rail Blade sat him down, and his helmet speaker said, "You can take off your suit. There's air in here."

Rail Blade moved and the metal flowed away from her face and hair, until she wore only the metal shell from the shoulders down. She watched him intently as he unsnapped the clasps of his helmet and twisted it off with a grunt.

"Jesus Christ," Richard said, lowering the helmet to the grass. He gulped in a big lungful of musty air with a scent vaguely reminiscent of a locker room. "I'm on fucking Mars!"

Amelia grinned. "Welcome to Xanadu."

"Xanadu?"

"You know, like the poem. This is my stately pleasure dome."

"Ah," said Richard. "Hi."

"Hi," she said.

"Which one of us gets to ask the obvious question first?"

"I'll go. What on Earth are you doing on Mars?"

"I like the way you phrased that," said Richard. "That's my first question also."

"I'm here to terraform Mars as a gift to the human race," said Amelia. "You?"

"Whoa," said Richard. "My answer isn't nearly as good as that."

"May I assume Father sent you?" said Amelia.

"No. He's dead."

"Oh," said Amelia. "Did my mother kill him?"

"What? Why would you say that?"

"I could see it in her eyes from time to time. That desperate look. And, no offense, but to my father, she was even more invisible than you. She was merely a vessel that Father used to give birth to us. Once we kids started flying around, Father's attention was entirely on us. Can you blame her for being resentful?"

"No," said Richard, relieved at her reaction. "That's why I put the gun in her hand."

"Bastard," said Amelia, her eyes flashing to anger.

Richard cringed, and threw up his hands, expecting her to hit him.

"What?" he said, relieved that she didn't hit him, and that metal blades hadn't popped out of nowhere and hacked him to bits. "Why are you mad? You tried to kill him yourself, once."

"He was still my father," said Amelia, turning away. "What you said about putting the gun in her hands, your tone . . . you were making a joke of it."

"I swear to God that was the most serious thing I've ever done," said Richard. "I still don't know if it was the right thing or the wrong thing, but it's the thing I did. I have to live with it. I didn't mean to sound insensitive."

"So, he's dead," said Amelia. "Has Rex Monday taken over the world yet?"

"In 100 percent seriousness, I killed him, too."

Amelia looked back at him, surprised. "How?"

"With the same gun," said Richard. "And a time machine."

"OK," she said. "I might need some more details later."

"I may have to draw a diagram."

"And you came all the way to Mars to tell me, huh?" said Amelia.

"I captured Rex Monday's space machine. Getting here was no big deal, except for the part where I went insane. It's just a hop and a skip back to Earth with this thing," said Richard. "I've come to take you home."

"No," said Amelia.

"I thought you might say that. Look, your father's dead. The whole war you've fought since childhood is over. You can be free."

"I am free," said Amelia. "Let's be serious. I can't imagine I'm popular back on Earth right now. I must be public enemy number one."

"Rail Blade is," said Richard. "But you don't have to go back and live the life of a superhero. You could retire, and live normally, quietly."

"Richard, take a look around you," said Amelia. "You are standing in the ruins of a lost Martian civilization."

"Wow, yeah, I kind was wondering about that. I mean, I thought maybe you had done it for decoration, but, wow, this is some kind of news, isn't it?"

"Do you know what you were walking in when I found you?"

"Dust?"

"A canal. The planet is covered with them. Ancient, empty, bone-dry canals, filled with thousands of ceramic boats."

"Oh my God," said Richard. "This is like some kind of science fiction novel come true. I mean, this is huge."

"No," said Amelia. "This is fiction."

"What do you mean?"

"This is my father's fiction," said Amelia. "There are canals on Mars because it was something that captured his imagination as a kid. There are ancient ruins here for the same reason that Sarah could fly and I could pilot that spaceship just by telling the steel frame where to go. There were never *any* Martians. These things are the evidence that this is my father's universe. And it's broken."

"Broken?"

"It's twisted. Corrupted. A parody of what reality must have been. We'll never know what Mars would have been like if my father hadn't triggered that bomb."

"I hadn't considered that," said Richard. "I guess I see what you're saying."

"Then you have to understand why I can't go back to Earth. It's too dangerous."

"Ah. Now that's the leap I'm not making in my head."

"Richard, do you know what I'm doing as we're standing here talking?"

"Looking good," said Richard.

"That's sweet, but no. Right now, even as we speak, I'm touching the entire planet. There are vast quantities of iron here, that's why the surface is red. And I'm slowly, steadily, driving the bulk of these iron ores to the core of Mars."

"That's quite a hobby," said Richard.

"This isn't a joke," said Amelia. "There's already a small rocky iron core at the heart of Mars, but it's cold, silent. I'm augmenting it by adding the surface ores, and I'm vibrating it now, warming it. It's a slow process. But in another decade or so, I'll have stoked it to a white-hot state. Do you know what this means?"

"Spell it out for me," said Richard.

"Once the core is excited, Mars will have a magnetic field. One reason Mars doesn't have much atmosphere is that it doesn't have a magnetic field like Earth's to protect it from solar winds. The high atmospheric particles can't be held by Martian gravity and get swept into space. I can put a stop to this."

"So what you're saying is, compasses will work on Mars."

"That's a trivial ramification, but yes."

"And it will have an atmosphere?"

"Within our lifetimes. The heated core will once again drive volcanic action. Subsurface gasses and water will be injected into the atmosphere as volcanoes begin to flow. And I'm stripping the iron in the rusty soil from oxygen atoms. It's where I got the atmosphere for this room."

"Within our lifetimes? What happens when you stop heating the core?"

"I don't know," said Amelia. "It should take thousands of years to cool down to the point where the magnetic field will fail. I figure it will be humanity's problem by then."

"Wow. I guess I shouldn't have been so flippant with that hobby comment. This is pretty impressive, Amelia. Where did you get the grass and plants?"

"And bumblebees, and worms, and dozens of other creepy crawlies. Father had made some do-it-yourself ecosystem kits when he was designing his domes. They fit nicely into the spaceship, along with about three years worth of MREs."

"Meals Ready to Eat?" said Richard. "I'm surprised your father never invented meals in a pill."

"Oh, I have those, too. And in another month or so, I should be able to start harvesting vegetables from the gardens."

As she spoke, the room grew darker. The sun dipped ever closer to the horizon, and without a high atmosphere to play against, the light faded away at a surprising pace. In moments, it would be night.

"Sounds like you've got it all planned out," said Richard. "But, it still doesn't answer my big question. Why are you on Mars?"

"I've crossed a line, Richard," said Amelia. "I've stretched my powers to a planetary scale. I'm never going to be normal."

"But normal is just—"

"Let me rephrase that. I am normal. *This* is my normal. I need a world to touch, to play with. And I think Father gave me Mars."

"Gave you Mars?"

"Think about it. It's a perfect match. It's a world covered in *rust*, iron oxides, waiting for someone to come along and free up the oxygen. It's a world that could support an atmosphere if it had a magnetic field, and I have the power to kick the core into motion. It's a world where canals that have never held water are already built, as if waiting for me to come along and fill them. On a more symbolic level, Mars is a world symbolizing war and violence. And I am a weapon. I was born to be an instrument of violence. Mars is the world where I can change from a sword into a plowshare."

Amelia sat down by the fountain. It was crafted from the same blue porcelain as the boat in the canal. It bore an eerie resemblance to the fountain on her father's estate. The look on her face was almost devoid of emotion.

"This is a broken universe. This is a broken world. And I am my father's broken child. This is home."

"You don't sound happy about it."

"I don't know what happiness has to do with it," she said.

"I know what happiness has to do with it," said Richard. "That's why I'm here. I've come to Mars to find happiness."

"And instead you found me," said Amelia. By now the light had faded to the point that her face was nearly hidden by the shadows.

"That's what I mean," said Richard. "I came to Mars to find you. Because you make me happy."

Richard sat down next to her at the fountain. The feeling of *déjà vu* grew stronger. "I love you, Amelia."

"Huh," she said. "How desperate are you?"

"Not as desperate as you might think," said Richard. "But it's pretty simple. I like you because you are broken. I like the way you've fractured. My God, this is a no-brainer."

"Really?"

"Really. You're the most serious person I've ever met. I'm someone who's always treated life as a joke. It must be true that opposites attract, because I recognize in you something that I'm missing. You have a certain magnetism, pardon the pun. It pulled me across umpteen million miles to find you."

"I can't believe you're saying this," she said. "Are you trying to trick me into going back to Earth?"

"I've a better idea," he said. "We can stay here. It will be nice to live on a world where everyone can see me. And I like the idea of our kids or grandkids waving at the first spaceships from Earth."

"Kids? You're getting a little ahead of yourself, Richard."

"Come on. Admit it. You've missed me."

"Yes," she said, softly. "But that still doesn't give you the right to come in here and start making plans for our children."

"Sorry," said Richard. "You're right. I should have brought roses. You deserve a real courtship. Although I guess moonlight walks holding hands on the beach aren't an option here."

"There are two moons," said Amelia. "You'll be able to see them through the windows in a few more minutes. You'd be surprised how bright they are."

"I may be all surprised out for the day, to be honest."

"This from a man who's just stepped across planets in hopes of getting lucky."

"Babe," said Richard, "all my life I've been lucky."

Above Mars, Phobos and Deimos crept silently through the void, reflecting the light of a distant sun to cast shadows on the undiscovered ruins of the world below.

In the bright moonslight, to the eerie bow-saw drone of wind whipping over a steel dome, two lovers held hands, and kissed.

MEANWHILE

A woman limped down the steps of the post office onto a nearly empty New York City sidewalk. Few people were out this Christmas morning, as a fierce wind whipped through the streets, blowing snow before it.

As the woman walked through the snow, a cloud of steam followed her, and a symphony of tiny hisses as the snowflakes vaporized against her skin.

She took shelter from the wind behind a dumpster in an alley. She dug around in the dumpster, grunting as she pulled out a large cooler, the battered green aluminum casing sporting several bullet holes.

"That you?" asked the cooler as she dropped it to the ground.

"No," she said, taking a seat on the cooler. "It's just the rats."

"Was there anything waiting?"

"Nope," she said, pulling out a pack of cigarettes from her coat.

"You sure you have the right P.O. box?"

"The key fit," she said, lighting the tobacco with a glowing fingertip.

"Are you smoking?" asked the cooler. "Christ, I'd kill for a smoke."

"You just finished regrowing a lung and the first thing you want to do is smoke?" said the woman, who without any irony took a deep drag from the cancer stick.

"So what next?" asked the cooler.

"We check again next year," said the woman. "Those are the instructions. If the boss disappears, we keep checking here until we get further assignments. You in a hurry or something?"

"If the boss were back in touch, I reckon he'd whip up some kind of ray or something that would make my arms 'n legs grow back faster," said the cooler.

"You are the last person who should bitch to me about missing limbs," said the woman, breathing out a cloud of smoke.

"Don't you ever worry that the boss might be dead?" asked the cooler.

"He probably has a plan for that," said the woman. "He has a plan for everything. We haven't heard the last from him."

A loud sigh escaped from the cooler.

"What?" the woman asked.

"Next time," said the cooler, "he should plan on robbing some banks."

ABOUT THE AUTHOR

James Maxey is the author of "Empire of Dreams and Miracles," a Phobos Award–winning tale that became the title story in the first Phobos anthology. Maxey started writing his first published novel, *Nobody Gets the Girl*, on November 15, 2000. His goal was to complete the book by New Year's Eve, so that he could claim to have written the last novel of the Millennium. Having tapped out the final words *on* New Year's Eve, he handed a dozen copies out, unread, at a New Millennium celebration, and was pleasantly surprised at the response.

Maxey has spent his time before and after the dawn of the 21st Century polishing his writing craft, starting with creative writing classes at Mars Hill College in North Carolina. For the last several years, Maxey has been an active member and sometimes coordinator of the speculative fiction critique group sponsored by the Writer's Group of the Triad in North Carolina. Maxey graduated from the

ABOUT THE AUTHOR

Odyssey Fantasy Writer's Workshop where he studied with Writer-in-Residence Harlan Ellison, and he is also a graduate of Orson Scott Card's Writer's Boot Camp.

James Maxey lives in North Carolina with a shockingly large number of cats. He spends his waking hours lost in daydreams, and during those rare moments when all the cats are asleep, turns his flights of fantasy into great stories. To research *Nobody Gets the Girl*, Maxey studiously read 1,312,017 comic books, starting in 1973 with a Superman comic book that guest-starred Batgirl.